The Afterthought

K.M. Baker

Copyright © 2024 by K.M. Baker

All rights reserved.

No part of this publication may be reproduced, stored in a retrieval system or transmitted in any from or by any means, without written permission from the publisher, except as permitted by U.S. copyright law. For permissions contact: kmbakerauthor@gmail.com

This novel is entirely a work of fiction. The names, characters, and incidents portrayed in it are the work of the authors imagination. Any resemblance to actual persons, living or dead, events or localities is entirely coincidental. All songs, song tiles and lyrics contained in this book are the property of the respective songwriters and copyright holders. Designations used by companies to distinguish their products are often claimed as trademarks. All brand makes and product names used in this book and on its cover are trade names, service marks, trademarks, and registered trademarks of their respective owners.

Cover design: Maree Rose

Editor: Taylor at Deliciously Dark Editing

Content Warning

This book is a Dark Romance and a work of fiction. It contains explicit 18+ content that I do not condone outside of a fictional world. Greyson Hayes is not a good guy. He's a ruthless criminal who likes to play with fire. The fact that he would burn down the world for Ava is just an added bonus. To my seasoned Dark Romance readers, please enjoy your shopping list.

If you have any questions or feel like anything should be added to this list, please do not hesitate to reach out via email at KMBakerauthor@gmail.com.

Your mental health matters.

Triggers:

Adult language, Addiction (Not the MCs), Anal, Arson, Assault (Not by MCs), Branding, Burning People Alive, Crooked Police Officers, Death of a Parent, Degradation, Drug Dealing, Dub-Con, Gangs, Kidnapping, Mentions of Cheating (Not the MCs), Mentions of Death by Drug Overdose, Mentions of Death by Terminal Illness (Not the MCs), Mentions of

Drug Use, Mentions of Struggling with Sobriety (Not the MCs), Mentions of Terminal Illness (Not the MCs), Mentions of Trafficking, Murder, Non-Con, Praise, PTSD, Public Sex, Pyromania, Pyrophilia, Spitting, Torture, Trauma, Underage Drinking, Violence

To anyone looking for a man
who would burn down the world for you,
and then fuck you like a god in the ashes.

Playlist

Prologue - Dial Tone - Catch Your Breath

Chapter 1 - Trouble - Iggy Azelea, Jennifer Hudson

Chapter 2 - Left Behind - The Plot In You

Chapter 3 - Hypnosis - Sleep Token

Chapter 4 - Unwritten - Natasha Bedingfield

Chapter 5 - You Give Love A Bad Name - Bon Jovi

Chapter 6 - Run This Town - JAY-Z, Rihanna, Kanye West

Chapter 7 - running to you - iamjakehill

Chapter 8 - Like A Villain - Bad Omens

Chapter 9 - Let's Go - Calvin Harris, Ne-Yo

Chapter 10 - IF YOU GO DOWN (I'M GOIN' DOWN TOO) - Kelsea Ballerini

Chapter 11 - Hey Girl - Stephen Sanchez

Chapter 12 - IDGAF - Dua Lipa

Chapter 13 - MAGNETIC - Wage War

Chapter 14 - Pac Ave - Diggy Graves

Chapter 15 - Addicted - Saving Abel

Chapter 16 - Medicate Me - Rain City Drive, Dayseeker

Chapter 17 - Panic Waves - Our Promise

Chapter 18 - Home - Phillip Phillips

Chapter 19 - Treacherous (Taylor's Version) - Taylor Swift

Chapter 20 - Paradise - Justin Timberlake, *NSYNC

Chapter 21 - I Chose Violence - iamjakehill

Chapter 22 - Take This Job and Shove It - Johnny Paycheck

Chapter 23 - Burn It Down - Silverstein, Caleb Shomo

Chapter 24 - Count on Me - Bruno Mars

Chapter 25 - Girls Just Wanna Have Fun - Cyndi Lauper

Chapter 26 - Your Love Is My Drug - Kesha

Chapter 27 - Villains Aren't Born (They're Made) - PEGGY

Chapter 28 - Gasoline - I Prevail

Chapter 29 - New England Palm Trees - Wind Walkers

Chapter 30 - Lose Control - Teddy Swims

Chapter 31 - I Was Alive - Beartooth

Chapter 32 - Give Me One Reason - Tracy Chapman

Chapter 33 - You've Created a Monster - Bohnes

Chapter 34 - Shackles - Steven Rodriguez

Chapter 35 - Still Into You - Paramore

Epilogue - (I've Had) The Time Of My Life - Bill Medley, Jennifer Warnes

Prologue
Avalynn

"Greyson? I don't understand." Tears stream down my face as I stare into the blue eyes of the man I love more than anything in the world. He turns away from me, running his fingers through his deep brown hair before fisting a handful and holding it in place out of frustration. "Why can't you just talk to me? We can work this out. You don't have to do this," I beg.

He frees his hands and throws them up in the air before turning back to face me again. "You don't understand, Ava. This has to be done. I can't do this with you anymore."

My stomach drops, and my heart slams in my chest as I try to process what he's saying. He's leaving me. Just like that, like I mean nothing to him. How can he walk away so easily? He said he needed to go off to do whatever the hell he was talking about for himself, but what about me? What about us? Did he just string me along and let me think we would be together forever? I have so many questions, but my head is spinning. I should have never believed him. He's just another lying disappointment.

I give in and let my hurt turn into anger because, in this moment, being angry feels so much easier than feeling the pain of him making this decision. We had plans. We were supposed to start our lives together now that we made it past high school graduation. We were supposed to escape this shitty town to start fresh somewhere new, the way we always talked about.

"We could do this together, but you're choosing to go off on your own. You're choosing to leave me behind, and for what!?" I yell, still trying to find some way to convince him to stay—to choose me.

"It's not that simple. My life. The things I do. The urges I have. It's not as simple as us working things out, Ava. I'm sorry, but I have to go." His jaw tics, but his face is stern. He takes a few steps away from me, grabbing a bag to gather some of his things out of the closet.

We spent the last three years splitting time between my mom's house and his, so he always keeps some of his things here. After he places a few of his shirts in the bag, something inside me snaps. I was so stupid. You don't find forever at fifteen, no matter how badly I wanted to believe he would be my forever. I should have known that he would leave me high and dry as soon as we turned eighteen and graduated. I should have never been naive enough to trust him.

"You're not sorry!" I grab the lamp from the bedside table and toss it in his direction. The glass base shatters against the wall next to him, but he doesn't flinch.

"You're going to hurt yourself. Stop throwing things. I hate seeing you upset like this," he tells me, and it pisses me off even more.

"You don't get to hurt me and then pretend to care, Grey." I bow my head in defeat, letting the sorrow consume me. Sobs wrack through my entire body, and the soul-crushing feeling eats at the pit of my stomach.

I hate that he's seeing me like this, but he just ripped my heart out of my chest and threw it on the ground. I built walls around myself to prevent this feeling. I let him through the walls, only for him to destroy them. I can't control my emotions. I keep bouncing between anger, sorrow, pain, hurt, loss, and heartbreak. It's like an endless circle of feelings that my body is rapidly cycling through.

He steps into me, gripping my chin and forcing me to look at him. I can't bring myself to look into his eyes, so I look to the side. It hurts too much to give him that part of me after he just crushed my world.

"Look at me, Ava." His voice is stern and serious. I want to comply, but it hurts too much.

"I can't," I admit.

'"Look at me, baby," he says, and my sorrowful gaze slowly meets his.

The way he looks down at me almost rips me to pieces. He looks so torn with this decision, but I can tell there is no convincing him to change it. I scan my gaze across his face, committing it to my memory.

"Please, just tell me why." I blink through the tears falling down my face. "Why does it have to be like this?"

"It just does. You've always been too good for me. This is your chance to get the hell out of here and make something of yourself. I would just hold you back. Go get that fancy degree and make a good life for yourself. You deserve to be happy." He doesn't understand that he's taking every last bit of joy from me right here, at this moment.

"We were happy. You ruined that." My face contorts in anger. I'm a fool. I was going to beg him to stay. Can I be any more pathetic?

"I was never your endgame, baby. You were always meant to get out of here. I was just biding my time with you until you were ready to go." He leans in and plants a chaste kiss on my lips.

FUCK HIM! I pull back and slam my hands against his chest, pushing him as hard as I can. "You don't get to do that anymore!"

"Ava," he says in warning, but I'm tired of hearing all of this. I'm done.

"Get out! Get out, Greyson! I hate you! I hope you look back on this moment, and it fills you with nothing but regret every single day for the rest of your life." I push against him again. "You had the world, and you're throwing it away." I scoff. "You're right! You don't deserve me, and you never did. Now, get the fuck out of my house! I never want to see you, ever again."

I bring my arm up to quickly wipe the tears from my face and stare him down. My gaze hardens as I try to calm my rapid breathing. There's a dull ache in my head, which I know will likely turn into a full-scale migraine once my emotions settle down. He goes to take a step into me again, but I shake my head and point towards the door.

"I mean it. Get the fuck out! I hate you," I scream at him even though I know it's not even a little bit true. I love him with every piece of me, but my love isn't good enough for him. I hate him for doing this. I'll never forgive him.

He sighs and turns to leave the room without any further fight. I watch as my entire world changes and feel physically ill. Our future was ripped away. I'm left with nothing except myself to pick up the pieces and figure out where to go from here.

I make my way back to my bed, climbing in to sit with my back against the headboard before pulling my knees to my chest and letting sobs wrack through my body. I'm not sure exactly how long I sit like this, but the tears have dried by the time I pick my head up. I've lost any ability to cry and have gone completely numb.

With an emotionless gaze, I glance around the room at the very few things I have and decide enough is enough. I grab a backpack and a duffle bag from my closet and fill them up, shoving in all the basic essentials along with a few mementos I can't bear to part with.

My hand slides under my mattress to reach for the cash that I've been stashing away for the last two years. The cash that Greyson and I were supposed to use for our fresh start. When I pull it out, my eyes go wide. There is triple what I had under here before. Greyson must have added to it without me knowing before he ended things. This makes me angry all over again. Fuck Greyson Hayes.

We were supposed to do this together, but I'll be fine on my own. That's what I'm used to anyway. I spent a good chunk of my life before being the one to make sure I had what I needed. It's not like my dead-beat mother ever gave a shit about me after my dad died. All she cares about is her next hit.

I fight off the tears again as I stuff the money into my bag before grabbing the last few things I want, including the picture of me and my dad when I was younger, to shove inside with the cash. With that, I give the room one last glance before walking out the door.

I can't get out of Dune Valley fast enough. It's time to start fresh and focus on myself. I'll never let someone hurt me like this ever again.

Chapter 1
Avalynn - 7 years later

I'm in line at the coffee shop I've been frequenting to get my daily caffeine fix when someone bumps into me. Why can't people just respect your personal space? I've never understood why they always have to stand so close to you. It's not like it will get them served any faster by being right next to you. I turn around, determined to tell whoever this is off, but I freeze.

Standing before me is a man who looks to be just over six feet tall, covered in tattoos, with a ball cap covering the shaggy blonde hair that's pulled into a low bun. I glare at him while also taking him in. He looks clueless about the fact that he just bumped into me. Life has taught me to stand up for myself regardless of the situation, or who puts me in it, so I square up to him.

"Maybe try to take a step back and be better at your situational awareness so you don't bump into people." I turn to give him my back without giving him a chance to respond.

I feel him lean down behind me. His breath hits my neck, and it makes me stiffen. "What if I did it on purpose so I could get a chance to talk to you?"

I whip back around. "If that's the case, I would tell you it's pointless. I'm not interested."

"I don't think that's true. I noticed the way you looked at me when you first saw me," he taunts.

I raise a brow at his audacity. "Listen, buddy. I'm really not in the mood. I haven't had any caffeine yet today. There is no outcome where you and I continue this conversation." I cross my arms over my chest. "Let me guess, you expect us to end up going on a date, and at the end of it, you end up in bed with me? Pass."

He raises a brow. Of course, he thinks I'm trying to play hard to get or something. It's always the same with guys like him. They believe that just because they're tall and decently good-looking, they can push until they get the desired answer. It's beyond infuriating.

A stupid smirk crosses his face. "You're thinking about how cute I am, aren't you?"

Seriously? Who the hell does this guy think he is? I scoff and turn away from him. I'm not even going to dignify that with a response. He's not wrong, though. The line finally moves forward, and it's my turn to order. I take my time ordering my usual iced caramel latte with oat milk, a splash of brown sugar syrup, and a shot of espresso. When the cashier asks for my name, I give them a generic name because I don't need the guy behind me knowing my real name.

They hand me the blueberry muffin I ordered, and I step to the side to wait for my drink. With any luck, it will be ready quickly, and I can find myself a table before the tall and handsome but full-of-himself man tries to talk to me again.

"Rachel," the person behind the counter calls out before setting the drink down. It takes me a second to remember that's the name I gave the cashier. I scurry over, grabbing my latte before heading to a table in the far corner.

Once seated, I pull out my phone to scroll through my emails and lose myself in my work. It's not always easy being a freelance private investigator, but it provides me with the freedom I want and a steady cash flow.

Legally, I'm not an official private investigator, but I'm as close as you can get without the schooling and proper licensing. I've done enough jobs over the last several years that I get most of my clients by word of mouth or through the website I have set up. I didn't think my life journey would lead me across the country to Massachusetts, but here I am.

Morality may say some of the things I do for work may not be right, but I don't give a fuck about that anymore. I'll stalk whoever I have to in order to give my clients peace of mind, carefully, of course. I don't need a repeat of the incident from a few years ago.

My dad would be ashamed of the career choice I've made. He was the sheriff in my hometown and always lived up to the highest standards. He was genuinely loved for his reputation. I'm sure he's rolling in his grave right now. I was his entire world. We did everything we could together when I was younger. I'm fortunate that he taught me how to protect myself, even though I've failed at that over the years.

My heart aches at thoughts of him. He was my best friend for the first ten years of my life and the only semblance of normalcy I had growing up. My mother was always too focused on finding her next high. I watched her struggle for the majority of my life with her addiction. She would be clean for a few months, only to fall back to the drugs again. I think that's why my father always made sure to spend so much time with me. The selfish bitch didn't even bother trying to reach out to me after I left Dune Valley.

I got a call a few months ago from some lawyer telling me that she had passed. The drugs finally won. Apparently, she left me the house in her will. I didn't even realize she had a will. I had him mail me the keys, but I haven't had the courage to show my face in that town again.

Someday, I'll find the strength I need to go back there. Until then, the house and whatever few belongings she didn't sell for drugs will be fine sitting there waiting for me. I make sure to have a friend check in on the place a few times a month to ensure there aren't any squatters who have claimed it as their own.

My phone rings, pulling me from my thoughts, and I look down at a number I don't recognize. I roll my eyes and contemplate whether or not I want to answer it. There's a 50/50 chance of this being either a new client or a bill collector. After dealing with the douche canoe in line, I don't really want to deal with either of these options. Reluctantly, I press the answer button and bring the phone to my ear.

"Hello," I breathe out cautiously.

"Hello, is this Miss Avalynn Blake?" the voice on the phone asks.

"It is. Who is this?"

"Hi, Avalynn. This is Sheriff Wolfe with the Dune Valley Police Department. I hope you're doing well. I was calling to inform you that your presence is required in our office as soon as possible."

My presence is required. That's weird. "I haven't been in Dune Valley in seven years. Why would I need to come in now?"

"You see, as it turns out, you have a half-sister. Her mother passed away this afternoon from a terminal illness that she has been fighting, and you are listed as Chloe's new guardian."

Shock floods through me. A sister? Guardian? I'm barely able to be responsible for myself. How the hell am I supposed to care for someone else on top of that? This would mean I have to go back to that town, where he is, where the memories are.

"You're going to have to explain this to me, Sheriff. You knew my father. Are you saying he had an affair while married to my mother?"

"I know this may be tough to digest. This is why I was hoping I could get you in the office so that we could discuss this in person."

"I can't take care of a kid," I state plainly.

"Chloe is seventeen, so she won't exactly require a ton of care. I know coming back here may not be something that you intended, but I'm asking you to consider it. If you do not take over as Chloe's guardian, we will have to contact the state. I would rather not subject her to the foster system at seventeen."

"She's seventeen?" I question, even though he clearly just said she was. I'm trying to rationalize this.

That would mean she was born when I was eight. Two years before my father died. How could I go all these years without knowing? She must have also just found out about me. Not only did she lose her mother, but she found out she has a mysterious sister. She probably thinks I didn't want anything to do with her.

"Yes, she would only need you to legally care for her for the next few months. I hate to push this on you so fast, but we really need your answer on how you wish to proceed. Chloe is my daughter's best friend, so I don't mind letting her stay with us for the night. If you accept the responsibility of the guardianship, you will need to be back in town within the next 24 hours. You will only need to stay until she turns eighteen or graduates high school and is able to take over the ownership of her mother's house. I will need you to fill out some paperwork, but I'm asking you to please consider this. The last thing this poor girl needs is another life change. You are her only chance at keeping what remains of any normalcy she's known."

I take a moment to think this through. It's only a few months. I can still do some investigating work around my hometown or find something under the table to make extra cash. There are plenty of shady people there, considering it's filled with not only drugs but also gangs.

I try to put myself in her shoes. She just lost her mother. Our shared father is also dead. Now she is facing the possibility of being uprooted from her entire life, oh, and she just found out about me. As much as I hate the idea of returning to that town, I'm not that selfish.

"I guess I'm coming home," I tell him.

"Great, thank you so much, Avalynn. Once you get into town, stop by the police station. We will go over everything else then."

Looks like I'm fucking going back to Dune Valley. I scan the coffee shop to see if the guy who was standing behind me in line is still here. If I'm going back to that town, I'm going to have a little bit of fun first to blow off some steam.

I spot him in the corner, and his eyes meet mine for a moment. They are filled with lust. I lift a finger and curl it, indicating for him to come over to me. He stands and walks over with a huge grin spread across his face. A surge of desire fills me at his obedience.

"It's your lucky day. I need someone to take my emotions out on."

"Is that so? What exactly did you have in mind?"

"My place, minimal talking, and no clothing," I tell him, getting straight to the point.

"I'd ask what made you change your mind, but I don't think you'd bother answering. I'll just take the win."

"Let's go. I live nearby." I reach down to grab his hand and pull him out of the coffee shop.

The idea of going back to Dune Valley has me feeling things I haven't felt in years. I need these feelings fucked out of me. This guy was just easy pickings since he was already interested in having me on my back. I won't be staying here any longer, so I don't give a shit if he knows where I live.

We make the quick three-minute walk to the apartment building just around the corner from the coffee shop, and I enter the code to open the building's doors. He follows behind me quietly, not saying a single word as we slide into the elevator.

The doors slide closed, and when I turn to look at him, he's grinning. He really thinks that he had this in the bag the entire time. I get a slight sense of satisfaction in knowing that I'm using him for my own needs, not the other way around.

"I like it rough," I say just as the elevator dings, indicating we've landed on the fourth floor.

"Well fuck, I wasn't expecting you to be such a spitfire, but I can't say I'm disappointed." He closes the distance between us as we approach my door.

I slide the key in and turn to look at him over my shoulder. "Don't be gentle with me, and don't make me regret inviting you up here. I can make myself come in five minutes or less." I grin and push the door open. "Do you think you can live up to the challenge?" I say as I step inside.

Within seconds, he's on me, kicking the door shut and using one of his arms to pin the top of my body to the wall. "I love a challenge."

He pushes up my black dress, not hesitating to slide his free hand over to my pussy. "So, Rachel? Is that your real name?

"Does it matter? I don't care what your name is, and you don't need to know mine. Now, the clock is ticking, big guy." I narrow my eyes and watch his darken.

His hand slides under my thong, ripping it as he pulls it to the side. Slowly, he slides his fingers through my center, taking in exactly how wet I already am. He wastes no time shoving two thick fingers into me, making me scream out at the intrusion. I clamp hard around them for a moment before letting my body relax to his touch.

"I like the way you sound when you scream." Chills spread over my body at his words. I wasn't expecting him to actually know what he's doing, but it looks like, for once, I may not actually be disappointed at the end of all of this.

He thrusts his fingers in and out of me, curling them at the perfect angle to rub against my sensitive walls. His thumb moves to make small circles over my clit, providing the perfect amount of stimulation my body needs to continually build my desire.

I find myself getting lost in the pleasure when suddenly he sinks to his knees in front of me and throws one of my legs over his shoulder. He pulls the hat off his head, sets it on the floor, and gets right to work. He dives headfirst into my pussy, wasting no time at all. His mouth finds my clit as he slides his fingers back inside me to pick up right where he left off.

I reach down and run my hands through his long hair, gripping it between my fingers to lead him right where I need him. I'm messing up his bun, but I don't care. His tongue moves in rapid motion, flicking over my clit and sending electricity through me with every lick.

I feel the pressure building inside, shocked that not only did he drop to his knees for me, but he also managed to build me so close to what I know is going to be an earth-shattering orgasm. My legs begin to shake. I'm so fucking close.

"More," I moan, making him pick up his pace.

I buck my hips, grinding on his face as the slurping sounds from my wetness fill the room.

"Yes, right there!" I cry out. He growls against me, determined to make me crest that peak.

His mouth closes over my clit, and I lose it. Stars flash across my eyes as my body gives in to the overwhelming sensation. Shock waves pulse from my center down to the tips of my fingers and toes as my pussy clamps around his fingers, and I explode. The pleasure consumes me. He continues his relentless pace until my body works its way through the climax, and he finally pulls his fingers out of me.

He stands in front of me as I struggle to catch my breath and pops both of his fingers into his mouth, making a show of him sucking my juices off. I quickly free myself of all my clothing, watching as he does the same, and walk the few extra steps from the entry hallway to the living room.

He grabs me by the back of the neck before I can make it any further and bends me over the arm of the couch. "If my count was correct, that was definitely less than five minutes. I'll take what I want now."

Fuck, I love it when men actually take control. He kicks my legs apart, and I freeze for a moment, turning my head to look back at him. "Condom," I state firmly, pointing to the bowl perched atop my entertainment center.

"I'm not even going to ask," is all he says before walking over to grab a condom from the bowl. He rips the foil off and slides it right over his cock.

"Good, because I wasn't going to explain. Are you going to talk or fuck me?" I challenge.

"You know, if you keep talking to me like that, I may just fall in love." He laughs, but my body stiffens at the words. I don't fall in love, and the last thing I need is someone getting attached. This is just supposed to be a random fuck to deal with my emotions before heading back to my hometown.

"Relax, it was a joke," he says as he makes his way behind me.

He pushes my head down on the couch and smacks my ass with his free hand. All of the tension in my body slowly resides. I feel him slide his cock up and down my wet center before pushing himself into me. He goes slower than I would like, but I can't ignore the pleasurable feeling of him sliding in, inch by inch.

Once he is fully seated, he grips my hips and pulls back before slamming into me hard. I whimper at the feeling as he continues his assault on my pussy, thrusting in and out, over and over. I find myself chasing that familiar high, the pleasure once again building in my core.

One of his hands releases from my hips, and he slaps my ass again, making me clench around him. He softly rubs the spot before repeating the action, and fuck, it feels so good. I can feel my body getting close.

"Just like that, don't stop," I tell him, making sure he knows just how close I actually am.

"That's it, take all of me, bitch," he says, which shocks me and briefly pulls me out of the moment. His hand slides under me to find my clit, and he pinches it slightly. My pussy convulses around him, and I lose myself to another climax. I hear him grunt and jerk in and out behind me, a telltale sign that he has also just found his release.

When he slides himself out of me, I stand and point over in the direction of the garbage can, indicating for him to toss his used rubber out. I gather his clothes quickly, and when he turns back to face me, I throw them over to him. I've been through this enough times to know the sooner you kick them out, the better. They're less clingy that way.

"Hey, so, um, thanks for all of this, but I think you should head out now. I don't do cuddles."

"You don't do cuddles?" he questions. "Well, I can't say I'm surprised."

THE AFTERTHOUGHT

"Yeah, and I have a good bit of things I actually need to do anyway." I give him a fake smile, pointing over towards the door.

He looks over at me with a mixture of amusement and disbelief. "You're kicking me out?"

"Yeah, I am, so if you could go without it turning into a big thing, that would be great. The sex was surprisingly great, but it was just sex." I watch as he makes his way to the door with minimal protest.

"So, I can't get your number then?" he asks.

"Afraid not," I say as he pulls the door open, laughs, and disappears without a fight. That was actually way easier than I expected.

Chapter 2
Avalynn

One day later, and here I am sitting in my car in front of the house I grew up in, as I try to muster up the courage to go inside. The house is mine. It's been mine for several months now, but I'm really struggling with facing all the memories waiting for me once I cross the threshold.

Time has a way of changing how we see things. As we change and learn through experiences, our thoughts tend to change according to any new information we learn along the way. I find myself thinking not only about my mother, my father, and my childhood but also about Greyson.

When I met him, I thought he was it. I thought he would be the be-all, end-all that you read about in books or see in movies. He wasn't. He left me alone without a care in the world to try and pick up the pieces of my shattered heart. The worst part about it is that he chose to end things. He made me feel like I wasn't enough. Feeling something like that is a pain I wouldn't wish on my worst enemy.

Hurt and pain have a distinct way of making a person grow. It's not always the most positive growth, but it's growth, nonetheless. I wouldn't change a single part of my experience that led me to this point. What he did shaped me into the strong woman I pride myself on being today. That doesn't mean I'll ever forgive him, though.

It's been seven years since I stepped foot in this town, but it hasn't changed one bit. I would have never even considered coming back if it weren't for Chloe, the mysterious new sister I'm now responsible for. I'm still not sure how I never knew about her, considering I spent ten years living two streets over from her. As much as I love my father, I can't help but feel disappointed in him. If he was still alive, I would give him a piece of my mind.

I am definitely not ready to take care of a seventeen-year-old girl, but I couldn't say no. She is my sister, after all. That simple fact alone is enough motivation for me to put forth every ounce of effort to try my best with her. I want to get to know her.

I know it's only a matter of time before Greyson and I run into each other since Dune Valley isn't exactly the biggest town, and I dread it. I have no desire to reconcile things with him, and I'm not the kind of person who needs closure. I got everything I needed all those years ago when he turned his back and walked away from me.

I've heard small bits and pieces about him over the years. When I check in with Wrenly, my childhood best friend, she always makes sure to give me an unsolicited update. Not long after I left, he joined the Crimson Rose, a gang in town. I've tried to tell her countless times to keep the updates about him to herself, but she is convinced we will end up back together one day. She's delusional. Greyson Hayes is the last person on earth I will ever trust my heart with again.

I hear a few screaming kids down the road playing at the park around the corner, and I take a breath to pull myself from my thoughts. The only way through this is to get it over with, so I push open the door and step out of the car. A strange sensation of someone watching me overcomes me, and I glance up and down the street to see if I can locate the watchful eyes. I don't find anything, but people are always watching in this neighborhood. I shake my head and open the back door to grab my bags before making my way to the front of the house.

The grass is overgrown, reaching just below my knees. I'm not the tallest, but at my five-foot height, that would make the grass roughly a foot tall. I'll have to see if I can find someone to cut it for me because I highly doubt my mother left a working lawn mower here.

I make my way up the creaky wooden steps and brace myself for what awaits me inside. My key slides into the lock, and I have to jiggle it a little bit to get it to disengage. Slowly, I push the door open and step inside.

I take in the sight of the old house filled with stale air. Just like the town, the house is completely the same. The puke-green-colored cabinets hang above the cream countertops in the kitchen. The old rust-colored floral couch still sits in the center of the living room next to the burnt orange lazy boy recliner. It's all the same.

I walk into the living room and run my fingers along the familiar cigarette burns filling the armrests of the chair. These were courtesy of one of my mother's boyfriends, who, looking back, I'm not sure was actually her boyfriend. Now that I'm older, I'm fairly sure he was her dealer.

I take a deep breath and make my way down the small hallway at the back of the living room that leads to the bathroom and two bedrooms. Turning to the left, I push open the door to my mother's old room. Piles of clothing lay on the floor, and small nick-nacks line her dresser. The small desk she has in the corner of the room seems to be the only thing that has changed since I left. I leave her room, making my way across the hall to my old bedroom, and hesitate for a moment before opening the door.

When I walk inside, my eyes fall on the full-length mirror in the corner. I'm unable to take my eyes off of myself. I've become a ghost of the girl who used to live here. Tears well up in my deep brown eyes at the realization that nothing here has changed at all except for me.

The room is the same, the house is the same, the town is the same, but the person in the mirror is vastly different. I used to have soft brown hair falling just above my shoulders. Now, I sport long, bright orange hair. The soft waves flow down and fall just below my chest. My skin has a soft tan to it compared to the general, pale look I used to have.

I used to let people in and give them a chance to prove they could be a decent person, but at the end of the day, it was all for nothing. Everyone always ended up hurting me. It took

Greyson leaving me to accept that painful fact. The truth is people are who they are, and it's just a matter of whether or not you can accept them for it. My mom was an addict, my father was a cheater, and the love of my life was a disappointment. It's fine. I'm better off alone.

I turn to the small desk in the corner of my room where I used to do all my schoolwork. Making sure I got good grades was always important to me. I wanted to ensure I had an opportunity to escape this house. The irony of me being back here to live for at least the next few months does not slip past me.

All of the various crystals I used to collect still sit in perfect rows on top of the desk. Greyson used to buy them for me every now and then, even though he had no clue what they meant. I grab a carnelian flame and hold it for a moment before setting it back down. My chest tightens when I pull open the top drawer, and a sorrowful feeling consumes me. In the corner of the drawer sits all the ticket stubs from when Greyson and I used to go on our movie dates.

This town offers little entertainment outside of the small drive-in movie theater and the few baseball fields with overgrown grass. I'm not sure how Greyson was ever able to afford to take me to the movies so often, but it became our thing.

I reach in to pull out the tickets and sit down in the old chair in front of my desk. I flip through them one by one, letting the memories of our date nights ravage my thoughts. The back of each ticket stub has a short little note. The first one I read says, "Grey held my hand." I can't stop the tears from filling in my eyes. I flip over another, and it says, "Grey whispered in my ear, and it gave me the chills." I was so young and innocent.

It's all too much right now, and my emotions are all over the place. Coming back to this town is so much harder than I originally thought it would be. Seeing the house and feeling all the things I'm feeling about my mom and Grey have me wanting to pack up my car and get the fuck out of here.

The alarm on my phone goes off, reminding me why I'm here in the first place. Chloe. I only have to be here until she graduates, I remind myself as I pull out my phone to get in touch with Sheriff Wolfe.

Chapter 3
Greyson

I sit at my desk, bouncing my knee while staring off into the distance. I've been on edge since hearing through the grapevine that Ava was back in town. I don't regret leaving her behind all those years ago, but I was banking on the fact that she would never come back.

I run my hand through my hair, holding the back of my head, before slamming my fist down on the desk. I don't have time to think about her. I have other things I need to be focused on, and quite frankly, I'm not even sure why she's on my mind. She was nothing more than a high school fling. That's what I have to tell myself. Those relationships never withstand the day-to-day struggles of life anyway. We would have never made things work when I told her I was part of the Crimson Rose. I walked away from her, and for good reason.

I've spent the last seven years making a name for myself with the most prominent gang in Dune Valley. We run this town. It hasn't been easy, but I've done a fairly good job of earning the respect and fear I deserve from most people here. Our boss, Knox, may be my brother, but I continuously make sure people know why he has me as his right-hand man.

I've been running with the gang, doing odd jobs here and there for extra cash since I was sixteen. Our family has a pretty steep role in this town, one that Ava thought I had no connection to. Any time she asked, I reminded her that we were planning to run off together. We were going to get away from the life everyone else in this town falls into. We were going to start fresh outside of Dune Valley.

I lied to her, but she would have never completely accepted me for who I actually am and enjoy being. It wasn't always easy keeping the gang life a secret from Ava when we were younger. She spent a ton of time at my house, but I made sure she was always kept out of it.

Sweet, perfect, fucking Avalynn Blake, dating the little brother of the head of the Crimson Rose. That was never something she deserved to be tied to. When things started getting more serious between the two of us, I knew I had to make a decision. It was either her or the gang.

I was too young to step away from the crew. How could I turn my back on my gang, my family? I've become the perfect secret weapon for the Crimson Rose due to my affinity for fire and burning shit to the ground. People fear us because of me, and it keeps them in check. I couldn't leave them.

I had to shut her out. I chose to push her away so that she could have a chance at a normal life outside of Dune Valley. She was supposed to forget about this town and everyone in it, yet she is right back here with the rest of us.

Anger floods through me. She shouldn't be back here. I gave her a chance, and she threw it away. Avalynn Blake will regret the day she decided to step back into my town because that's exactly what Dune Valley is, mine. My brother may be the boss, but his empire would crumble without me.

I hate that she has me here thinking about all this stupid shit. I need to figure out why the fuck she's here and find a way to make her leave. I won't let her get under my skin, and I have absolutely no intention of seeing her. She's already fucking with my head, and I can't stand it.

I clear my thoughts and grab my keys to head out. It's been a while since I've been afforded the opportunity to kill someone. We don't really like to draw that kind of attention to the crew if we don't have to, but there are a few special instances where someone fucks up and crosses a line that the only way to deal with them is by death. Luckily, today is one of those days. I need the outlet.

I wonder if this guy I'm about to end will beg like the last one did before I lit him up and watched him burn to a crisp. I hope he does. That always makes it so much more fun.

The 45-minute drive to the city has me on edge. I haven't had enough caffeine to deal with this day, so I find my way to a drive-thru coffee shop and order a black coffee. When I take the first sip, I'm immediately disgusted by the bitter taste.

I lean back in the seat of my car and run a hand through my hair as her brown eyes fill my thoughts yet again. The memory of the first time Ava made me try her favorite latte flashes in my mind. I hated it and immediately spit it out, making her laugh. She grew up drinking coffee, but I never started drinking it until I met her.

I shake my head. What the fuck is wrong with me? Fuck Ava and all these stupid memories of her. She could have stayed, but she chose to leave. If I told anyone about the thoughts I've been having since hearing she was back in town, they would call me a little bitch. I won't have people thinking differently of me because of a piece of ass I had years ago. I convince myself the reason I'm even having these thoughts at all is because it's been a solid month since I've fucked someone. I'll have to reconcile that.

I pull up to the front of the tall building that was noted on the slip of paper Knox handed me and step out of the car. This asshole is expecting a car service, so I make my way to the back door and patiently wait with my hands placed in front of me, one hand wrapped around my wrist. I made sure to wear a long-sleeve black shirt to hide the tattoos that run down the length of my arms. The hat tilted low on my head covers the main view of my face from any cameras pointing in our direction.

As soon as the man I'm supposed to make disappear leaves the building, I immediately recognize him from the picture Knox showed me. Mr. Myers doesn't pay any attention to me as I open the back door for him. He slides right into the seat, and a grin crosses my face when I close the door, securing him in the car. Poor bastard doesn't even realize he's on a ride to his death.

I make my way around to the front and start the drive. Men like him won't even realize we aren't going the right way. A quick glance in the rear-view mirror confirms my suspicions. He's too consumed with his phone to pay attention to his surroundings. Business is his life, and doing business with the wrong people will be his death.

I don't know the specifics of what he did to garner this sort of resolve from the Crimson Rose. I don't handle much of the business side. I prefer to stay on the side where I get to torture the people that fuck with us. I'm betting this guy's crime has something to do with the money laundering, or hell, maybe he borrowed money he wasn't able to repay. When it comes down to it, I really don't care. He will be dead soon, anyway.

A short 10-minute car ride takes us far enough outside of the city that I feel comfortable enough not to get caught with what I'm about to do. I reach my hand over to the passenger seat to slide it into my bag, pulling out the black balaclava mask and slipping it over my head. The mask really isn't necessary, but it adds to the theatrics.

I grab the bag with the rest of the things I need, tossing it over my shoulder before opening the driver's door and making my way to the back passenger seat. I smile at how easy this is really going to be and open the door for Mr. Myers. He still has no idea we're not sitting outside his lavish home. The dumb fucker would need to take his eyes off his phone and acknowledge the world around him for that.

He steps out of the car and finally glances up, sliding his phone into his pocket. Big mistake. Confusion washes over his face as he looks around at the vacant field in front of us. His body turns to face me, and his eyes widen in realization. He begins to back away from me frantically with one hand raised, like that's going to keep me from getting to him.

I step forward, keeping up with him pace for pace until he trips over his feet and falls backward onto the ground. I tilt my head to the side and just stare down at him for a moment. More theatrics. I twist the bag around my body, reaching my hand in to grab the bottle of fire-starting fluid before twisting off the cap and dousing it all over him. He chooses now to try to scramble back to his feet. Of course, he's unsuccessful.

"What the fuck is going on?" He questions as the fluid splashes all over him. What a stupid question. "I have money. Is that what you want?" He manages to get on his hands and knees, and I kick him in the side, forcing him back to the ground.

"I definitely don't want your money," I tell him with a laugh.

"What do you want then? I can get you anything. Please. You don't have to do this."

Aaaah, there it is. I love it when they beg. I squirt the liquid in his face, and he coughs. "Right now, the only thing I want is to watch you burn to death. Knox said to let you know he's disappointed your business deal didn't work out."

I reach into my pocket and pull out the lighter, holding it where he can see it in my hand. I'm in the mood to play with my prey today. I flick it on and off a few times, watching as the flame appears and disappears.

"Knox? You have the wrong person. Please don't do this," he begs, and I toss the empty lighter fluid bottle at him.

I continue flicking the lighter on and off, kicking him back to the ground every time he tries to stand. "Gary Myers? The Crimson Rose doesn't ever get the wrong person. I can assure you of that." I squat in front of him, bringing the lighter to the ground next to him and igniting the fluid on the ground.

"You're crazy!! I paid him back! He's lying! He must have lost the money." He screams as the ground around him burns. Ah, there it is. I knew it had to do with money. The flames find their way to his clothing rather quickly. The flammable liquid he is drenched in sped up the process a bit.

Mr. Myers is frantic now, rolling around and trying to bat the fire away. All he's managing to do is stroke it to burn faster. The flames consume his body as he screams and cries out for help.

"You should know better than to call Knox a liar. This is my favorite part, you know." I smile behind the mask as it burns through his clothing and begins to scorch his skin.

He desperately tries to roll to put out the flames, but it is useless. Even now, if he did manage to put the fire out, the burns on the length of his body would be enough to kill him. As they consume him, I feel my cock straining in my pants. The smell of burning flesh isn't something I enjoy, but the sight of the flames alone is enough for me to disregard the disgusting stench. He smells especially foul.

Fire has always had the power to draw me in. The way it dances freely is intoxicating. The mixture of the sight of this fire and adrenaline from the kill has me needing to find my release. I've become a bit more unhinged over the last few years.

I reach down to unbutton my pants and pull my cock free and stroke it as I stand next to the scorched body. I tilt my head back in pleasure as I stroke myself over the sight of the orange and yellow blaze dancing over the now-dead Mr. Myers and the ground next to him. "Fuck," I say as I stroke faster. I close my eyes, and Ava fills my mind. I imagine her on her knees in front of me, basking in the orange glow of the flames. She licks the length of my cock before covering it with her wet mouth. The way the fire illuminates her skin in my mind is enough for me to blow my load almost instantly.

I tighten my hold on my cock as I begin to feel the pleasure building up in my body from thinking of her sucking the life out of my cock. My balls tighten, alerting me to my near imminent release. I picture Ava gagging on my cock again, and it's all too much. I lose it all, surrendering to the sensations coursing through my body. My come shoots out all over my hand in spurts as I try my best to ensure none of it falls to the ground. I reach into the bag on my shoulder with my free hand to grab the towel and wipe myself clean.

I'm a bit annoyed that Ava came to mind while I was jerking off. I need to make a point to get her out of my town. Having thoughts of her in my head isn't something I want. The last item I need from the bag is the small fire extinguisher I carry because

I'm a responsible criminal. I'm not about to start a brush fire in the middle of this field, although it would be fun to watch. That would draw too much attention to Mr. Myers' dead body.

Once I'm sure the flames have made their way through the entirety of his flesh to leave behind only charred bones, I pull the pin on the fire extinguisher. I feel disappointed as I grip the handle to spray the contents and douse out the fire. Just like always, the remains of the piece of shit appear to be black like coal.

With that, I clean up everything possible, ensuring there is nothing left that would connect me to the crime scene if it's ever found. Who knows how long this sorry piece of shit will be out here before someone finds him.

Chapter 4
Avalynn

I park my car along the street across from the Dune Valley Police Station, giving myself one last moment alone before everything changes. When I walk into the building, I'll be walking out responsible for someone besides myself. I'm still not entirely sure what this dynamic is going to look like, but here goes nothing.

I cross the street and climb the stairs to the police station. The door sticks as I struggle to pull it open, and I curse under my breath. A smiling face appears on the other side of the door, pushing it open for me.

"Sorry about that. We have someone coming to fix it later today." He steps to the side, and I slip into the building, anxiously twiddling my fingers. I'm not sure who he is, but there is nobody else around. He's wearing a blue pinstripe shirt tucked into beige khakis. The lines along the sides of his eyes and forehead tell me he has to be close to his mid-40s, but I never know for sure. Judging by the way he's looking at me, I have a feeling he knows exactly who I am.

"Thank you. Can you tell me where I can find Sheriff Wolfe?" I glance up at him cautiously.

"You're looking at him, young lady. You must be Avalynn." He gestures for me to follow him down the hallway, which I'm guessing leads to his office.

"Yes. It's nice to see you, Sheriff." I say nervously. I'm so on edge with the idea of meeting Chloe.

"Your sister should be here soon. I'm having my wife bring her, but I wanted to have a few moments alone with you first to go over some things."

"Absolutely."

We step into his office, and my eyes find the gray chair seated across from the L-shaped oak desk in the corner of the room. I head over to the chair and lower myself into it, waiting to see what exactly he needs from me. He takes a seat in his chair and grabs a substantial stack of papers out of the drawer, pushing them toward me. A large birthmark in the shape of a moon between his thumb and pointer finger catches my eye.

"There are a few papers you will need to sign in order to assume guardianship if you wouldn't mind," he says, gesturing towards them.

"I was kind of hoping I could meet Chloe before signing anything," I confess, which sounds pretty stupid now that I think about it. It's not like it would change anything.

"I'm sorry. I was under the assumption from our phone conversation that you would be taking her in. We fast-tracked this process due to the special circumstances. Are you unsure whether you will be caring for her?" He gives me a condescending look.

"No, that's not it at all. I was just thinking maybe she wouldn't want to end up with me."

"I can assure you that my wife, daughter, and I all talked with Chloe last night, and she is excited to meet you. She thinks the two of you will hit it off just fine." He tries to reassure me, and it relaxes my mind a bit. "Are you ready to sign then?"

"Yes, sorry. This is all just a lot to take in. I didn't think my father was capable of keeping a secret like this from me," I confess.

"Even the best people have secrets. I'm sure you have a few of your own as well," he says while smiling over at me.

"That may be true, but those secrets don't include an entire family member I never knew about." I shake my head. "Can I have a pen?"

He hands the pen over to me to sign away the next few months of my life. Fuck. I really hope this all works out and the two of us don't butt heads too much. I skim through the first few pages of the stack in front of me before deciding it's just too much legal jargon and sign the last few without even bothering to look at them. The sooner I can meet Chloe, the better. My nerves are basically eating me alive with anticipation. I sign the last page and set the pen on the top of the pile, pushing the stack back towards him.

"Thank you so much, Avalynn." He takes the stack of papers and sticks them in a large folder. As if on cue, a phone rings from his pocket, interrupting whatever exchange was about to continue between us. I thought he had questions for me. "Yes, please go ahead and bring her in. We have been waiting for you to arrive." He hangs up on who I assume is his wife since he said his wife would be bringing Chloe here.

"That's it? I just sign a few papers?" I ask.

"That's it. Legally, you now have guardianship over Chloe until she turns eighteen. You aren't required to stay here in town, but after what she's been through, I would highly suggest staying here to prevent her from any further trauma. In the last few days, she lost her mother and learned about a sister. I don't know how she would handle the prospect of being uprooted from her friends and hometown when she is so close to graduating."

"I don't have any intention of making her leave town," I respond, my tone shorter than usual.

Before any further words can be exchanged between us, there is a soft knock on the door. Both of our heads turn towards the doorway when two people enter the room. Immediately, I stand to take a step towards them and reach my hand out to introduce myself.

"Hi, I'm Avalynn. It's nice to meet you," I say while shaking the hand of the first woman. She appears to be older, likely Mrs. Wolfe. Her long brown hair has a few grays sprinkled in here and there, and the bags under her brown eyes suggest she's had quite a few sleepless nights.

"It's nice to meet you, Avalynn. I'm Susan Wolfe," she says briefly before stepping aside to reveal the girl behind her.

The girl steps forward, and I reach my hand out to her, just as I did to Susan. "Hi, I'm Avalynn, but you can call me Ava. I'm so happy to meet you."

She smiles and shakes my hand, although I can tell she is a bit apprehensive. "I'm Chloe. So, you're the secret sister, then?"

I wasn't expecting her to be so blunt, but I suppose the two of us have that in common. Hopefully, that won't be an issue going forward. Her blue eyes meet mine, and a slight furrow creases her brow. She doesn't trust me. I don't blame her.

"Yeah, I suppose I am. Your mom never mentioned anything about me or my dad at all?"

She scoffs at that statement. "Nope. It was always just the two of us. She said he left her high and dry when she found out she was pregnant. We only ever needed each other anyway."

"I'm sorry you never got to meet him."

"Yeah, so kind of him to leave my mother to raise me on her own."

I can't tell her she's wrong for feeling like this. If I were in her shoes, I would likely feel the same. We are both angry at the same man but for different reasons. I had him up on a pedestal, but he proved with his secret that he never deserved to be there. I wish he were still alive so I could introduce her to him, and we could sit down to ask him why he did what he did. Did he even know about her? I guess it doesn't matter much now.

I turn to Sheriff Wolfe. "Is there anything else you need from us, or can we go ahead and get going? I'd really like to have some time to get to know Chloe. I'm sure she has a ton of questions for me, too."

"Not particularly," she mumbles under her breath. Luckily, it's not loud enough for Sheriff Wolfe to hear.

"Chloe, are you good to head out with Avalynn?" he asks her. "You know if you ever have any problems, Susan and I are only a phone call away. You're more than welcome to come over to see Andrea any time."

"Thanks. I think I'll be fine, though," she says with a smile.

"Don't sweat it, kiddo." He steps in to give her a quick hug before pulling back and turning to face me again. "You two are free to go on your way. Do not hesitate to call me if you have any issues."

"Thank you. Enjoy the rest of your day. It was nice to meet you, Susan," I say before stepping out of the room and making my way back down the hallway. I glance over my shoulder to see Chloe following silently behind.

When we get to the car, I pull out my phone to shoot a quick text to Wrenly, letting her know that the entire day has been like ripping off a giant band-aid. I ask if she is able to stop over at the house soon. It would be nice to see her. The last time I saw her was nearly two years ago when she flew out to meet me for a weekend at one of the jobs I was doing in Miami.

"You're not supposed to text and drive," the teenage voice next to me says.

I ignore the hostility in her tone. I'm sure she must be going through some rough emotions with her mom just passing away. I finish up my text and set my phone in the cup holder.

"Do you need to grab anything from your house before I take you to mine to settle in?"

I see the way her jaw clenches when I mention stopping at her house. I recognize the pain in her face. I guarantee she hasn't been inside the house since her mom passed away.

"I don't want to go there. Can't you just take me to buy a few things?" she asks.

I really wish I could, but all the money I have is needed to keep us afloat until I can find a way to bring in a steady income. The savings I have need to be used for household things and food.

"I'm really sorry, but I don't have that kind of extra cash right now. For now, I can let you borrow some of my clothes if you want."

Her brows furrow and she raises one of them. "If what you're wearing is any indication of what the rest of your closet looks like, I think I'll just suck it up and go get some of mine." She pauses for a second. I can see why she doesn't want to wear my clothes. My style is mostly black, and hers seems a lot lighter. "I'll give you the directions. Just drive."

I nod my head and start the car, heading back toward my mother's house. The Sheriff told me that she only lived a few streets over from me, so I'll wait for her to point me down the right street. We make a few turns, and I pull to a stop outside of a small brick house. It's not much, but it's in way better shape than my house. The front of the house has all kinds of pretty flowers and bushes landscaped around it.

I turn off the car and glance at Chloe to find her staring blankly up at the house. It's so similar to the look I had earlier today when I drove up to my house.

"I get it," I say softly. "I don't know the specifics of how your mother passed, but I know that look. It's going to be weird going in there for the first time, knowing that everything is different now, but I'll be there with you for support if you need it."

"I just need a few minutes, that's all," she says while letting out a breath.

"Take all the time you need," I say, hoping that just maybe she will let me in, even a little bit. Having someone to talk to about some of this would be nice. Someone else who knows what it feels like to be alone in the world.

I hate that I even have that thought. She's seventeen. She shouldn't ever feel alone. We sit here for a few more minutes before she unbuckles her seatbelt and looks over at me with a stone face.

"I need you to carry some of my stuff. Let's get this over with." She opens the car door and slams it shut before hearing my reply.

Chapter 5
Avalynn

I run across the street to follow Chloe down the sidewalk to the house, annoyed. She slips the key into the lock and freezes momentarily before turning the handle and stepping inside. She doesn't even hesitate to run up the stairs and disappears from my sight.

I'll just wait here. I look around the house and take it all in. It's nothing high-class, but you can definitely tell that she was raised with more opportunities than I was.

None of her furniture has burn marks on them. You can tell everything is in newer condition, and someone actually spent money to ensure there is an equal level of both comfort and style. The lamps on the end tables match, and the TV is one of the biggest ones I've ever seen in Dune Valley.

There are throw pillows on the couch, and a recliner that complements it, and matching blankets laid over the backs of both pieces of furniture. It feels warm here, safe, and very homey.

Pictures line the walls of each room that I wander through. Different versions of Chloe stare back at me as I take her in over the years. There are a few of her in cute dresses with pretty bows on the top of her head and others with her in fancier dresses. It looks like she had a happy and fulfilling childhood despite all of her circumstances. She grew up in a single-parent household with a terminally ill mother, but this home screams love.

We both had our own reality checks that forced us to grow up faster than we should have. I was dealing with my mother's addiction, and Chloe was dealing with her mother's illness.

I walk down the small hallway, looking at the pictures of her and her mother smiling back at me. Both of them have the same shade of auburn hair. You can tell in these pictures that as Chloe grew older, her mother grew weaker. I can't help but notice that Chloe bears a striking resemblance to my father in her younger pictures. My heart aches a bit, seeing him in her.

"HEY!" I hear her yell down the stairs. I make my way back over to them and glance up at her.

"Uh, yeah?" I question.

"Are you going to keep creeping around in my house, or are you going to come up here and help me get my stuff? I thought you said you wanted to make this quick."

"You ran up there and didn't say anything. I just assumed you wanted me to wait down here. I didn't want to invade your privacy," I tell her.

"Aren't you invading my privacy by wandering around my house?" she says, and I must admit this girl is too smart for her own good.

I make my way up the carpeted stairs and follow her into a small room with the cutest color of lilac painted on the walls.

Her room is not what I expected at all. From her attitude toward me, I expected it to be more harsh and jagged around the edges, but it's the exact opposite.

There are a few stuffed teddy bears sitting on her bed that look to be about as old as she is. The nightstand next to her bed houses a lamp the same shade as the walls, with crystals dangling from below it. In the corner of the room, a small table holds a vinyl record player and a bunch of records.

She catches me looking at it and walks over to the record player, pulling the tonearm over to play it. Music fills the room, and I freeze in place. My eyes go wide. Out of all the things she could have possibly played, it had to be You Give Love A Bad Name by Bon Jovi.

Chills spread over my body, and my heart rate instantly increases. My eyes well up, and tears threaten to fall from them. Panic begins to fill my chest, and I'm pulled into memories of that day—one of the many days that shaped who I have become.

His eyes bulged out of his skull when he saw me with my camera in the corner of the window. It was a stupid mistake on my part. I know it was sloppy, but it was the anniversary of my father's death, and I wasn't in the right brain space to be at the best of my ability that day.

I watched through the corner of the window as his eyes turned cold and brutal. He stomped out of the house, and before I could gather my things to run away, he raced toward me. He grabbed me by my throat with his fingernails digging into my skin. I dropped my camera as he kicked my feet out from under me and slammed me on the ground.

He straddled my waist, and my fingers clawed at his hand on my throat as I struggled to breathe. His cell phone rang in his pocket. You Give Love A Bad Name by Bon Jovi played around us as I continued to struggle beneath his grip on my throat. The song continued to play, but he didn't answer the call. He was too preoccupied with trying to make sure I paid the price for snooping on him.

"You little fucking bitch. Did my wife hire you to follow me? Did she think it would be that easy to get rid of me? Sending some pathetic girl to trail me and try and catch me in a fuckup." Spit from the intensity of his words came down to coat my face.

The sound of my phone falling to the floor pulls me from the memory. My hands are violently shaking, and tears freely flow from my eyes. I run over to the record player to stop the song from playing and place my hands on either side of the small table to try and calm my breathing.

"Are you okay?" Chloe asks cautiously.

I shake my head no and turn to run past her, picking up my phone on the way out of the room. I have to get out of this house and get some fresh air to gather myself. I'm supposed to be keeping my shit together, but here I am, falling apart the first day we meet. I've been doing so good about not letting the memories from that day affect me.

I push open the front door and flop down on the top step of the porch stairs, letting myself stare out into the distance.

Taking a few deep breaths, I let the cool spring air fill my lungs. I shut off all my emotions because feeling what I felt that day is too much. I can't go back to those memories. I'm not that girl anymore. I'm stronger now.

"Hey," Chloe says before sitting on the stairs next to me. "Clearly, you're not okay. You don't have to tell me what happened, but at least come back inside. The people around here are too nosey for you to be sitting out here."

My eyes look up and down the row of houses lining the street for the first time, and she's right. Several people stopped what they were doing in their front yards and are now peering in our direction. They aren't even trying to hide the fact that they're staring.

"Okay," I say, standing up and walking back inside with her. She makes her way into the kitchen and grabs a glass from one of the cabinets. I don't miss how the glasses all match one another, unlike the cups in my house that are all mixed.

She goes to the faucet to fill the cup with cold water before coming over to me and handing it to me. This isn't the same cold-hearted girl she was earlier.

"I recognize it, you know," she says as I take the glass from her, looking at her with a questioning look. "The trauma response. My mom used to have episodes, too."

I look at her, refusing to let her know of this potential weakness in me. "I'm fine. Let's go get your stuff so we can get you settled into my house."

Part of me knows it's a mistake not letting her in when she is giving me an olive branch, but I don't ever plan on telling her, or anyone, about that day. Talking about it makes it more real. The scar on my chest aches, and I bring my hand up to rub it briefly before walking over to place the empty glass in the sink.

"Come on." I leave the kitchen and back up the stairs to her room. She follows behind me silently until we enter her room. When I turn to face her, she crosses her arms in front of me.

"You go ahead and keep your shit to yourself. Don't expect me to be willing to open up to you if you aren't going to do the same. I was just trying to be nice." She grabs the backpack filled with clothes off her bed and tosses it in my direction. I reach out to grab it, bending at the knees with its weight. What the fuck is even in here? "I can handle the rest. You're more than welcome to go wait in your car."

I roll my eyes at her, refusing to be told what to do by a seventeen-year-old girl. I pull the strap of the backpack over my shoulder and stand there, watching as she walks over to the closet to slide the door open.

She grabs a duffle bag from the floor and starts filling it before looking over her shoulder at me. "Will I have a closet at your house, or do I need to take these off the hangers?"

"There's a closet. I'm putting you in my mom's old room. I haven't packed up all of her stuff yet, but I'll get enough of it in boxes today. You can put your clothes in there, and I'll do my best to pack up the rest throughout the week."

"Your mom's room?" she questions.

"Yeah, she died a few months ago."

She starts laughing hysterically. I side-eye her, wondering how the hell me saying my mother died could possibly be amusing.

"So dead moms club then. Well, actually, orphan club because our dad is dead too." She shakes her head and pulls the clothes out of her closet, leaving the hangers on them and stacking them in a pile on her bed. I'm still not entirely sure how I feel about her acknowledging the fact that we share a father.

"Alright, this should be enough for now. I don't have to bring everything, do I? Can you bring me back here if I need to grab something else?" She throws the duffle strap over her shoulder and grabs the stack of clothes off the bed.

"Of course, I can bring you back anytime you need anything."

She nods, and we make our way out of the house and back to the car. Getting her set up in my mother's old room should be fun. I wonder how she is going to react to my house, considering how vastly different hers is from mine.

We make the short drive, and I park in front of my, well, our new home for now. "Come on. I'll give you a quick tour, and then I'll leave you to get comfortable."

We grab her things out of the car and step inside. I eye her carefully as she looks around at the condition of the furniture and just overall cold feeling of this house. She keeps her opinions to herself, but I can read them all over her face. She doesn't want to be here. I give her a quick tour of the small home, and she just takes it all in without saying a word.

We walk down the small hallway toward the bedrooms, and I push open the door to the bathroom on the right before opening the door to my room. She peers in, letting curiosity get the best of her briefly, and then she looks back at me. We step across the hall to open the door to my mother's old room. Chloe's new room.

"Don't you want the bigger room?" She turns to me and asks.

"It's fine. I don't really want to move all of my stuff. You can have the bigger room."

"Good, because clearly I have more stuff than you do." She remarks before dropping the handful of things she's carrying onto the bed.

I shake my head as I step in front of the closet, slide open the door, and pull the hanging clothes out to make space for Chloe's things.

"I'll get the rest out of your way tomorrow. Make yourself comfortable and let me know if you have any special requests for dinner. I'll be across the hall if you need anything."

I leave the room with my mother's clothes and walk back into mine, tossing them into a pile in the corner and flopping down on the hard mattress. It's been a long ass day already, and there's still half of it left. I just need some time to let my brain relax for a bit. I pull out my phone and scroll through some social media accounts before quickly getting bored and texting Wrenly. Maybe she can come over and ease the tension between me and my new sister.

She doesn't answer my text. It's weird, actually. I haven't heard from her all day. We aren't as close as we used to be, but I was really hoping that she would find a way to make time to see me today. She better have a damn good excuse.

Chapter 6

Greyson

"Hey, bro. Are you ready for tomorrow night?" Kai asks as he steps into the kitchen to open up the refrigerator. He grabs the half gallon of milk before snagging his go-to bowl and box of cereal from the counter next to it.

Kai has been like a brother to me over the years. He was the first person who really took me under his wing when I started to officially run with the crew. He may look big and mean, but deep down, he's a softie. He's a few inches taller than me, and I find myself having to look up at him even though I'm 6'2.

He pulls his hair back into a ponytail, and I roll my eyes at him. His hair is his pride and joy right now. One of the other guys in the crew bet him that he couldn't grow his hair out to be long enough to cover his nipples when it's pulled over his shoulders. Of course, he can't resist a bet. It's been two years since he's cut it, and I'd say we've got about another year before he wins the bet. He's committed; I'll give him that.

"I told you I didn't want to make tomorrow a big deal. I don't know why you insisted on throwing something together." I roll my eyes with annoyance.

"It's your birthday, asshole. Of course, we're going to use that as an excuse to throw a banging ass party. Knox can take advantage of the crowd and sell some extra product. That's less the crew has to worry about pushing out the rest of the week."

He's got a point. Parties in Dune Valley have been known to be a bit extreme. What starts as a small get-together always ends up turning into nothing but drugs, sex, alcohol, and loud music. The cops don't bother us because they don't want to deal with the paperwork.

Most of them are on our payroll anyway, save the few that the Cobras managed to get in their pockets. Nobody in Dune Valley thinks they are going to stop the gangs, drugs, or overall lifestyle of this place. The few people who did decide to make an effort to join the police force only did so in order to have their fancy badges and a false sense of security.

The only person we really seem to have any issues with outside of the Cobras is Sheriff Wolfe. He's got his panties in a bunch lately because his daughter started hanging around the gang. He should have raised her better if he didn't want her involved in this lifestyle.

"Fine. A party. What did you have in mind?" I ask because with Kai, I really never know what to expect.

"Nah, it's nothing crazy like that. Just a regular party. I'll grab a few kegs and cups. We can make everyone pay $2 for a cup, and we're golden."

"You're managing the funds this time, then. Last time, you had what's-his-face do it, and he skimmed a bit off the top for himself. I ended up having to beat his ass for Knox."

Kai raises his hands in defense. "I'll handle everything. All you have to worry about is having a little fun and letting loose. You seem super fucking uptight today. What's going on with you?"

I'm not about to tell him that I've been on edge because the girl I dated seven years ago is back in town, and it's fucking with my head. No, if I tell him that, he will for sure call me a pussy.

"You're not all up in your feels about getting older, are ya? I hardly think twenty-six is that big of a deal. You're still young," he jokes and pours the milk into his lucky charms.

"Do not even try to talk to me about age while you're eating Lucky Charms," I joke.

"Hey, don't come for the charms. They're magically delicious." He laughs and shovels a spoonful into his mouth.

"I gotta run and do a quick job for Knox. Do you think you can handle all the party shit without my input?"

"I've got you. It's already planned anyway." A sly smile crosses his face as he shoves more cereal into his mouth. Milk drips down his chin, and I shake my head at him.

"Keep it simple. I don't need any dumb shit like a cake or anything. The less attention there is on me, the better." I step over to the counter to grab my keys.

"Come on, we gotta have cake. What's a birthday party with no cake?" He brings the bowl to his mouth to drink some leftover milk.

"Don't waste your money on that shit," I say before walking out of the door and closing it behind me. I know there's no point in arguing with Kai. He will do whatever he wants. Nobody will convince him otherwise, and nobody fucks with him. It's one of the reasons I have him as a roommate. That, and he has a steady flow of income that keeps the rent paid and the lights on. It means I can funnel more of my money into my savings.

I pull open the door to my car and make my way to Adam's Garage. It's where a lot of the crew spends their downtime. Our home away from home. We have no clue who the fuck Adam is or why this place was named after him. One of the guys managed to buy it from someone he knows, and it became a safe haven for the Crimson Rose. It also helps that we can launder our drug money through an actual business.

Knox told me to meet him here for a job because he doesn't trust any of the others to handle it. I don't usually handle this part of the business anymore, but this one is important. I enter the garage bay, saying hi to a few of the guys before turning and making my way to the office. I know that's where Knox is going to be. When I push open the door, he is leaning back in the chair with his feet propped up on the desk. He doesn't look like he belongs here. The ambiance and general vibe of the room is dirty and unkempt, but he is wearing a navy suit with the jacket folded carefully over the computer in front of him. He always dresses so formally as opposed to my usual black T-shirt and jeans.

I shut the door behind me and sit in one of the chairs in front of the desk. He's wrapping up his phone call, so I pull my phone out to clear my messages and shut it off to place it on the desk for him to see. Knox may be my brother, but he doesn't trust anyone. He always says that cell phones are the easiest way to betray people.

He nods at me in approval, and I roll my eyes. His blue eyes roam over me when he hangs up, eyeing me up and down. If I were anyone else, I'd be freaking out. I'd be wondering if this was my last day, but because he's my brother, I know he's fucking with me to try and make me nervous.

"Cut the theatrics. What do you need from me?" I ask him, and he laughs.

He runs his hand through his well-kept beard and raises a brow. "You're so sure I'm messing with you."

"Come on, Knox. I have other things I could be taking care of right now. What's going on?"

"You always have to be such a buzzkill. We have a new client that could change everything. I need you to meet with him and give him a sample of the product."

"This isn't something one of the other guys can do?"

"I don't want any of the other guys knowing who he is. I can't risk word getting out and the Cobras swooping in to take him from us. We need this, Grey."

"Is there something else going on that I'm not aware of? Why would one deal be a make-or-break thing? We have enough of a stronghold to keep the Cobras out of our territory," I say.

Knox sighs and puts his feet down on the ground. He scoots into the desk and places his elbows on it with his hands clasped in front of him. "We lost a big client to the Cobras last week. I didn't want to make a big deal about it because I knew I had this lined up, and I think I can get them back. If this doesn't go well, we could really be in trouble though. Alec has been pushing his men closer and closer to our territory. Without the strong backing this client brings in, we may lose our edge to them."

I run a hand through my hair. "Fuck, you should have told me."

"Look, Greyson, I know you've done well over the last few years. You've more than earned everyone's respect, but the Crimson Rose is my responsibility. I am not obligated to disclose everything to you. You're important to the organization. You provide a specialty to your torture that nobody has been able to match thus far, but that doesn't mean you're privy to all the information."

Leave it to Knox to put me back in my place and make me feel worthless. I've always had to live in his damn shadow. "Understood," I tell him, not wanting to even bother wasting my breath. He's right. He is the leader of the Crimson Rose. I have no desire to lead this crew anyway.

"Good, now that we've got that all squared away, here are the details of the meetup. You will meet with him tomorrow near the coffee shop in town and follow him to the nearby park. Once he knows for sure that you are alone, he will ask you for the bag, and you will hand it over to him. Make sure he knows that we will be professional and discreet about his business. And for the love of fuck do not say or do anything that would make him want to back out of a deal with us." He sits back in his chair and stares me down.

"I can handle it. Is there anything else I need to know?"

"You may be a bit surprised by who shows up."

"What the fuck is that supposed to mean? Who am I meeting?" I ask, concern lacing my tone.

"Just make sure you're on your best behavior. This is important, Greyson. Do not fuck this up."

"Relax. I've got it under control." I'm not really sure why he's being such a whiny bitch about this.

"One more thing. Your ex-girlfriend. The one who used to come over to the house all the time before you officially joined the gang. She's back in Dune Valley." He pauses to take in my expression and get a read on me. I don't give him anything to go off of. I manage to keep my face blank.

"And?" I question.

He eyes me cautiously. "Is this going to be a problem?"

"Why would it be a problem? I haven't seen her in seven years." The defensiveness in my tone seeps through.

"Yeah, but you also haven't had another serious partner since she left. Why did she leave anyway?" he asks, not knowing that she left because of me. I ended things, not her.

"Does it really fucking matter why she left? My dating life is not your concern. I've never let it get in the way of business before, and I'm not about to start now. I haven't been with anyone because I don't fucking want to be with anyone."

He throws his hands up, laughing at how annoyed I am. "Don't shoot the messenger. I just wanted to make sure she wouldn't be an issue."

"She's not an issue," I state plainly. "She doesn't mean anything to me."

"Good. So, tomorrow. Get this taken care of for me, and I'll get you that fancy new shed we talked about."

I raise a brow at him. I've been asking him to find me a place to torture my victims for years. All of the gang's usual businesses are too flammable to risk me using a blowtorch in them, so doing all my work outside has had to suffice. It really limits my abilities, considering Mother Nature isn't always on my side. I've been itching to have a place for myself, and this is finally my chance.

"I'll get it done." I nod briefly and then stand up to make my way back to the car. Tomorrow will be easy. I'll get it done and finally have my nice new torture shed because of it.

Chapter 7
Avalynn

It's early, too early, but I'm happy this little shit town actually has a small coffee shop now. This is one of the few uncomplicated things to come from this week. Between Chloe and my quickly draining savings account, I really need to get it together and figure out my finances. I hate the idea of getting a concrete job here. The reality is, if I'm staying for a few months, I might as well have a steady income.

I bet one of the local bars is looking for a bartender. Drunk assholes aren't my favorite people to deal with, but it beats being a server. At least in a bar, I can tell people to fuck off without being at risk of losing my job. I make a mental note to make the effort to go talk to the bar owners. My PI work isn't going to be bursting with possibilities here. I doubt the people of this town want someone snooping around in their business. I had to ditch the last job I was doing in Massachusetts to come back. Maybe I'll get lucky, and someone will reach out with something relatively close to town.

I grab the ponytail from my wrist and tie up my hair. I hate how it feels when it rubs along the back of my neck sometimes. My roots have started to grow in, and the brown at the top of my scalp is more visible than I'd like. I just don't have the extra cash to buy the dye to freshen it up right now. Another reason I need to get a more permanent job.

I feel a sudden urge to look over my shoulder and see a familiar ghost cross my path. He doesn't notice me because he's focused on something else, but there he is—the man who broke me all those years ago. My stomach sinks at the sight of him. He looks so much different than before, but there's no mistake—it's Greyson.

I feel sick. I hate him for what he did. One night, we were in bed confessing our love for each other while making a plan to leave this town, and the next, he left me. I thought I did something wrong. I cried over him for months. I tried to find another guy to swoon over, but nobody could ever live up to him. Despite what he did to me, he is the only guy I've ever let breach my walls to see the real me.

His gaze trails my way, and I catch sight of those beautiful blues that I used to get lost staring into. He doesn't see me. He looks right past me before turning his head and focusing on someone walking in front of him. I can't see exactly who it is from where I'm sitting. I tilt my head to the side, narrowing my eyes to watch as he trails the person with just enough distance to ensure that he won't be caught.

He turns the corner of the street at the end of town and disappears from my line of sight. I quickly gather up my things, toss my coffee in the trash, and chase after him. I'm not sure why I feel the need to confront him at this moment. After all these years of not seeing him, I can't help but follow him. It's been seven years, but what better time than now to rip off the band-aid and tell him he's a massive piece of shit for dumping me the way he did.

I turn the same corner he went around, but nobody's there. This street has a few closed businesses, and the end of it leads straight into the state park. My eyes trail around the small parking lot of the park to see which way he could have gone. There's nothing else out here except a path through a line of trees that leads into the woods.

A feeling in my gut tells me this is a bad idea, but I ignore it and walk down the path between the trees. My steps are quiet as my eyes dart around to take in my surroundings. This has to be the way he went, but there's nothing around. I stop in my tracks to listen for any kind of sound but hear nothing. What the fuck am I even doing out here?

There are a few vacant buildings scattered around the wooded area of the park. Tiny little one-story log cabins that I don't think were ever really lived in. I peer around a few of them, but nothing stands out. I spend the next few minutes searching for some kind of clue that he came this way, but come up empty-handed. Finally, I give up and decide I've put way too much effort into finding someone that I shouldn't give a shit about, especially after what he did to me.

As I make my way back down the path, I lose my footing on a loose rock on the cobblestone walkway. My body flails forward, and I land on my hands and knees, scraping them off of the hard surface. Pain shoots through me while I try to assess the damage. This is so sloppy. When I try to stand, my ankle throbs, so I crawl to the side of the path near a tree.

There are small rocks in the bloody scrapes on my knees. I pull my sleeve down over my hand to try and wipe the debris off, wincing at the pain when I swipe over the cuts. My left hand has a pretty good slice in my palm, and I look down curiously as blood drips out of it. I stand and place a hand on the tree to try and steady myself.

My vision begins to blur again as the memories of a night long ago threaten to pull me in. Blood has been a trigger for me since that night, and I haven't felt safe since. Before I can stop it, the thoughts consume me, and I'm right back there with him.

The blade came down across my chest, cutting my shirt open and slicing me down the center of my body. I felt the warm blood almost instantly, pooling around the cut.

I tried my best to kick around and free myself from him as he held the knife above me, watching as the blood flowed freely from me. He laughed at my attempt to speak. His hand tightened further on my neck, threatening to completely cut off my airway.

"You can't report back to my wife if you're dead, you fucking bitch," he yelled as I felt the blade slice into my stomach this time. I was too worried about trying to breathe to focus on the pain of each cut. Over and over, he cut into the skin of my stomach and chest, marking me up. The wetness of the blood was all I could feel as the tears flowed freely down my cheeks. Time seemed to go on forever, an endless loop of suffering in hell.

I'm yanked from my memories in the blink of an eye when something pushes me roughly against a tree, face first. I try to push back when a hand wraps around my ponytail. My head is shoved into the bark with enough force to keep me from turning to look at my assailant. I grimace as the rough surface scrapes against my face.

A body fills the void behind me as someone presses into me, holding me in place. Based on the massive hard-on pressed into my back, I know it's a man. I try to breathe, remembering that staying calm might be my best way out of this mess. I just have to wait until his guard is down, and he will loosen his hold. A man is just a man at the end of the day, and there are countless ways to make them fall.

He leans into me, and I take in his scent—burnt leather with a hint of mint. The kind of mint that comes from those little chocolates. It's so familiar, but I can't explain why. I feel him inch down further until he is close enough to whisper in my ear. "You thought you were being sly, didn't you? Like a little shadow."

I swear I recognize that voice. I shake my head and open my mouth to tell him to fuck off, but a hand covers it, silencing me. His nose trails along my neck like he's breathing me in before grinding himself further against my back and letting out a growl.

"This is my town. You shouldn't have been sticking your fucking nose in where it doesn't belong."

I push back against him to try and get him off of me, but it doesn't help. It's hard to get the right angle with the way he has me pinned up against the tree. He pulls the hand from my mouth and manages to grip both of my wrists, pinning them against my back.

A deep chuckle erupts from his chest. "Did you want to play, little shadow?"

"Get off of me!" I yell out, but the only response I receive is laughter. Fuck him. If he thinks I'm going to be meek, he's wrong. He got lucky and caught me off guard when I was lost in thought; that's all this is.

I catch sight of him for the first time from the corner of my eye, and nothing but pure rage flows through me. "Greyson! Get the fuck off of me!" I yell out, and he freezes.

He releases my hands and whips me around so that my back is now pinned against the tree, a look of shock painted across his face. "Ava?" he questions.

"Yes, you fucking asshole. Now get your hands off of me."

"What the hell did you do to your hair?" His eyes narrow.

I didn't start dyeing my hair this color until after I left. I needed a change, a new identity, and this became part of that. I don't owe him any kind of explanation, though. He's changed just as much as I have. His hair is still long on the top, but it's less styled now, as if he just lets it lie wherever he wants it to. His once bare face now has a shade of stubble around the entire lower half. Tattoos cover almost every part of his exposed arm, and I find myself wondering where else he has them. What do each of them mean? Do they even have a meaning? One in particular catches my eye, a flaming rose. A stark reminder of who he is now.

"You left me and joined a gang. That's where you had to go all those years ago. What a joke." I laugh right in his face like it's the most outrageous thing I've ever said out loud.

"Keep fucking laughing at me." His jaw tics.

"I spent years being upset over you, and you shut me out so you could run around with a bunch of dudes in a gang. It's funny."

His eyes narrow, and I catch the moment when the look in them changes from curiosity to pure hatred. He shoves me harder against the tree, and a whimper leaves my lips. This is not the same man I knew before. He would have never hurt me. Except, he did hurt me. He hurt me worse than any other person has throughout my entire life. It was like I was nothing to him, like I'm still nothing to him.

"You need to get the fuck out of Dune Valley. I thought I made it perfectly clear seven years ago that you aren't meant for this town. I was nice about it then, but I won't be as nice now," he seethes.

"You were nice about it? We spent years together, and you fucking crushed me."

"I was nice about it, Ava. Get the fuck out of my town."

"I can't," I admit. "Trust me. This is the last place I want to be, but I'm stuck here for the time being. Now, get the fuck off me before I scream."

He leans in with a sadistic smile. "People around here are used to me making people scream."

He frees me from his grasp, and I fall to the ground. My twisted ankle wasn't anticipating the added pressure. It's nothing serious. I'm able to stand up after a few moments, although it still hurts. When I look around to tell him off, I notice he has disappeared, just like he did when I followed him here earlier. I'm left here staring out at the empty space, thinking the same thing I thought all those years ago—fuck Greyson Hayes.

Chapter 8
Greyson

Kai was right. This party is exactly what I need to get my mind straight and unwind. Out of all the people to run into today at the park, it had to be fucking Ava. She really needs to keep her nose out of my business and get the fuck out of Dune Valley. Luckily, I had already met with the client and passed the drugs along to him. I was extremely surprised to find out his true identity.

I flip open my lighter and close it over and over again, watching the flame light and then extinguish. Why did she have to go and dye her hair the perfect shade of flaming orange? When I noticed someone following me, I never would have guessed it was her. I expected her to stay as far away from me as possible, not seek me out.

She was turned away from me, so I didn't see her face until she called out my name, and I turned her around against the tree. It was the hair that drew me in. I've never seen a girl with hair as close to my favorite shade of fire.

She looked so much different than the way she did before. She has a hard exterior to her now, like life hasn't exactly been kind to her. I guess I'm partially to blame, but I don't give a fuck. She was angry, and that's how I need her to stay so she will leave.

I still have no clue why the fuck she decided to come back here. Her mother is dead, and the only person she has left in this town is Wrenly, who, at the moment, is conveniently across the room, throwing herself all over Kai. I shake my head. That right there is a disastrous match.

The music pounds through the speakers, and everyone seems to be having a good time. I finish my beer and slip through the sliding glass door in my living room to the backyard. I need to get to the keg to fill my cup. A group of gang sluts hang off to the side of one of the kegs. Great, just what I need to deal with tonight.

The gang sluts are what we like to call the women who show up to all the parties with the clear hopes of getting with one of us. In their minds, if they fuck us, then it's an easy way for them to get their hands on some drugs or find themselves a quick baby daddy. Some of the guys are dumb enough to fall for it, but when I need to get my dick wet, the last place I'll be sticking it is in a gang slut.

I step around them to get to the keg, but one of them steps into me. "Oh, I'm so sorry. I didn't mean to bump into you."

I eye her up and down, slightly annoyed at her tactic to try and get me to talk to her. "Get the fuck out of my way."

"Well, that's no way to talk to a lady." She attempts to place her hand on my arm. I pull away from her before she gets the chance.

"If you were a lady, you wouldn't be desperately trying to get me to give you attention. Now get the fuck out of my way before I have you removed from MY house," I say, watching as her eyes almost bulge out of her skull. She steps to the side, telling me how sorry she is blah, blah, blah. I really don't give a flying fuck.

The sound of laughter has me turning my head to the round table with chairs set up around it. Two younger girls sit on one side of the table, and two younger guys on the other. I only recognize three out of the four of them.

One of the two younger guys has been running with us for a few years now. I think he is the younger sibling of someone in the crew. The other younger guy has been around for a few months. He is dating one of the younger girls—the blonde one, who also happens to be the Sheriff's daughter, Andrea. I've told them countless times not to let her over here. She's going to stir up trouble I have no interest in. The other girl is one that I haven't seen before. Her auburn hair shines in the light, and she looks familiar. She reminds me of someone, but I can't for the life of me place who.

The girl I don't know gets up and walks over to me, pointing in the direction of the gang sluts. "They just have absolutely no shame, do they?"

I raise my brow, curious as to where she plans to take this conversation. She is clearly underage, and I have no desire to be her trophy for the night. I'm not into younger girls.

"They try every time," I say as I reach for the keg's tap. All I want to do is get a drink, but people feel the need to keep bothering me. What part of my face tells them I want to be approached right now?

"They must not know who you are," she states plainly while holding out her cup for me to fill it up.

"You're underage," I say, pushing her hand with the cup away. "Besides, what do you know about who I am?"

"I know you're Greyson Hayes and that you own this house. I also know you run most of this town. Knox is the boss, but people look up to you. You're highly respected. I'm Chloe, by the way," she states, proud of herself for knowing.

"And why does a little girl like you know all of these things?" I ask her.

"Oh, uh, my boyfriend, Matt, he's been running with the crew," she says, rubbing the back of her neck nervously. Again, I get the strange feeling that I know her from somewhere. She looks so damn familiar.

"Yeah, well, tell Matt he needs to keep his bitch on a leash." I reach out and grab the cup from her. "I don't know who gave you this, but if you're underage, you don't drink at my house." The look of shock on her face doesn't go unnoticed.

I march over to the table where the rest of the group of underaged assholes sit and grab the cups from each of their hands too.

I look directly at Andrea. "You need to find somewhere else to be. I don't need to have trouble with your dad."

"My dad thinks I'm at Chloe's house. It's fine." She shrugs and leans in to whisper into the ear of the guy sitting next to her. His eyes light up with desire, and I can almost guess what she told him. I was his age once, young, in love, and dumb as fuck.

"Ten minutes. Wrap things up and get out," I say. "If you expect to keep running with the Crimson Rose, get her the fuck out of here."

I turn on my heels and make my way back into the house, determined to find Kai and lay into him for giving them cups. He knows better than to allow underage drinking here. Given his height, he's pretty easy to spot. He's in the kitchen talking to some random dude, so I walk up and pull him aside.

"Dude, what the fuck?" I say with zero context.

"You have to be a little more specific than that," he tells me.

"You were in charge of the cups tonight, remember? It was supposed to be your job to keep track of the money and ensure nobody underage got them. You know I don't want that shit happening here."

"What did you want me to do, check everyone's IDs?" He laughs.

"This is serious, Kai. The Sheriff's daughter has a cup for fucks sake. When I ask for something to be a certain way in my house, I expect that to be respected." My eyes narrow at him. Typically, he and I don't have any issues, but this isn't something I'm not willing to budge on. My dad used alcohol a lot to cope with things when I was younger, and I know what that can do to someone. I don't want it happening in my house.

"Look, I'm sorry. I didn't think it was that big of a deal. I got distracted for a bit, so some people might have slipped in and helped themselves," he says.

"It's a big deal. Figure out who's underage and get them the fuck out of here. I don't need Sheriff Wolfe on our asses because you wanted to get your dick sucked." I'm probably being harsher than I should be, but he pissed me off, and right now, I don't really care.

He steps out of the kitchen and into the garage. I'm assuming it's to figure out who shouldn't be here and do what I told him to do. This was supposed to be a birthday party, but it's been nothing but pure stress. The one thing I am actually grateful for is the fact that there is no cake.

I sip on my beer and turn to look towards my living room. I catch sight of someone with fiery orange hair pushing their way through the crowd of people and then disappear into the hallway. You have got to be fucking kidding me. I know this bitch did not just show up at my house after I told her to get out of town.

I slam my cup on the counter, and the contents slosh over the edges, wetting my hands. After wiping them on my pants, I push myself away from the counter and toward the hallway to track her down.

Countless people slap their hands on my back as I walk past, telling me happy birthday. I just nod at them and push my way through to my destination. She's never been inside my house, so she has no clue where she's going. I started renting it a few years after she left town. My question is whether or not she knows who this house belongs to.

It's not uncommon to end up at a random party on this side of Dune Valley. She's not supposed to be out at parties, though. She's supposed to be packing her shit. I step into the hallway but can't see the bright orange hue of her hair anywhere.

"Did you see a girl with orange hair?" I ask the girl standing outside of the bathroom, waiting for her turn to go inside.

"Yeah, she went in there. I told her that room was off limits, but she didn't care," she says nervously.

I raise a brow and turn my head over to the door she is pointing at. Avalynn Blake is in my bedroom. Oh, this is going to be interesting. I push open the door to see her looking around my room. She is staring at a picture on my dresser, and almost immediately, I know what she's looking at. I slam the door behind me, causing her to turn in my direction with wide eyes.

"Grey," she says as I stalk towards her.

I grab her by the shoulders and push her against the wall. "What the fuck are you doing here? I told you to leave. What part of that did you not understand?"

"I'm looking for my sister." She tries to push me off of her.

"Come on, Ava. Don't treat me like I'm stupid. We dated for three years. I stayed at your house all the time when we were kids. You don't have a sister." I can't help but find myself a bit intoxicated by her presence. Having her so close to me does things that I hate to admit I enjoy.

"You don't know shit." Her lip curls up, trying to emphasize her distaste for me.

She's trying to test my patience, and I'm not about to let her get the upper hand. I lean in closer, changing my grip so that my entire left arm is pinning her shoulders in place. My hips block her in, and we are dangerously close.

"I can find another way to make you tell me the truth." A fun little idea crosses my mind.

My now free hand trails up the tights covering her thigh. She's wearing a black mini skirt with lace-patterned fishnets, a pair of knockoff Doc Martens, and a band tee tucked into the skirt. It's a very gothic style choice, which is completely different from what I remember her having. I continue to trail my hand up her leg until it disappears under her skirt.

"Greyson," she warns. "What are you doing? Stop it and let me go. I need to find her."

She is sticking with this sister story, and it's really pissing me off. "Tell me the truth, and I'll stop. Why are you here?" I say as I get dangerously close to her center. I can feel the heat radiating off of her and can't help but admit it has my heart racing in my chest. I hate what this girl does to me. I hate how much power she has over me after all this time.

"I already told you. I'm looking for my sister." Her eyes are wide. She doesn't actually think I'll keep going, but I'm here to prove her wrong. It's a party, in Dune Valley, on my birthday. She must have come here to look for me.

"You showed up here like a needy slut, expecting me to do something about it. Well, here I am. Beg me to stop."

I kick her feet apart, giving me the access I need as I swipe my finger across her center. Even through her panties and tights, I can feel that she's soaking wet. I tear open her tights and pull the thong to the side, sliding my finger along her clit and making her hips buck in response. She tries to push me off of her again.

"Grey, please," she says, almost like she's confused about whether she is asking me to continue or to stop.

"Want to tell me the truth now?" I ask again.

"I already told you," she states firmly. Stubborn. She has to be so stubborn.

I push one finger inside her and pump it slowly in and out, watching as the look on her face transforms from hate to lust. Her eyes go heavy, and I can feel the way her breaths quicken. I add a second finger, keeping up my slow pace.

"This is why you came back here, isn't it? You show up in my town. In my house. In my bedroom. You're so desperate to get my attention."

"I didn't know this was your house. I don't want anything to do with you," she breathes out. I see the fight in her eyes. She is trying to decide whether or not to let this continue or to try harder to get me off of her.

My fingers pick up the pace, and her pussy tightens around them. She doesn't make a sound, but I can tell by the way that her breathing has increased that she's enjoying herself. I keep my eyes on hers as I curl my fingers in just the right spot. I spent years with her. I know exactly how to make her pussy sing.

A whimper leaves her lips, and I feel her clench around my fingers again. I have her right where I want her, right on the edge. I slow my pace, letting the high I know she was chasing recede.

"You don't have a sister," I repeat. Her eyebrows narrow in fury. The look of pure hatred plastered back onto her face.

"I do! Not that it's any of your business, but it's the only reason I came back to this piece of shit town." She tries to push at my hold on her again, but I keep her in place. "Get the fuck off of me so I can go find her and get the hell out of here. I can't stand the sight of you."

My fingers begin working her up again, and I feel the slight lift of her hips when I rub them against her inner walls. A moan leaves her. She's so fucking wet. My thumb finds her clit, and I know I have her right where I want her.

"The truth, little shadow," I say while moving my fingers in and out of her steadily.

"She's seventeen. I just found out about her," she says through ragged breaths.

Dots connect in my mind, and suddenly, I know why the younger girl in my backyard looked so familiar. She has the same eyes as Ava. Maybe not the same color, but the same almond shape. A sly grin crosses my face when I decide she's telling the truth and should be rewarded for it. I rub my thumb faster on her clit while curling my fingers inside her until her pussy clamps around them.

"That's it. Come on my fingers. Just like old times. Be a good little slut." I lean in and whisper in her ear.

A soft moan falls from her lips, and I let her ride out the orgasm before I pull my fingers out of her and wipe them on the front of her shirt. I step back and take in the perfect pink color on her flushed cheeks. She is trying to calm her breathing, and her eyes meet mine.

"Go find your sister and get the hell out of here."

Her eyes narrow, and she pushes herself off the wall, shoving me with her shoulder on the way out of my room. Immediately, I regret putting my hands anywhere near her. She's like a drug. Now that I've had another taste, thoughts of her are going to consume me, and I hate her even more for it.

Chapter 9
Avalynn

Fuck Greyson and all of his stupid bullshit. I had no idea when I showed up here that it was his house. That was the truth. I'm only here to find my sister. He didn't have the right to touch me.

Chloe was supposed to stay in her room, but when I pushed open the door earlier to see if she and Andrea wanted to watch a movie with me, I noticed they were gone. Fucking teenagers. I should have expected it. Of all the people my new sis could have as a best friend, why does it have to be the Sheriff's daughter?

The last place I want to be on a Saturday night is at a house party in Dune Valley, but that's all anyone in this town does. Sex, drugs, gangs. This isn't who I am. This is the lifestyle I ran from when I packed up my shit and left without a second thought. This was what Greyson and I were supposed to leave behind before he decided it would be easier to just leave me instead.

Every weekend, it's always the same. They find some sort of reason to party. Here I am, right back with the rest of them, just waltzing into a strange house, trying to find my sister. I know how things go in this town, and I know she has to be here somewhere.

I was so wrapped up in my own mind over the last few days that I didn't even realize what today was or why there might be a party happening in this specific house. The puzzle pieces connect now. It's Greyson's birthday. This is his house. It's his damn birthday, and I showed up at his house to his birthday party. I'm sure he thinks I'm nice and pathetic; no wonder he hates me.

I push through the crowd of people and find my way to the sliding glass door in the living room. It's pulled open so that people can come and go freely. I haven't checked the backyard yet, so I step out and look around the yard quickly to see if my eyes can catch her.

My eyes find her at a small table with Andrea and two random dudes. Absolutely not. I storm over to the table, crossing my arms as I stop in front of her and glare down. She looks up at me cautiously, unsure how this entire exchange is going to go.

"Car. Now," I say to her before turning to Andrea. "You too, unless you'd prefer I give your dad a call."

I hate that I have to be a buzzkill, but I'll be damned if these two girls will be out partying with a bunch of gang bangers and drug dealers. If they want to step into this life once they turn eighteen, that's on them. As long as Chloe is under my roof, and I'm in charge of her, she will keep her underage ass away from them.

"Ava, can you relax? We're just hanging out with our boyfriends. It's not a big deal." She laughs and doesn't make any effort to get up.

Some of the people close by have turned their heads and are now watching over our heated discussion. I don't care if I embarrass her. I need to get the hell out of Greyson's house. Not because he told me to but because I don't want to be anywhere near him. I recognize Wrenly out of the corner of my eye, walking over to me.

"Hey, Ava, I, um, didn't expect to see you here," she admits with a bit of guilt.

"Yeah, obviously, I didn't know whose house it was. Thanks, by the way, for not texting me back earlier. I thought we were doing something tonight." I'm not really sure what the hell has gotten into her. She was supposed to be my friend, but I don't have time to deal with her shit right now. I need to deal with Chloe because I'm a responsible adult these days.

"I didn't really know how to bring up the fact that there was a party for Grey's birthday. I'm sorry," she confesses.

"It's fine." I'm a bit short with her, but at the moment, I don't care.

Another figure approaches us, and I can already tell without looking that it's Greyson. His burnt, minty leather scent gives him away. As if this wasn't already infuriating enough, now I have to have him standing there and watching as I try to convince the seventeen-year-old sister I've only known for a few days to leave a party on a Saturday night.

"You're Ava's sister?" he asks her.

She rubs up and down her arms nervously. "Apparently."

"Good, get out," he states plainly before looking over at her friend. "You too. I already told you once. Go the fuck home."

Both of their mouths drop at how blunt he is. Without another word, he turns and walks back into the house. The two of them quickly gather up their things and kiss their boyfriends, and the three of us then walk right out of the house in complete silence.

I made the executive decision to take Andrea home. She can tell her dad whatever excuse she wants for not spending the night, but I can't have her at the house right now. I look over at Chloe in the passenger seat and find her staring out the window, deep in thought. Within no time, we are back at my house. I drop my keys on the table, sighing as I take off my black boots.

Chloe turns to face me once she gets inside. "Do you have any idea how embarrassing that was? Everyone at school is going to be talking about it."

"Embarrassing?" I question.

"Yeah. You don't even know me. You don't have the right to tell me I can't go to parties with my boyfriend."

"I get it. You're young. You want to have fun and fall dangerously in love with whatever the hell your boyfriend's name is." She goes to interrupt me—I'm guessing to tell me his name—but I stop her. "I don't care what his name is. It doesn't matter because he is just going to leave you high and dry and choose the gang over you. That's what they all do." I try not to let some of my feelings about Grey seep into this, but I can't help it.

"You don't know anything. You haven't even been in this town for the last seven years," she says to me, rolling her eyes.

"I know enough. I was you," I admit.

This seems to get her attention because she lets her guard down a bit and eyes me curiously. I pull out one of the chairs from the kitchen table and sit down, giving her a moment to sit next to me.

"Look, this whole situation is still new. We are both two different people trying to figure all of this out. I'm not your enemy, but I won't sit back and blindly let you make decisions that could change your life. At least for the next few months." She stares at me, still silent, so I continue. "When I was seventeen, Greyson and I were supposed to graduate and leave this town. We spent years together and saved up money. He told me everything I wanted to hear until he didn't. He tossed me aside like I was nothing but an afterthought and moved right along with his life. I was angry, so I packed up and left, half expecting him to try and come find me, but he never did. I was crushed. That's one of the reasons I haven't been back in this town since. It hurts to be here and be reminded of what he did."

"You didn't come back to visit your family?" she asks.

"My mom wasn't like yours. She was a drug addict that I never had a relationship with. The only thing she cared about, especially after my dad died, was her drugs. We didn't have nice things or live a nice life. Anything nice I did manage to get for myself, she ended up selling for her next hit. So, no, I didn't feel the need to come back here to visit her."

"You said she died," Chloe says, looking around at the noticeably empty house.

"Yeah, an overdose a few months ago," I state coldly. I think at this moment, she realizes the only reason I came back to this town was for her.

"I'm sorry." She actually looks like she feels bad, which annoys me a little bit. I don't need people feeling bad for me because I had a bad childhood. Lots of people go through their own shit. I picked up and moved on from it.

"Can we just agree to try and find some sort of common ground? I would really like to get to know you." I finally feel comfortable enough to admit it to her.

"Sure, I guess that wouldn't be terrible. The rest of my family is dead. You're all I have. I'm not breaking up with Matt, though."

I laugh at how straightforward she is. "Just be careful and protect your heart. Some lessons just have to be learned. I think we've had enough breakthroughs for tonight, though. Do you mind if we call it and just start fresh tomorrow?"

"Yeah, we should sleep. The bags under your eyes are really hideous right now," she jokes, and I find myself laughing with her before the two of us go our separate ways into our bedrooms. Maybe things will all work out after all.

It's probably shitty of me to compare my past to her current situation, but I can't help it. The only real difference between her situation with Matt now and me being with Grey all those years ago is that she at least knows he is running with the Crimson Rose. He was at least honest with her about that.

Today has been such a roller coaster from Greyson to Chloe to my dead mother. I find myself missing my life from a few weeks ago when the only person I had to worry about was myself.

Chapter 10
Avalynn

The vibe at the house this morning was definitely less hostile than it has been since showing up at Dune Valley. Chloe got up and went to school with zero issues. I'm hoping that after the incident last weekend, we have finally found some sort of common ground. Maybe we can ride out the time until she graduates without any other intense events. I'm not really trying to be her parent, just a sister.

My phone dings in my pocket, pulling me from my thoughts. It's Wrenly. She's been trying to get a hold of me since seeing me at Greyson's party, and I've been ignoring her. Her going to that party and not telling me really pissed me off. I understand she has her life here, but I just came back to town. You would think she'd make an effort to see me instead of partying at my piece-of-shit ex's house.

> Wrenly: Come on, Ava. I said I'm sorry.

> Wrenly: Let me grovel and buy you coffee today.

THE AFTERTHOUGHT

Coffee does sound good, and not having to pay for it sounds even better. I've been cutting corners to try and stretch my savings. Fancy iced coffee is one of the luxuries I've gone without. Fuck. Am I really going to let her buy forgiveness just like that? My mouth starts watering just thinking about the caramel latte I could be drinking right now. Yep, I sure am.

> Me: I'm getting the biggest size.

> Me: And a blueberry muffin.

> Wrenly: Totally fine by me. Meet me in 10?

> Me: Fine. But I expect heavy groveling. That was a real shitty move over the weekend.

> Wrenly: I knoooowww... I'll be on my knees waiting for your forgiveness.

> Me: Don't be weird. I'll see you in a few.

I swear to God, if I show up and she is on her knees, I'm turning around and pretending she doesn't exist. I grab a black sweater and throw it over my shoulders, snagging my keys on the way to the door. The spring air is a little chilly today, but the drive to the coffee shop is short and quick.

When I walk in, Wrenly is sitting at a table in the corner with a ridiculously large iced coffee and muffin across from her. I smile at the sight of both her and the bribe and make my way over to her. She spots me and stands up to close the distance between us, pulling me right into a hug.

"I'm sorry, Ava. I know you probably think I'm a terrible friend."

I can't deny she was a lousy friend over the weekend, but she's been my ride-or-die since before I can remember. "It was a dick move. But you've bought my forgiveness with that." I tilt my head toward the table with the coffee and muffin on it.

She sighs and lets go of me, stepping back to the table. I sit across from her and pull the coffee up to my lips. The first taste sends chills through my body. Fuck, I missed this. There really isn't anything better than feeling that first taste of caffeine spreading through your veins.

Once I'm confident the coffee has successfully calmed part of the bitch inside me, I look at her. "Okay, explain."

"Do you know that guy I was with at the party? Kai?" She smiles.

"I don't really know him, but yeah, I saw you with him."

"Well, we've kind of been talking." Her cheeks blush slightly at the confession. Interesting.

"Talking or fucking?" I shoot a brow up and giggle.

Her eyes go wide, and she shakes her head at me. "Maybe both. I know I should have texted you and told you that I was going there. I just know you still get uncomfortable when I bring up anything about Greyson. I didn't want to tell you about the party, and then you get excited about a night out, only to find out it was for him."

"It's fine. I've been so caught up in my own shit with Chloe that I completely forgot it was his birthday. I can't believe I ended up at his freaking birthday party."

"Yeah, how the hell did that happen?"

"Chloe decided to sneak out. Trying to manage a seventeen-year-old is weird. I remember what it was like being her age and all the parties we were invited to. Even if I never went to any of them, there was always a party every weekend. This town is the same as it's always been. I figured if I drove around the area, I would find out where she ended up. She could only go so far on foot. I just didn't really expect it to be his house."

"You didn't know?"

"How the hell would I know where he lives, Wren? I've been out of town for the last seven years, and I don't exactly keep tabs on him. The little bits I even know are things that you told me without me asking."

"That's true. He's hot, though, isn't he?" She wiggles her brows, testing the waters.

"He's an asshole," I state plainly before grabbing my muffin and taking an aggressive bite.

"Something happened." Her head turns in question.

"He..." I trail off. How the hell will I even begin to explain what happened? Oh, you know he pinned me to a wall and made me come on his fingers before he told me to get the hell out of his house. I'm so angry that he felt like he could put his hands on me. He doesn't deserve to touch me after everything.

"He what, Ava?"

"He... it was nothing. He told me to get the fuck out of his town, like he has any say over who can and can't be in Dune Valley."

"He does sort of have a say, though."

"What are you talking about?"

"He's been with the Crimson Rose since you left. I don't know if you know this or not, but his brother, Knox, is the boss."

"Wait, what? I knew Knox was his brother, but I didn't realize he was the leader of the Crimson Rose."

"Yeah, and Greyson's sort of his right-hand man. An unofficial second in command. He runs this town, and people are afraid of him, for good reason too. Last year, he sent a man to the hospital with third-degree burns all over his body. They couldn't prove he was the one who did it, so nothing happened. It's not like the cops in this town would even care."

The Greyson I remember wasn't like that. He was always super protective of me, and he liked fire, sure, but he wasn't the kind of person I thought would ever hurt someone else. I guess I was wrong about that, too.

"Be careful around him, Ava. He's not the same guy he was when we were kids. If he's intent on getting you out of town, he won't stop until you leave. He always finds a way to get what he wants."

"Yeah? Greyson Hayes can eat a dick. I'm not leaving town." I never wanted to be in this town, but for some reason, knowing what I know now makes me want to stay. If it's something that is going to piss him off, I'm eager to do it. My mind is free from every thought of leaving at this moment. Greyson doesn't get to choose what happens to me. Not anymore.

"Tell me about Kai since I have to share you with him now." I take another bite of my muffin, and she smiles.

"He's sweet. I've never met someone like him before. On the outside, he seems like this mean, unapproachable brute, but he's been so kind to me. He actually bought me flowers last week."

"Does it not bother you that he's part of the Crimson Rose?" I'm glad she's excited about him, but I'm not going to hold back my questions.

"I'm not like you, Ava."

"What the hell is that supposed to mean?"

"This town, it's always been my life. I don't want to leave. The gang life is part of Dune Valley. You either end up involved with the Crimson Rose or the Cobras. I'm okay with it."

I take a moment to think about what she's telling me. I know that Dune Valley is all about gangs, but some of us get out. I didn't think she would want to live the gang-wife life, but if she's okay with it, then I have to accept her wishes, even if I don't like it.

"If he hurts you, I'll cut his balls off myself. I don't give a fuck who he runs with." I finish the last of my muffin and watch as her eyes light up.

"Thank you for always being supportive, even though I can tell you hate the idea of him being in a gang." She reaches out to touch my hand reassuringly.

"I mean it, Wrenly. He better not fuck with you."

"You have to hang out with us one of these days. Maybe we can hit up the drive-in movies sometime soon. I think they have a few really good ones playing right now."

My heart aches a bit at the mention of that place and the amount of date nights Greyson and I had there. One of his friends would always drive us, and we would lay out the same blanket and pillows to enjoy our night while his friend made out with his girlfriend in the front seat of his truck.

I realize the strong possibility of said driver being a member of the Crimson Rose. If he was running with them back then, it would make sense. It fuels nothing but pure rage in me. How dare he bring me around his gang and not bother to tell me about it.

"... and he took me to see that one like a month ago. It's still new, but I really like him." Wrenly finishes her coffee and waits for me to respond, but I missed most of what she was saying because I can't get that asshole out of my head.

"Maybe you can just bring him over to the house for dinner or something. I don't know if I want to go to the drive-in." I drop my head and fiddle with my fingers.

"Yeah, we can definitely do that. I bet he would even cook for us if I asked him to. We could sit on the couch and let him wine and dine us." She giggles, and it reminds me why I love her so much. She didn't even hesitate to say yes to dinner instead.

"Now you're talking. Do you think he would go for it?" I smile at her.

"I'll ask him today and let you know. Actually, I have to get going. I have to be at work in like 15 minutes." She gets up to throw away her empty cup and comes back over to me.

I stand to give her another hug, happy that we were able to figure out our issues. When it comes down to it, she is the closest thing I have to family, except for my newfound sister. Before leaving me there to finish my coffee, Wrenly promises to call me later.

I'm feeling happy and content when I look towards the door again and notice a familiar face walking inside. What the hell?

His eyes meet mine, and he walks over to me. "Looks like we have a habit of running into each other in coffee shops, huh?" He laughs.

"Are you stalking me or something?" Why the hell is the random coffee shop guy that I fucked in Massachusetts in Dune Valley?

"Definitely not stalking you. I live on the other side of town. I was actually going to ask if you were stalking me."

"Alec," the girl from behind the counter calls, and he turns to go grab his coffee from her. He must have ordered ahead. I see him pause for a moment as if he's trying to decide whether or not to sit with me, and I wave him back over. He doesn't hesitate to come over to my table and sit in the seat Wrenly just vacated.

"Alec, is that your real name then?"

A soft chuckle leaves him, and a huge grin spreads across his face. I'm still being cautious because he gives off weird vibes. I felt it before in Massachusetts, but it didn't bother me as much because I thought I would never see him again.

"It is my name, yes. Do I get the pleasure of knowing yours this time?"

I study him, trying to decide if I should tell him or not. I don't know anything about him. For all I know, he could be one of Greyson's little spies. The only way to find out is to be straightforward and ask. Fuck it. "Are you in any way associated with the Crimson Rose?"

His eyes go wide, making me a bit anxious. "Uh, definitely not."

"And why were you in Massachusetts?"

"Business," he says.

I look at him curiously. What the hell are the chances of him showing up at another coffee shop on the other side of the country? "It was all chance when we ran into each other at the coffee shop?"

"I can honestly say that I had no idea who you were when we ran into each other at that coffee shop. After all, you were the one who approached me to come home with you. I was simply getting a cup of coffee."

I take a moment to think over his words. He chose them carefully, almost too carefully. I decide he's being truthful, though.

Reluctantly, I hold my hand out to shake his. "My name is Avalynn."

"Nice to meet you, Avalynn. How have I never run into you in Dune Valley before? This town is small. I would have remembered someone as beautiful as you."

"I just moved back." I glance down at the time on my phone, not really wanting to get into my whole life story with him right now. I need to go to the police station and talk with the Sheriff. I want to see if they need to hire anyone for PI work or bounty hunting. I'm sure I can figure out the whole bounty hunting thing. "I should probably get going. I have to go talk to someone about a job."

"Do you need a job?" He raises a brow.

"That depends on what the job is." I'm not about to tell him how desperate I am for a reliable income.

"I own a club just outside of town. It's called Temptations."

"That sounds like a strip club. Not exactly the kind of work I'm interested in, but thanks anyway." I push the chair back and stand up. "Sorry to cut this short, but I have to go." I turn and take a few steps in the direction of the exit.

"Wait." He reaches out to grab my wrist to stop me, and I see red.

"Don't touch me." I rip my arm out of his grasp and keep walking. Ever since that incident a few years ago, I'm not keen on strangers touching me. We had sex, but I still barely know him.

"I need a bartender, not a stripper," he calls out, and I stop in my tracks. I turn back to face him.

"A bartender?"

He closes the distance between us and reaches into his pocket to pull out a business card.

"Yeah, I would have told you that, but you freaked out. If you're interested in the job, stop by later tonight. The address and phone number for the place are on the card."

I eye him carefully before grabbing it from him. "This isn't your phone number?"

"No. If you wanted my phone number, I'm sure you would have asked for it. You seem to have no issue stating your thoughts, opinions, or wants."

That makes me laugh. "At least you're smart enough to figure that out. I'll give you that."

"I'm anything but stupid, Avalynn." His eyes narrow slightly. If I hadn't been paying attention, I probably wouldn't have noticed.

"Right, and the uniform for a bartender at your club is what?" I seriously hope he doesn't expect me to wear something too exposing.

"Whatever you're comfortable in. If you want to let your tits hang out, have at it, or don't. You don't have a uniform."

I relax a bit and smile at him before walking toward the door. "Thank you for this. I'll stop by tonight." He follows me, and we exit together.

Chapter 11

Greyson

When I told Knox that Ava coming back to town wasn't going to be an issue, that's what I honestly believed at the time. I thought I would be able to convince her to leave again. The fact that she refuses is really getting under my skin. I'm letting her affect me.

My thoughts go back to last night when she was pinned up against the wall. She didn't fight me as much as I know she could have. Ava has never been a weak woman. The fact that she let me make her come must mean that at least a part of her wanted it to happen.

Fuck. Part of me has missed the look she makes when she falls apart. It's been so long that I almost forgot how her gorgeous cheeks redden. The way that her tight little cunt squeezes my fingers. I can almost imagine what it would feel like to be inside her again.

I play with my Zippo lighter, flipping it open and closed over and over again. I've had this lighter for eight years now, and I'll never get rid of it. The silver has a few scratches, and the waterfall design on the front doesn't exactly fit my persona, but this is one of the few possessions I have that is invaluable.

My phone ringing pulls me from my thoughts. "Yeah, Knox?"

"Come to Adam's Garage. I've got a surprise for you."

"Be there in a few." I end the call and pocket both my phone and the lighter.

I wonder what he has up his sleeves today. It could be anything from a joint to a new person to kill. I never really know when it comes to him. When I pull up to the garage, he's standing outside with a huge smile on his face. What the fuck is going on? I park and walk over to him.

"I have a surprise for you," he tells me before I can get any words out.

"Yeah, you already said that. Why are you standing out here smiling? It's freaking me out."

He rolls his eyes. "It's more like a double surprise. Remember the douchebag from last week that was going around and running his mouth?"

"Yeah, I'd love to burn that smug look right off his face." I reach into my pocket to fiddle with the lighter again.

"What if I told you that you can?" He elbows me in the side and tilts his head to prompt me to follow him.

We go behind the garage and step a few feet into the tree line. The garage is on the outer edge of town, so it's pretty secluded. There are a few acres of woods behind it that I've used a time or two. It was the perfect place to torture a couple of assholes who felt like they had the balls to speak out against the Crimson Rose.

A structure in the woods catches my eye. This definitely wasn't here the last time I was back here. We walk closer, and I notice it's a large dark brown building. It's the size of a small warehouse. It's much bigger than your typical backyard shed, which I was expecting Knox to place back here for me. This has double doors on the front. The color of the metal blends with the browns of the trees surrounding it. If you weren't looking for it, you would never even notice it's here.

If this is here for what I think it is, then I'm beyond excited. Knox has been hinting about getting me a place to carry out my work so we don't have to tie these fuckers to trees anymore.

"Is this what I think it is?" I ask him.

"It sure as fuck is. What do you think?" The smile on his face should be alarming, but I can tell that he is just excited to be able to give me this.

My brother doesn't always understand my desires, but he still supports me. I can't even count the number of things that belonged to him that I destroyed when we were younger. I used to go into the house to grab things just so that I could light a fire in the backyard and stare at it while it burned.

There's just always been something so transfixing about watching the flames dance. The older I got, the better I became at trying to keep my urges in check, but they were always there. Times like right now, when I am extra stressed, have a tendency to make them worse. I won't lie. I've been really struggling to keep my shit in check since Ava came back into town.

"How the hell did you manage to get this here so quickly?"

"I've had something in the works for a while now. They were able to rush the setup with minimal questions. I told them we needed a place to store the cars we work on at the garage. We needed a more permanent solution to what we were working with before. It wasn't cheap, but I think it'll be worth the investment."

"Is it fire resistant?"

"It is. I paid extra for it. Wait until you get inside; your second surprise is there waiting for you," Knox says as he pulls the door open.

I'm practically jumping with anticipation now. We step inside, and I take it in. Immediately, my eyes are drawn to the person secured to the chair in the middle of the room. Their head is drooping down as if they are unconscious with a bag over it. I look over at Knox and point my thumb toward the mysterious third party.

He walks over and rips the bag off to reveal a man with duct tape over his mouth. His entire face is covered in sweat. He looks like shit, but I instantly recognize him.

This is the fucker who was running his mouth last week. He is conveniently tied to a chair inside my new fireproof torture shed. I know it's not a shed, but that's what I'm going to call it. This is exactly what I need today to get my mind off of Ava and her presence in Dune Valley.

"Thank you, brother." I give him a sinister smile, and he nods at me before walking back toward the entrance.

"Make sure he knows who he fucked with, but don't kill him, Grey." Without another word, he steps out of the shed and leaves me alone with my prey.

I look around the room to acquaint myself while the guy quietly watches me. He knows what is coming and isn't wasting any energy trying to fight his fate. I can almost respect that a little. Too bad for him. I'm in a mood today, and I need to release some pent-up energy.

I turn to the right and notice some large shelves filled with various torture devices. My eyes instantly go to the shelf filled with the different blowtorches. I'm so giddy I practically skip over to grab one of the butane torches. Now that I'm closer, I eye up the metal pieces on one of the other shelves and grab one that is about twelve inches long with a rounded point to it. The last thing I grab is a glove to hold the metal bar with. I can tell these are specific for holding hot metal. They couldn't have been cheap.

The excitement coursing through my bones almost makes up for the fact that Ava hasn't left town yet. Next to the shelves is a small stool with a round seat on wheels, and I kick it in the direction of my tied-up victim. I decide I have everything I need for now, so I walk over to smile down at him.

I set all of my things down on the floor and rip the duct tape off of his face, not caring whether or not it pulls off some of his beard. It definitely pulled off some of his beard.

"Fuck you and the Crimson Rose." He spits, making me laugh hysterically in his face.

"You're awfully brave for a guy who is tied up and about to get tortured. Do you know who I am?"

"Trash," he replies, spitting toward my feet.

I lean in with a cocky smile on my face. "Sometimes the guys on the street call me Coal. I've come to wear it like a badge of honor."

His eyes widen, and I know he knows who I am now. My reputation speaks for itself. People call me Coal because of how I like to torture my victims. It was the main reason I wanted to join the gang life, to finally have a way to express my urges. I've been known to do as little as brand people and go as far as burning them alive. This guy is lucky I'm not allowed to kill him. Today, he will only have to withstand a few burns. It's really nothing the body can't handle.

"Not so tough now, are you?" I chuckle. "Want to know why you're here? I shouldn't bother telling you because I don't need a reason, but I think you might be a bit curious."

He keeps a straight face, refusing to say anything further. I expected this. He won't betray his gang by speaking to me. He knows every word I get is a small victory. The Crimson Rose and Cobras have been at each other's throats for years. Just like their name, they're a bunch of snakes.

I pull out my small pocketknife and make various cuts along the fabric of his shirt, causing it to fall to the ground. When I'm done with him, he isn't going to want that irritating his skin anyway. I'm really doing him a favor. I lean down to grip the small butane torch in my hand, admiring how perfectly my fingers fill the grooves of the handle. This one might become my new favorite toy outside of my lighter.

My eyes light up as I flip on the torch. Flames woosh out of the end, and I watch as the moment the look on this asshole's face goes from cocky to pure terror. He shakes around in the chair to try and free himself, but he isn't going anywhere.

I flip off the torch to grab the glove off of the floor and slip it on before bending down to grip the metal bar with the glove. I turn the torch back on and bring the bright blue flames over to the tip of the metal, watching as one end of the metal heats and turns a vibrant orange hue.

I step behind him and lower the hot metal onto his back. His screams tear through the room as I focus on the sound of his sizzling skin. The smell of burnt flesh fills the air around us. I make a mental note to wear a mask next time, so I don't have to smell it. I repeat the process over and over again, listening as he screams out in terror. Chunks of melted skin stick to the end of the metal. I can't help but feel increasingly at ease with every burn inflicted on him. It's like I'm transferring everything I feel directly through the scorching metal.

Time goes on, and I lose myself in my work. I didn't notice that he stopped screaming at some point. His head is slumped forward, likely passed out from the immense pain. Pussy. I just have one last thing to burn into him before I'm satisfied with this job.

I toss the hot metal aside and pull the glove off my hand, letting it fall to the floor. I place the torch next to it. The lighter that resides in my pocket finds its way to my hand, and I flip it on. For a brief moment, I stare into the dancing orange flame before bringing it to my finger to heat the end of the ring on my middle finger.

This has become my signature. Nobody gets away from my torture without carrying my mark. Once I'm sure the ring is warm enough to sear his skin but not hot enough to burn mine, I step forward and shove my fist into the back of his neck, searing my mark into him. I give it a few seconds before stepping back and admiring my work.

A small skull with my initials in its empty eye sockets now sits near the burn marks I left on him. It's my own personal signature for my artwork. God, it feels fucking good to focus on what I love again.

Finally, I feel relaxed. I definitely needed this. I'll have to make sure that Knox has someone else lined up for me soon. I have a feeling I'm going to need to scratch this itch more often than before.

As long as Ava stays in town, I'm going to be on edge. I'm going to have to get myself together because if Knox thinks she is any kind of issue, he will have to intervene. He can't have his star pupil being distracted.

I leave my new friend in my torture shed and walk to the front of the garage. Briefly, I wave goodbye to a few of the guys before deciding to head into town. I'm sure Knox will be sending someone over to pick up the snake I left behind and take him back to the Cobras. It will be interesting to see if they retaliate against us because of this.

A hot coffee sounds pretty good right about now, and there's only one coffee place in town. I could make it at home, but I'm just really not up for the effort; plus, I think Kai used the last of the milk with his damn cereal addiction.

I park and make my way to the coffee shop, but what I see inside stops me dead in my tracks. Ava is having coffee with Alec. My ex-girlfriend is having fucking coffee with the leader of the Cobras.

Rage consumes me. My blood boils, and it takes everything in me to not rush inside and beat the shit out of him for going anywhere near her. When I see them laughing and smiling, I tighten my fists at my sides. Alec glances out of the coffee shop window and spots me. A sly grin crosses his face. He knows exactly what he's doing and who he's fucking messing with. He wants me to retaliate, but I can't. Knox would kill me if I escalated things over a piece of ass.

She isn't mine; I remind myself. I hate the way she makes me feel. It's more than infuriating not to be in control of your own emotions. Everything was fine without her here, but now that she's back, I have this insane desire to make her mine again.

She stands up from the table and looks upset. He reaches out to grip her wrist, and immediately, I'm subconsciously walking across the street toward the shop. Nobody puts their hands on what's mine. Fuck what I've been trying to convince myself.

Regardless of whether or not we are together, Avalynn Blake is mine. She has always been mine.

I freeze when she rips her arm from his grasp. Good girl. She starts walking away from him toward the door, but she stops and turns back to him. He reaches into his suit jacket and hands her a business card. I know exactly what he's up to. This fucker is going to offer her a job at Temptations. It will be over my dead body that I allow her to work for him.

They walk out of the coffee shop, and she finally sees me. The two of them stop, and she takes a small step away from him. That's right. You know you're mine even if you don't want to admit it. Fuck. I told myself I wouldn't think like this, but seeing her with him, of all people, makes my skin itch.

"Ava. Come here," I grit out while locking eyes with Alec.

"No. Fuck off, Greyson. I have nothing to say to you." She steps closer to Alec to try and prove a point to me. I close the distance between them and reach out to her, but she moves away before I make contact.

"Did you not understand me telling you to fuck off? Let me spell it out for you. I don't want to see you, talk to you, or be around you. Go away." She tries to wave me off, and anger flashes through me.

"Is there a problem here?" Alec asks.

This piece of shit has the nerve to open his mouth. If it were up to me, I would wrap my fingers around his throat and watch as he takes his last breath. I have to think about my crew, though. I can't kill the leader of the Cobras. Not right now, at least.

"There's no problem. I'm going home." She walks away from us and gets in her car.

I turn to Alec, who has a stupid fucking grin on his face. "Stay the fuck away from her," I grit out.

"Yeah? I don't think I'm going to. She's quite the spitfire. We had a nice little rendezvous in Massachusetts before she came back to town."

"What the fuck are you talking about?" Pure rage pulses through me. It's taking everything in me right now not to retaliate.

"You should ask her about it," he says before he laughs and walks away.

You can bet your ass I'm going to ask her about it. I march back to my car, rip the door open, and slam the car in drive. My mind is focused on one thing and one thing only, getting to Ava's house and finding out what the fuck he was talking about.

Chapter 12
Avalynn

I'm completely annoyed as I drive back to my house. Who the fuck does he think he is? One minute, he's telling me to get out of his town; the next, he's trying to tell me what to do. I'm not about to let any man tell me what to do. I've spent too many years on my own to let one man from my past take over my future.

I park in my usual spot across the street from my house and head back inside. There are still a few hours before Chloe comes home from school, and I want to go through some more of my mom's things. I've been putting it off for way too long now.

A few minutes after I'm inside, I'm startled by a loud pounding on my door. For a moment, I let terror flood my body. I don't have any weapons in here to defend myself. My gun is in the glove box of my car. Knives. I grab a knife from the silverware drawer in my kitchen and point it toward the door. I'm not about to let someone scare me.

"AVALYNN BLAKE. OPEN. THE. DOOR. I know you're home."

"Greyson?" I call out.

THE AFTERTHOUGHT

"Let me in this fucking house, now, or I'll kick the door in," he says while continuing his assault on my door. "One way or another, I'm coming into this house."

"You're fucking insane." I keep the knife in hand and walk to the door, flipping the lock free and stepping back.

He steps inside, anger written all over his face, but he just closes the door and stands there. He doesn't make any effort to walk toward me or say anything. He's just huffing and puffing like a raging bull.

"If this is about the coffee shop, I'm going to stop you right now. You lost the right to have a say in my life seven years ago."

"You let him touch you," he states. It's not a question, and he looks pissed.

"That's none of your business," I state firmly, and he steps closer to me.

"Not here. In Massachusetts. You let him touch you." His nostrils flare, and he takes another step toward me.

"What?" My eyes go wide. How could he possibly know about that? He takes another step closer to me, and I take a step back, holding the knife up between us. He eyes it and laughs.

"Cut me, baby. It'll only turn me on." He tilts his head to the side, silently daring me.

"What are you doing here, Grey? You made it perfectly clear that you want nothing to do with me." I shouldn't care, but part of my heart aches at that admission.

"You're going to tell me exactly what happened in Massachusetts." Again, he takes a step forward, and I step back. The look in his eyes is feral. I'm not sure why he thinks he can talk to me like this after all this time, but I'm not having it.

"I'm not telling you shit. You can leave." I step forward and push against his chest, the knife still in my right hand but pressing flat against his chest as I push. He grabs my wrists.

"Did. He. Touch. You? I want to hear it from you. Did you let him touch what's mine?"

Those words make me snap. I'm not his. "He sure fucking did. He pushed me up against a wall and had me falling apart on his fingers in less than five minutes. The second time he sent me barreling over the edge, I was bent over my couch with my pussy squeezing his cock hard enough to—"

I'm cut off. Within seconds, he's on me, twisting the knife from my hand. It falls to the floor with a clank. I push at him, but he pulls me to the floor next to the knife and straddles me. I slap and claw at him, but he grips my hands, roughly pinning them above my head.

"Do you even realize who he is?" He hovers over me. The proximity of his body to mine is doing things to me.

"It doesn't matter who he is. I don't belong to anyone, Greyson. I can fuck whoever I want."

"If you insist on staying in Dune Valley, then you belong to me. This town is mine. As long as you are here, so are you. If I have to put my mark on you to prove it, I will."

He leans in, and before I know what's happening his lips crash onto mine. I gasp, giving him the invitation he needed to allow his mouth to consume mine. I should stop him, but

I don't. Our tongues dance for dominance, and he nips at my lip. I lose myself a little bit and let an accidental moan slip free. I was hoping he wouldn't notice, but he pulls back and smiles. Fuck.

He adjusts the hold on my hands so that he has a free hand but is still able to keep my wrists pinned down. His eyes stay locked on mine as he slides his now free hand under my shirt and across my chest. He watches me carefully when he grabs my breast briefly before releasing it and pinching my nipple.

My brows raise at the sensation. I arch my back in response, letting my mouth fall open. He alternates between twisting my nipple between his two fingers and lightly flicking it. His eyes never leave mine the entire time. He's intently watching every slight reaction from me.

He pulls his hand out of my shirt and shoves two fingers into my slightly open mouth. I gag around them, and he pushes down firmly on my tongue. Tears well up in my eyes as my throat constricts around his thick fingers. He leans forward to whisper in my ear.

"Tell me you're mine."

"Fuck you," I mutter around his fingers.

He pulls them out of me, and I cough. In a swift moment, while I'm trying to recover, he flips me onto my stomach and pins my hands behind the small of my back. He straddles me lower this time, giving him some access to my lower half.

"Tell me what I want to hear, little shadow," he repeats.

"Get the fuck off of me." I squirm under his grasp, but he only holds me in place tighter.

He pulls my leggings down enough to sneak his hand into them and swipes his finger across my panties.

"Even your pussy knows who she belongs to. So wet for me." He's not wrong. That traitorous bitch is aching for him. My heart pounds in my chest, and my breathing is heavy.

I should tell him to stop touching me, but I don't. He pulls my panties to the side, and electricity shoots through me when his skin meets mine. A deep groan leaves him as he runs his fingers along my wet center.

"Let me remind you who I am to you," he grinds out.

A finger slowly slips inside me, and immediately, I clench around him. He touched me at his house, but this is different. He is trying to own me. I hate it, but I love it at the same time. He slides a second finger in and splits them inside me, rubbing against my sensitive walls. His pace is slow, and the ache in my core builds, but it's not enough. He is purposely keeping me just below my peak. It's more than infuriating. I hate him, but my pussy wants, no needs, the release he is teasing me with.

He pulls his fingers out and flips me over onto my back, pulling my leggings and panties down to my ankles in one swoop. I pull one leg out of them so that my legs spread easily, and he settles between them.

"Such an obedient slut for me when I want to taste you." He licks his lips, and his eyes land on my glistening pussy.

I shouldn't let this happen. I should kick him out, but I'm blinded by the lust. He leans in, and I almost lose my mind when I feel his hot tongue glide up my center. Immediate pleasure courses through me as he feasts on me like I am his last meal.

"Grey," I moan.

He pulls back and looks up at me. "Tell me what I want to hear."

"No," I state firmly.

He dives back in with a renewed passion. His eyes locked on me the entire time. I can't help but watch as he loses himself in my pussy. He sinks two fingers back inside of me, pumping in and out while sucking on my clit and flicking it lightly with his tongue. Shocks course through my body with each flick of his tongue. It's all too much. I intertwine my fingers in his hair, gripping hard and pulling him exactly where I need him.

He groans against me, causing vibrations that send me over the edge. Tingles spread from my core, slowly making their way to the tips of my fingers and toes. My hips buck beneath him as I cry out in pleasure. My pussy clamps hard around his fingers as I completely lose myself. My eyes roll into the back of my head, and the high consumes me. He doesn't let up until I look him in the eyes again. My chest heaving as I try to catch my breath and regain my reality.

"Tell me," he repeats.

"I don't belong to you. Not anymore." Sadness fills me, but anger crosses his eyes again.

He reaches out to grab the knife on the floor, holding it in his hand, and my eyes widen in panic. No, no, no, no. He wouldn't. My heart rate picks up again but for a different reason this time. Memories pull me back to that day.

I struggle to breathe with his cold fingers wrapped around my throat. He tightens his grip, and I claw at his hand to try to get free. He's too big, and I can't get away from him.

"You little fucking bitch. Did my wife hire you to follow me? Did she think it would be easy to get rid of me? Sending some pathetic girl to trail me and try and catch me in a fuckup." Spit from the intensity of his words came down to coat my face. He was angry, and his face was a deep shade of red as rage radiated from him. He was going to kill me. I saw it in his eyes.

His grip around my throat tightened when his other hand moved to his pocket. He pulled out a knife, and my eyes went wide, silently begging for him to let me go. The small breaths I was able to take quickened when I caught sight of the blade. I tried to get away from it, but my body was tired from the lack of oxygen, and he was bigger than me. This was it. This was going to be my last moment.

The blade came down across my chest, cutting my shirt open and slicing me down the center of my body. I felt the warm blood almost instantly pooling around the cut.

I tried my best to kick around and free myself from him as he held the knife above me, watching as the blood flowed freely from me. He laughed at my attempt to speak. His hand tightened further on my neck, threatening to completely cut off my airway.

I desperately tried everything I could to get away from him, but it wasn't enough.

"You can't report back to my wife if you're dead, you fucking bitch," he yelled as I felt the blade slice into my stomach this time. I was too worried about trying to breathe to focus on the pain of each cut. The intrusion of my flesh was nothing to him. He smiled down at me while he cut into me.

Over and over, he cut into the skin of my stomach and chest, marking me up. The wetness of the blood was all I could feel as the tears flowed freely down my cheeks. I was in too much shock to keep trying to get away. I accepted the moment. Time seemed to go on forever, an endless loop of suffering in hell.

When he stood up, he looked down at my motionless body. I was frozen, afraid that if I tried to move away from him, he would lean back in, and it would all start over again. His lip curled up in a snarl, and he spat on me before kicking my leg.

"Stay the fuck out of my business, you useless bitch."

I can hear someone calling out to me as the sound of their voice pulls me from the memory.

"Ava?" Greyson asks cautiously. "Are you okay?"

He seems genuinely concerned. I look over at the knife still in his hand, unable to speak. My eyes are glued to it.

"I was never going to hurt you, I swear. You were close to the knife, and I didn't want you to get cut with it." He tosses it into the kitchen.

A renewed sense of clarity courses through me, and I use my full strength to buck him off of me. I push him to the side, freeing myself, and pull my leggings and underwear back on. I close myself off to anything I may have been feeling. My walls are securely back in place. Greyson Hayes can go fuck himself.

"Get out." I point my finger toward the door.

"Ava, what was that all about? Talk to me."

"No, I said get out," I assert.

"Did someone hurt you?" He says while standing. A look of tenderness in his eye.

"You don't get it, do you, Greyson? You hurt me. You crushed me. I had to pick up the pieces one by one. I was alone. I carried that hurt with me for a long time before I was able to move on. My life hasn't always been the best over the years, but it's MY life. You don't get to know anything about me now. I don't owe you anything."

He looks at me in disbelief. Did he really think I was going to cave and just fall back into his arms so that he could toss me aside again when he was done with me?

"You don't know who he is, Ava. Alec isn't a nice guy," he says as I push him toward the door.

"I don't give a fuck about that guy at the coffee shop." It's not a lie, although I'm still considering the job because I could use the steady income.

"Just talk to me."

"I don't want to." I walk around him and pull the door open, waiting for him to leave.

He doesn't fight me anymore, and I'm thankful. He steps out and turns to look at me one last time. I slam the door in his face and lock it before he has a chance to say anything. Slowly, I turn around and press my back to the door, sliding down and pulling my knees to my chest to let myself fall apart. Memories from that day always destroy me.

Chapter 13
Greyson

I was so confused by her reaction to me holding the knife that the entire reason I went there in the first place slipped my mind. I was supposed to be putting her in her place, but somehow, she managed to get the upper hand. She was supposed to be explaining how the fuck she ended up letting Alec slip his slimy cock inside her. The thought of it makes fire burn through my veins. He had to know who she was. This was to get under my skin, and it fucking worked.

The only reason I left her house was because I knew something else was going on. Something in her shifted when she saw me holding the knife, and she slipped into some kind of memory. I wish she would have talked to me about it, but she shut herself off and refused. That's fair, I suppose. It's the treatment I deserve after everything.

How the fuck did this happen? I slam my fist on the steering wheel, staring back at her house, and debating whether or not to go back in. How did I let her get inside my head this fast? I was supposed to be making her leave town, but the only thing she hasn't been able to leave is my mind. I walked away from her all those years ago, but I don't know if I'm prepared to do it again.

THE AFTERTHOUGHT

The moment I saw that fiery orange hair and those deep brown eyes after so long, I knew any hope of getting her out of my mind was ruined. The image of her is burned into my brain. Every time I close my eyes, I see her. When I drive through town, I see the things we used to do together. I was fooling myself when I said I could keep her at a distance.

Maybe I could have kept up the act long enough for her to leave town, but something in me awakened when I saw Alec put his hands on her. Something that I haven't felt in a long time. I thought I needed to give her up to give in to my needs. I thought she would never understand why I had to join the Crimson Rose. They are my only way to be my true self and fully embrace the flames without ending up in prison. Maybe I was wrong all along.

The idea of having her so close but not being able to have her has only made the urges worse. Today was supposed to cure my craving, and it did until I laid eyes on Ava. I fucking love the way she looks when she falls apart for me. I forgot about so many of the tiny details about her. I've had a taste, and now I'm obsessed. She is my new urge.

Things have changed. I need to talk to Knox and make sure he knows where I stand with her. Alec's involvement adds an extra layer of complexity to this, and it can't be allowed.

I'm worried about what Knox is going to say about Ava. He knows how connected we were when we were younger, which is part of why he ensured I was in check when she returned to town. She's always been the one person to keep my urges both in and out of control, depending on the state of our relationship.

Ava thinks she doesn't belong to me, but she's wrong. She's mine, whether she wants to be or not. I'll just have to make sure I remind her every time she forgets. I'll burn anyone who tries to come between us alive and spit on their charred bones.

I glance back at her house one last time before pulling my phone out of my pocket and dialing Knox's phone number. It rings three times before he picks up.

"Hey, everything okay?" he asks.

"I need to meet you. We need to talk."

"I'm at the garage. Does this have to do with the Cobras?" His tone goes cold. I can tell he is trying to prepare his mind for how to retaliate against whatever they did.

"No. Yes. Sort of. I'll explain everything when I get there. They didn't strike us directly. Not officially."

"Okay, I'll wait here for you. Dad's nursing home called, though, so I can't be long. He's having a bad day today, and I have to make a trip out there."

Guilt wracks through me at the idea of keeping him from going to see Dad. Our dad had a nice twist of fate with the drugs he was trying to manage back before Knox took control. Dad was still in charge, and he sampled the wrong thing, which sent him into a fit of seizures. Something in his brain chemistry changed that day, and he hasn't stopped regressing from the brain damage since.

It was enough to land him in Dune Valley Nursing Home. Some days, he's more lucid than others, but he barely knows who we are most days. I don't bother stopping in anymore. Knox handles everything that has to do with him, so I don't have to.

"If Dad is having a day, it can wait," I say.

"It's fine. Just hurry up."

He ends the call, and I drive over to the garage, wondering what he ended up doing with that asshole I tortured earlier. Was that why Alec ended up at the coffee shop with Ava? There's no way he could have known the shape of his man by then. He only would have known that he was missing. Is that enough to encroach on another man's woman? Can I even call her my woman? I know I'm grasping at straws, but him being with her doesn't make sense.

I pull up to Adam's Garage a few minutes later, parking the car and strolling right inside. Two guys huddle in the corner, whispering when I walk past, and I narrow my eyes at them. These are newer members of the crew. I don't like whispering. Whispering is suspicious, but I don't have the mental fortitude to deal with that right now.

I push open the office door that I've come to know so well and find Knox sitting behind the desk, scrolling through his phone. He looks up to meet me and nods to acknowledge my presence. I do my normal routine of powering off mine and placing it on the desk for him to see.

He looks up at me after a moment, and I can see the concern on his face. He's able to clearly see that something is bothering me. He glances back down at his phone to finish whatever he is doing before placing it on his desk next to him.

"What's going on Grey?"

"There's no way for me to go about this besides spitting it right out. The dynamic between me and Avalynn has shifted." My jaw clenches at the thought of Alec having his hands on her.

Knox sighs. "I figured it was only a matter of time until that became the case. I remember you following her around like a lost puppy all those years ago."

"It's become more complicated than that."

"Fucking hell Greyson. What did you do now?"

I run my hand through my hair, letting the frustration flow through me. "I had no intention of getting close to her. When I found out she had come back, I wanted her to leave. I tried to make her leave. She followed me last week when you sent me to meet with our new client for that job. It was the first time I saw her face to face again."

This gets his attention, and he slams his fists on his desk. "What did she see?"

"I don't think she saw anything. I walked into the park for the meeting and found her wandering around after meeting with him. I think she was looking for me but got lost when she lost sight of me."

"You think, or you know? You need to be sure of what she knows. We can't have this getting out. It could ruin everything if the Cobras find out who he is. If they get the leg up on this, it could be the end of the Crimson Rose. You know Alec has been trying to find a way to overrun us for years." His voice is stern. "This is exactly what I was worried about. Some bitch comes back to town, and shit fucking goes to hell."

"Don't talk about her like that," I seethe. "I respect you as my brother and my boss, but you won't speak about her like that."

"I'll say what the fuck I want! You're supposed to be my right-hand man, Greyson. Now, I have to worry about whether or not you will be by my side when I need you to be. In seven years, I've never had to question your loyalty until-"

"That's just it. You've never had to question my loyalty," I interrupt. "It's not going to start now. I can be loyal to the Crimson Rose and still pursue things with Ava."

His eyes narrow. "You think you can do both without issue? What is your precious lady going to think when she finds out what you do for us? How will she react when she finds out you traffic drugs, kill, and torture people? What do you think she will say when she hears that you burn people alive?"

"She will just have to accept it."

He laughs. "Accept it? Brother, you truly have no idea how women work, do you? I can't say it's entirely your fault. It's been a long time since you've been in a relationship, so let me give you a spoiler. Women never just accept things."

"It will be fine," I insist.

"This is on you. If things go sideways, you know what will have to happen to her."

Anger courses through me. The fuck it will. "You won't fucking touch her!"

"You're so willing to choose a woman who hasn't chosen you over your brother and your gang already. Do you see why this could be an issue for me?" His brow raises.

"You don't have to worry about my loyalty, and you don't have to worry about her. I will make sure she is in line, and I will find out if she knows anything about who I met with last week." I hesitate to continue because if Knox has an issue with this, he's really not about to like what I have to say next.

"For fuck's sake. There's more, isn't there? She's been here for like a week. How can one woman cause so much trouble in such a short amount of time."

"Alec knows what she means to me. I tried to play it off, but I can tell he's up to something."

"What are you talking about?"

"Before she came back to Dune Valley, she had a run-in with him. I don't know all the details of it yet, but I know they slept together. I saw them having coffee at the coffee shop earlier today. By the smug look on his face, I know he's trying to involve himself with her to intentionally get at me."

I sit and look at Knox, waiting for him to say something, but he stays quiet for a moment. I watch as he processes the information, and different thoughts cross his mind. He pinches the bridge of his nose before leaning back in his chair.

"Is she worth it?" He looks at me with a stern look.

That question confuses me. I have no clue why I feel the way I do about her. She's a completely different person than she was before she left town all those years ago, but something about her just pulls me in. It's almost as though there is an invisible thread connecting us that I can't seem to clip. She consumes all my thoughts, and I barely even know who she is anymore.

I can't admit to Knox that she has no desire to even be in the same room as me. He will want to take the easy way out of this whole mess and have her killed. That way, he gets his town back in order and his little puppet back at his side to do all his bidding.

I would gladly light it up and watch it all burn for her. This whole town could burn for all I care. Just a few interactions with her have me acting like an eighteen-year-old boy again. She has this uncanny control over me. I made a mistake letting her go before. She will be mine this time, whether she wants to or not. This life, this town. She doesn't get to leave again.

I look back up at Knox and nod. "Yes."

"Keep her in check, and don't make me regret this decision," he says, making me nod again. "If Alec's up to something, get your girl in line and find out what he's planning. The Crimson Rose has run this town for the last thirty years. I won't let it fall to the Cobras over some piece of ass. I'll put out some feelers to see if I can find something."

"Okay." I take the win, even though I hate him referring to her as a piece of ass.

His phone starts buzzing next to him, and he clicks it to voicemail with a clear look of frustration. "Is there anything else I need to know, or are you done fucking up my day?"

"She has a younger sister that's still in high school, Chloe Marshall. She's been hanging around some of our younger recruits."

"I'll put the word out for the guys to be respectful to her." That's his way of saying he will make sure they stay away from her.

"Thank you," I say before making my way to the door to head out.

"Greyson," he says, and I stop to turn back at him. "You owe me one. I hope she's worth it."

He gets one more nod from me before I turn and head back to my car. That went better than I expected. I thought he would lose his shit and tell me to kill her. I think he knows that could never happen. I smile as I pull open my car door and slide into the front seat. I'm sure, at some point, he will want to cash in on the debt I now owe him, but that's a problem for another day. It's time to get my precious flame and officially make her mine again.

Chapter 14
Avalynn

As soon as Greyson left, I gave myself some time to wallow in my feelings before pulling myself together and moving on with my day. I wonder if he was telling the truth when he said he wasn't planning to hurt me with the knife.

Why did I let him touch me like that? I fought him, sure, but not nearly as hard as I could have. Part of me wants to submit to him, but I won't allow that. I can't believe he had the audacity to ask if I was okay. Like he really gives a shit if I'm okay. It has to be part of whatever game he's playing to get me to leave town.

He hurt me before; what's stopping him from doing it again? I won't allow Greyson into my heart this time. A sly smile spreads across my face. He seemed very distraught at the idea of me and Alec spending time together. There is something off about that guy that I can't seem to place, but knowing it will piss Grey off has me wanting to run right into Alec's arms.

I should probably keep my distance from him. He can't be a good guy. Most people from this town are involved in gangs or drugs in one way or another. The only people who aren't are the stupid ones who enjoy living in poverty. There are no opportunities in this town outside of the criminal organizations.

That was one of the many reasons I never wanted to stay here. It was why we were supposed to leave. Even Chloe has been running around with some of the crew. Part of me worries for her. She is stubborn, and most of those guys get immense joy from breaking people like her. I have to trust that her boyfriend wouldn't let that happen, even if I don't want to.

I wonder if I'll be able to convince her to come with me after she graduates. If the two of us sell our parents' houses here, we could have enough money to establish ourselves somewhere decent. We could move to a big city where I could do my PI work, and she could go to college. She could get a real education and go on to really make something of herself. We wouldn't have to worry about the men of this pathetic town.

Memories of what Grey said hit me like a sack of bricks. *Do you even realize who he is?* What the hell did he mean by that? Who is Alec? I make a mental note to be more cautious with him going forward, at least until I know what I'm dealing with.

I do a quick Google search, and boy am I surprised by the results. This man has a rap sheet a mile long. He's never been arrested or formally charged, but there are a bunch of articles about… no fucking way. The Cobras. He's part of the Cobras.

As soon as I see that, I know I won't find the information I'm looking for on the internet. The media only ever gets their hands on basic things regarding the gangs in this town. Most of the time, they manage to pay them off before anything too demeaning hits the papers. The only way I will get information on this guy is from a local who makes it their job to be involved in all the town gossip. Wrenly.

I scroll through my contacts before landing on her number and pressing the call button. It feels wrong to get her involved in this, but I need to know exactly what I'm getting myself into. The call goes to voicemail, so I send her a text asking her to give me a call when she gets a chance. I'll have to figure this out myself then.

I head back to my room to change my clothes and put on something a bit more comfortable. I've settled on black high-waisted leggings, a black cropped sweater with skull hands making a heart, and my black and white Converse—cute but comfortable.

I decided to make this easy on myself and go to Temptations. I know Alec will likely be there because it's his club. I'm a bit nervous at the idea that it could be a Cobra hangout, but I need to know. I could pretend I'm there for that job and do a bit of digging. He expects me to show up there anyway.

Anxiety courses through me at the thought of letting myself get close to Alec. If I'm staying in this town for the next few months, I'll have to choose a side. Greyson is part of the Crimson Rose, and he's made it clear that he doesn't want me around. His only goal is to get me out of Dune Valley. I'm going to one-up him. I'll fucking glue myself to his damn enemy and shove it down his throat. He thinks he has some claim on me because we dated when we were kids, but he's wrong.

With my mind made up, I grab my keys and head to my car once again. Getting involved in any gang could be one of the dumbest decisions I've ever made. I left this town to get away from this shit, but here I am, willingly driving to a club owned by someone in the Cobras. The direct enemy of the Crimson Rose. They're not nearly as big or powerful as the Crimson Rose, but they have been trying to gain traction to take down the Crimson Rose for years. It's a bloody feud that I should avoid, yet here I am, placing myself right in the middle.

I try to find a reason to talk myself out of this as I make the drive across town to the club. I tell myself I can find another job somewhere else. Do I even want to work at Temptations? It's true, I could find a job somewhere else, but where's the fun in that?

I pull up to the address listed on the card Alec gave me and park in one of the spaces directly in front of the main door. The building is long and rectangular in shape. A few deep purple stripes flow along the building to break up the monotone black color. There are no windows. Above two blacked-out doors, a sign that says Temptations hangs with a martini glass next to it.

There are quite a few cars in the parking lot, which is a bit surprising for the time of day. I raise a brow as I watch someone else pull into the parking lot. He parks in one of the far spots and looks around cautiously before entering the building. My eyes have to be playing tricks on me because there's no way Sheriff Wolfe just walked into this club. Maybe he likes strippers. Who am I to judge?

I take a deep breath, trying to gather my thoughts. Am I really going to do this? Am I going to get a job in a strip club to piss off my ex-boyfriend? I know from the coffee shop incident that they don't get along. I only came here to creep on Alec, but the opportunity to make Greyson mad is enticing. A grin crosses my face. I most certainly am. It's now or never, I suppose. I push open my door and walk up to the front door of the club.

I step into an entryway with a large man sitting on a stool, scrolling on his phone. I immediately catch sight of the snake tattoo on his neck. He must be a Cobra. He finally pulls his gaze from his phone and raises a brow, not bothering to hide the way he looks up and down the length of my body.

"I need your ID." He holds his hand out, waiting for me to place my driver's license in it. After a quick glance, he looks at me again. "You're good to go. No pictures." He hands my license back to me, and I roll my eyes.

When I push open the door to the club, it takes my eyes some time to adjust to the lack of light. It's dim, with low lights surrounding each stage. Once my eyes adjust, I take a moment to look around at my surroundings. A soft bumping sound fills the club. This isn't my first time in a place like this. In my line of work, there are a lot of shitty men out there, and shitty men like naked women.

To my left is a stage with a woman in a thong sliding up and down a pole. The look on her face tells me that she is lost in thought as a group of men sit in seats around her, eyeing her. I turn my gaze directly in front of me, where another stage sits with a large mirror behind the entirety of it. Two more women on poles dance on this stage in various forms of undress.

I look past the stage in front of me to find a set of doors leading to the bathroom, another set of doors that are roped off, and one final door that is not labeled. To my right, I find a long bar, filling up the remaining length of the room, and walk over to it.

Two men sit on barstools at the bar, talking to the person working behind it. I'm surprised to find a man working behind the bar. With this being a club, you would think a woman would be back there getting the drinks. I suppose that's what I'm here for.

When I approach, the bartender locks eyes with me, and the three of them go quiet. The two sitting on the stools turn to look at me, and I have to control the shock on my face when I see Alec sitting there and having a calm discussion with Sheriff Wolfe. I ignore their eyes on me and slap a $10 bill on the bar.

"I'll have a vodka soda."

The guy behind the bar laughs and reaches out to grab the money before turning to make the drink. I wait patiently, watching out of the corner of my eye as Alec leans in and whispers something in the sheriff's ear. He nods and looks over towards me.

"Keep your men in line, Mr. Boone. I don't want to have to come back here again." He says it loud enough for me to hear. It feels like he's putting on a show, and I wonder why he's really here.

He takes a step away from Alec and stops next to me. "Avalynn, I trust you are settling into town nicely."

I turn and face him, keeping my face blank. "Yep. Here for a job."

"You don't strike me as the type to work somewhere like this," he admits, and I can see the way his eyes burn through my clothing.

"I'll be behind the bar. Fully clothed," I clarify.

"Ah, well, I will leave you to it. I have to be on my way. Give your sister my best."

I give him a weak smile. A glass lands on the bar beside me. I reach out to grab the drink, noticing that Alec has turned in his chair and is now looking at me. I casually smile at him while sipping on my drink.

"I expected you to call before showing up," he says with a look of irritation. He doesn't like being caught off guard. I wasn't supposed to see the Sheriff here talking to him.

"What can I say? I like to be unpredictable."

He takes a moment to study me before I see his features visibly relax. "Let's go to my office so we can talk without the noise and distraction."

Alarm bells ring out. This is a bad idea, but still, I follow him as he hops off the stool and goes straight to the unlabeled door I saw earlier. The door opens to a big office. Half of the office has a large circular couch with a pole in the middle. The other side houses a large oak desk. Bookshelves with assorted items line the wall behind the desk. Several bottles of what looks like expensive whiskey and glasses sit on one of the shelves.

Alec steps up to the desk, pushing the large black chair to the side to grab himself a glass and pour some of the amber liquid into it. I take it upon myself to fill one of the seats across from the desk with my vodka soda in hand. When he finally turns to look at me, he smiles. It seems fake, but he smiles.

"I'm happy that this morning's little run-in didn't scare you away." He takes a seat in the chair behind his desk, making himself comfortable.

"In case you haven't picked up on it yet, I'm not the kind of woman who lets someone else tell her what to do."

"Indeed. You are a rare gem, Avalynn. One I'm happy I had the chance to indulge in."

A blush meets my cheeks when I remember him dicking me down. Clearly, he is still interested in pursuing something outside of the usual business relationship. I need to be cautious with this. He's a Cobra, I remind myself.

"So, this job?" I question attempting to bring the conversation back to part of the reason I'm here.

"It's yours if you want it." He brings the glass to his lips, taking another sip, never letting his gaze leave mine. Something about it seems a bit sinister.

"That's it? No interview? No questions? It's just my job if I want it."

"That's what I said, is it not?"

"And no uniform?"

"Correct. You are welcome to wear, or not wear, whatever you like. You could bring in some pretty big tips from some of the regulars if you wore something... less." A chuckle escapes him. "I might prefer it if you covered up a bit, though. I would rather not have to fight off my customers to get to you."

Here we fucking go. Another man who thinks that just because we fucked he now has some weird claim on me. What the hell is going on in the minds of the men in this town? I belong to myself and myself only, regardless of who I let put their dick in me.

"If I were to start working here, this would be a business-only relationship between you and me going forward."

"I am a bit disappointed. Are you sure that's what you want?"

"Yes. I need to have some type of respect from the other people here. I can't have them thinking I only got the job because I slept with the boss."

"But that's exactly why you got the job." He throws the glass back, downing the last of the drink and setting it down on the desk in front of him.

"Not funny," I state.

He throws his hands up in defense. "If it makes you feel better, I've slept with most of the women who work for me."

That definitely does not make me feel better, but I really need a job that provides a reliable source of money right now—for Chloe. He stands up slowly and walks over to me. His hand comes up, and the back of his finger trails across my skin from my ear down to my chin. He keeps moving it down to my chest, and I reach up to push his hand away.

"I mean it, Alec. It's not happening again."

"Very well." He admits defeat and goes back to his chair.

"When can you start? Bruce has been working behind the bar, but he's terrible and has a tough time keeping his opinions to himself."

"I can start as soon as today if you want."

"Great. I'll show you around, and you can get comfortable behind the bar. I'll let you shadow Bruce for the rest of his shift, and then you can dive in from there. You have bartending experience, right? I don't have to worry about you mixing weird shit?"

"Yes, I have experience. I'll manage just fine." It's not a lie. I've worked in a bar a time or two when the jobs were slow coming in. It was always a quick way to make money under the table. There's always a bar somewhere looking to hire a pretty face.

"Great. Let's get this tour done. I actually have somewhere I need to be." He stands and leaves the room. I make a point to purposely leave my glass of vodka on his very nice wooden desk. I hope it leaves a ring in its wake, asshole.

We walk back out to the main room, and he points over to the two different stages and tells me briefly about them. I nod, taking it all in. When he turns to go toward the roped-off area, the man standing next to it pulls the rope aside to let us pass.

"These are our VIP rooms. You should never need to come back here for anything. If someone from back here needs a drink, one of the girls who works in these rooms will grab it from you at the bar."

"Got it."

I take in all the rooms we walk past—six in total, three on each side of the hallway. One of the doors is closed, so I only get a good look at five of them, and they are all the same: a pole, a couch, some cheap lighting, and a small table to place drinks on.

When we exit the VIP section, he brings me to the bar and introduces me to Bruce. I eagerly dive into each task he asks of me while Alec stands there watching. Once Bruce is convinced I know what I'm doing, he nods over to Alec.

Alec smiles. "Great. Now that you're all set, I'll be on my way."

He turns without saying another word, leaving the club. I wasn't expecting to have to work today, so I pull out my phone to send a quick text to Chloe, letting her know that I won't be home until late and that there are leftovers in the fridge that she can eat for dinner. She texts me back with another one of her smart-ass remarks about how gross my food is, and for a brief moment, it seems like everything might actually fall into place. Maybe.

Chapter 15

Greyson

I go back to her house, but she's not there. Chloe will be home from school soon, so Ava has to come home at some point, right? I decide to sit outside, parked across the street from her house, until she does.

Time passes, and nobody shows up. I begin to get more and more frustrated. Where the hell could she possibly be? She doesn't have a job, and she's only been in town a short while. Her only friend is Wrenly. I know the two of them aren't together right now because she's with Kai.

When Chloe comes home from school and makes her way into the house alone, I decide enough is enough. I march right up to the front door. Her sister has to know where she is. I just need to have a conversation with her so that we can figure out how to make this work.

She says she hates me but hate and love aren't really that different. Both inspire passion. Both require you to think of that person often. My little shadow says she hates me, but I'll just have to remind her exactly why that's not true at all.

I politely knock on the door and wait for Chloe to answer. When it swings open, I can tell I'm not who she expected.

THE AFTERTHOUGHT

"Is your sister home?" I ask.

"No," she says.

"Do you know when she's going to be home?"

"No." Again, a one-word answer.

"Do you know where she is?"

"None of your business." She folds her arms across her chest.

Great. This is exactly what I wanted to deal with today. Another version of Ava, except this one is younger and seems to hate me for no apparent reason.

"Do you mind if I come in to wait for her?"

"Are you sure that's a good idea? You are, after all, the person who made it clear that the crew needs to stay away from me, right?"

Well, fuck. There it is. The reason that she's being so cold and standoffish toward me. Knox didn't waste any time getting the word out about Chloe. It's only been a few hours since I talked to him.

"Chloe."

"Save it for my sister. I don't need to hear your bullshit excuses. You aren't going to keep me away from him, you know. He loves me." She pokes me in the chest with her finger. "You were the person saying he should keep me on a leash. I'm a bitch remember."

"If he loves you, then he will fight for you."

"You mean like you did for Ava? Yeah, I know all about that now. You two dated for a few years, and you broke things off so that you could join the Crimson Rose. You threw her aside like she meant nothing to you. Now, you want to insert yourself back into her life. She moved on, so you want to punish everyone else because she doesn't want you anymore."

"Whatever is going on between Ava and me is none of your business. You have no idea what the fuck you're talking about. Are you going to let me inside, or do I need to wait in my car?"

She seems a bit taken aback by how firm I am in my words. I didn't come here to get scolded by a teenager. I'll wait outside if I have to, but I'm talking to Ava tonight. I stare at her for a few minutes while she decides whether or not I'm good enough to come into the house.

"I don't know when she's coming back. If I let you in, you're ordering me pizza for dinner. I'd rather not eat Ava's shitty leftovers."

"Pizza sounds good." This seems to pacify her enough to step to the side so I can enter the house.

I gaze at the entryway floor, remembering the look on Ava's face as she came around my fingers there. Her pussy gripped them so tightly, and she made the sweetest sounds. She can say she didn't want me to do it all she wants, but we both know that's a lie. I can't wait to see her fall apart again.

I turn towards the living room to get comfortable on the couch. This thing has to be at least fifteen years old and is complete shit. It's the same one they had here when we were younger. The floral pattern reminds me of something that I would find at my grandmother's house when I was a kid. Why is she still living like this?

My phone dings in my pocket, so I pull it out to check who it is. It's Kai. When I read what he sent, my blood boils. It takes everything in me not to march back to my car to drag her home.

> Kai: Wrenly said Ava got that job at Temptations.

I told her not to go there, but she didn't listen. She never fucking listens. Temptations, really? The one place I can't freely go. Of course that's where she is.

I lean forward on the couch, debating what to do. I don't really have any options here. My foot taps anxiously on the old carpet while I stare out blankly. I can't just waltz into Cobra territory and take someone who wants nothing to do with me. It would be different if she agreed and gave me a chance, but she made it known in Alec's presence that we aren't together.

This is exactly why I wanted to stay away from her. She is nothing but an added complication. Everything was fine until she turned up, and the feelings I had buried started coming back to the surface. I still don't understand why I feel such a deep-rooted need for her. I was able to step away so easily all those years ago. She still crossed my mind daily, but it didn't feel like this.

Chloe comes out of her room and narrows her eyes at me. "Where's the pizza?"

Fuck. I've been so stuck in my head that I forgot about the pizza. "I'll go get it now. If I leave to pick it up, are you going to let me back in?"

"I don't care what you do as long as you get the food. You're Ava's problem. I like pepperoni." She turns on her heels and shuts herself back in the bedroom. Teenagers. There's no way we were that bad when we were younger.

I called the pizza shop and ordered a medium pepperoni pizza and a large buffalo chicken pizza. I'm sure Ava will be hungry when she gets home, so she can eat some of mine. I can't get my mind off of her and what she's doing at Temptation right now.

Who is touching her? Who is she talking to? If someone hurts her while she's there, I have no way of getting in to help her without starting an all-out war. Is that what Alec is trying to do? Does he want a war between the Cobras and the Crimson Rose?

I pick up the pizza and drive back to Ava's house. Chloe sticks to her word and lets me in, and the two of us eat in silence at the kitchen table. She has her phone out and hasn't stopped texting. I'm guessing it's her boyfriend. I need to figure out this kid's name and what his deal is. He must care about her if he is willing to go against a direct order from Knox.

We finish up, and she eyes me cautiously before deciding her next words. "Tell Ava I went to Andrea's. Her dad is on the way to pick me up. I don't want to be here when the two of you have whatever fight you're about to have."

"Aren't you supposed to stay here?" I have no clue if the two of them have rules they agreed on.

"So I can listen to you hate fuck after you fight with each other? I think I'll pass. I'll have Sheriff Wolfe bring me home in the morning." She flips her hair over her shoulder and retreats to her bedroom to gather a bag. Before I know it, she's out the door, and I'm waiting for Ava alone in her house.

By the time I hear a car pull up outside, it's well after midnight. I've had plenty of time to run this conversation through my mind, but I still have no clue what I'm going to say. She's going to be pissed when she finds me here. She's already said countless times that she wants nothing to do with me, and that was fine before. Before she got stuck in my head, and before she started to consume my every waking thought. This really isn't healthy.

The door creaks open, and I turn to look at her from my place on her couch. She hasn't noticed that I'm here yet. She seems tired. There is an extra sag to her shoulders, and her general aura is giving off an 'I've had a long day, stay away from me' energy. She turns toward the kitchen and freezes at the sight of the pizza.

"Chloe?" she calls out, not knowing that Chloe isn't going to answer her because she's not here.

She grabs a slice of the pizza from the box and takes a bite, groaning as the first taste hits her mouth. The buffalo chicken pizza. She eats the whole first slice, cold, and goes for a second before she stops dead in her tracks. It's as if she had some sort of realization of where the pizza is from. I made sure to get it from the less popular joint in town. She always loved this one the most when we were younger.

"Chloe!" she calls out again.

When she turns and finally sees me on the couch, she jumps and yells out, making me grin. "Hey, little shadow."

"Greyson?" She questions as if to make sure it's really me and not someone else sitting in her house without her permission.

"Yeah, baby, it's me."

"Don't call me that. I'm not your baby." She stalks past the living room and pulls open the door to what I'm assuming is Chloe's room now because it's across the hall from the room Ava stayed in when we were kids. She marches back out here and stops in front of me with her arms crossed. "What the fuck are you doing here, and where is Chloe?"

"We need to talk." I reach out to grab her hips to pull her toward me, but she swats my hands away.

"No, we don't. I've had a long day. Where is my sister?"

"She went to Andrea's and will be back in the morning. She didn't want to be here when you got home, and we started hate fucking. Her words, not mine." A smile crosses my face, but hers turns to a scowl.

"When we what? We are not having sex. I'm not in the mood for this, Greyson. Can you just leave?"

I stand and step into her, grabbing her hips before she can swat my hands away this time. I pull her close and lean in, running my nose along her neck and taking in her sweet citrus smell. I know better than to push my boundaries right now, even though all I want to do is throw her against a wall and fuck her senseless.

I turn her and push her toward the couch. She falls onto it, and I sit down next to her. "We're talking," I insist.

"There's nothing to talk about."

"At the very least, we can talk about how, on two different occasions, you've come apart on my fingers."

Her cheeks blush, but the rest of her body and face remain stiff and unreadable. She doesn't stop me from talking or attempt to get up from the couch. I'm taking this as my go-ahead to shoot my shot.

"You can't hate me forever." I try.

"Greyson, I've barely been here a week. You've told me to leave countless times. Now you're telling me I'm not allowed to hate you?" She crosses her arms in front of her chest. "Why don't you tell me what exactly you expect at this point? I'm getting whiplash from your mood swings."

"Watch the way you talk to me. I'm trying to have a nice conversation with you," I grit out. The only thing I want to do right now is throw her down and fuck that attitude right out of her. Nobody talks to me like that.

She laughs. "I don't know if you realize this or not, but I'm not like the rest of the people in this town. I don't give a shit about your feelings or whatever fear I'm supposed to have for you. You can't hurt me any more than you already have. Say what you need to say and get the hell out so I can go to sleep."

That's it. That's enough right there to make me snap. I tried this the nice way. I tried to be the chivalrous man who gave her a choice. She doesn't want to talk. Fine, we don't have to talk.

Before she has a chance to react, I reach down and grab her ankle, pulling it onto the couch and tugging her tiny body down so that she is lying on her back on the length of the couch. I grip her arms and pin them above her head, placing my body on top of hers.

Her narrowed eyes are filled with challenge. "Are you going to hurt me, Grey? Do your best."

She's playing with fire. As much as she tells me she doesn't want this, I can tell she does. I run my nose along her neck, similar to what I did earlier, but this time, I bite down on her lower earlobe before whispering in her ear, "Tell me you hate me."

I grind my now-hardened cock against her center. Her legs slide apart for me, letting me settle right where I belong. I use my free hand to tug the belt from my jeans before grinding down on her again. "Tell me, Ava. Be a good slut, and tell me how much you hate me."

Her eyes light up. "I hate you."

There's my girl. She wants to play. Who am I to deny her?

I straddle her and pull her hands up to wrap my belt around them. After making sure they are nicely secured together, I push them back down over her head. "These stay here, or you'll be punished."

She goes to say something, but I bring my hand over her mouth. "Don't ruin it. You know you need this. Just let me use you, and you can hate me through the whole thing."

"I do hate you," she mumbles again behind my hand.

"You know what hate is, baby? Passion. I'll make sure you're screaming my name, don't worry."

I slide my hands under her cutoff sweater, pulling it up over her head until it rests on her wrists. Her hands are tied, so I can't pull it off completely. My gaze goes to her chest, and I freeze when I see the scars.

I trail my hand along the first one that goes between her breasts. Her body goes rigid. She goes to pull her hands back over her head, but I grab them and slam them back down to where I told her to keep them. "Don't fucking move them."

I stand up next to her on the couch to grip the top of her leggings, but before I can pull them down, her bound hands swing up to stop me.

"Put your hands back, or I'll tie you to something else so you can't move at all."

She seems a bit reluctant, but she slowly puts them back. She eyes me cautiously when I pull her leggings and panties off. I'm shocked by what I see. The leggings were so high up on her waist that they concealed all of her scars.

Countless lines cross the entirety of her abdomen and chest. My brows furrow, and I look up to meet her glare. "Who did this to you?"

I see the tears well up in her eyes, but she refuses to speak. Slowly, I lean down and tenderly kiss each one of the scars. I hear her whimper under me, and a piece of me breaks. Somebody hurt her. Somebody hurt her because I made her leave.

"When I find out who did this, I promise you they will pay. I will fucking burn them alive for hurting you."

She stiffens under me. "It was a long time ago. It doesn't matter."

"Someone hurt what's mine. They will pay for that." I bring her to a seated position on the couch, kneeling in front of her and pulling her ass right to the edge. She keeps her hands above her head and rests them on the top of the couch, letting me settle between her legs.

"I wasn't yours when it happened, and I'm not yours now," she says just before I lick up the length of her.

"Oh baby, that's where you're wrong. You've always belonged to me. Let me remind you how good I am to what's mine."

I dive into her without saying another word. I want to feel her fall apart from my tongue before her tight cunt squeezes my cock. Her hips grind into my face as I lick and suck her pussy. She's so wet. I dip my tongue in and out of her while also sliding up to her clit to keep her stimulated.

She's breathing heavily, and a loud moan leaves her lips. I glance up to take in the look on her face. Her eyebrows are pinched together, her mouth is slightly open, and her eyes are squeezed shut, so I pull back.

"Eyes on me," I tell her.

She opens them, and reluctantly, they meet mine. It makes my heart bloom in my chest. I pick up right where I left off, devouring her one lick at a time. She gasps when I nip at her clit with my teeth. My pace is steady as I watch the way the pleasure builds on her face. Her breathing picks up more and more.

I can tell by the way she keeps bucking her hips against my face that she's close. I latch onto her clit, sucking and flicking my tongue until her hips shake uncontrollably. She's so close to letting go for me.

"Grey!" she cries out, bringing her hands down to rest on the top of my head as I claim my prize. I want to tell her to be a good whore and come on my face, but I don't dare let up my pace. Her hips jerk under me while she writhes beneath my tongue.

Slowly, her movements slow, and she starts to come down from her high. I pull back and wipe my face with my arm. It's not enough. I need more of her. I need to feel the way she comes apart on my cock.

Chapter 16
Avalynn

He looks up at me, his eyes filled with darkness, before standing. I watch as he pulls his shirt off. My gaze immediately lands on his washboard abs. I look him over carefully until something pulls my attention directly to it. Tattoos cover his entire chest, but I can't take my eyes off the one directly over his heart.

To a normal person, this would have no meaning, but I immediately know what it means. Two movie ticket stubs are directly over his heart. One is front-facing with the word 'cinema ticket' tattooed on it, and the other appears to be the back of the ticket. Instead of the usual blank backing, this one has words on it—words in my handwriting.

He catches what I'm staring at, and he steps into me. His hand reaches down to the bottom of my chin, tilting my head up to look him in the eyes. "If you're wondering what I think you are, then the answer is yes."

I shake my head at the thought. I don't want to think about why he has this specific tattoo over his chest. My eyes land on the three words again, I love you. The first time we told each other we loved each other was at the drive-in. I came home that night and wrote these exact words on the back of the ticket stub so that I could look back and always remember the importance of this particular movie night.

He didn't have this before I left. Those memories, the things we did together. He ruined all of that. He was the one who pushed me away and wanted me to leave. I should tell him to leave now, but he's already got me so worked up. Just one touch from him is enough to send electricity to my core. I just want this to be easy right now. Uncomplicated sex. So, I lie. I close off my thoughts and lie to him.

"I wasn't thinking about anything except for why you haven't fucked me yet. Either do it or leave." I need to keep him at a distance. I can't let him in again, not after how badly he hurt me last time.

Thankfully, he lets it go and sits on the couch next to me. He leans over to grab me and pull me on top of him. I straddle his hips, and he grabs my bound hands and lifts them over his head so that one arm is on each side of it.

This is too intimate. I should stop this. He knows what I was thinking, regardless of how I try to play it off. I know it's a bad idea, but for some reason, I can't. I want him. I don't say no. I let him use my body the way that he wants to. One time won't hurt. That's what I tell myself, at least. It's just sex. I'm not letting him into my heart. That will never happen again.

"Condom," I say.

"I put one on while you were staring at the tattoo on my chest."

His hands reach down to grab my hips. He lifts me up and slowly lowers me onto him, inch by inch. I almost forgot how big he was. He gives me a moment to adjust to his size. My eyes focus on the wall behind the couch as he finally begins moving inside me. He pushes and pulls at my hips, making me grind on top of him.

"Look at me, Ava."

"No," I state firmly, and he stops. I'm not looking at him. I can't. I won't allow this to be intimate. Looking him in the eyes in this position would be exactly that.

One hand leaves my hip, and he reaches up to pull my face towards his. "I want you looking at me when you come apart on my cock."

"No," I say again while staring into his eyes.

He pushes me off of him, making me fall to my side on the couch. He stands and pulls me up so that I'm on my knees, facing the back of the couch. My bound hands hang over the back of the couch. He grabs my hips and pulls me towards his cock, slamming inside me with zero hesitation.

"You want me to take it from you then?" A hand comes down to slap my ass hard, and I clench around him. He laughs at the feeling of my pussy clamping down on him as he continues to alternate his slaps between each ass cheek. "Do you want me to use you like my dirty slut?"

"Yes!" I cry out. This is what I need. No intimacy, just pure lust.

He pushes my head down and grabs my hips again, slamming into me harder and harder with each thrust. I push back into him, silently begging for more. With each movement, I can feel the heat building in my core, inching to the pure bliss I seek. When I feel myself getting close, he stills inside me. He grabs a handful of my hair and pulls my head back. I whimper as my back meets his chest, and I look up at him.

"You don't get to come without begging for it. That's your punishment for not looking at me. Beg me to make you come like the desperate slut you are."

Chills spread through my entire body. "Please."

He pushes me back down forcefully. My bound hands land in front of me, sliding into the crack of the couch cushions. He holds my head down with one hand and grabs my hip, thrusting into me again with his relentless pace.

"Beg, baby. Make me believe you."

"Please, let me come, Grey. I need it." I almost forgot what it was like to be with him. Our bodies just know each other so well. His cock rubs against the perfect spot inside of me, making my heart pound in my chest.

"Not good enough. I can feel the way your greedy pussy is gripping my cock."

A smack lands on my backside again, and I cry out in pleasure. "Please, please, please." I try, but he pulls out of me. Instantly, my body cools down again, and anger floods through me. I need him to make me come.

"You can do better than that." He plunges back into me.

His fingers grip my hips with so much force that I know there will be bruises there in the morning. I don't care. All I want at this moment is whatever he is willing to give me. I'm too far lost in sexual bliss to think logically anymore. He smacks me again.

"Greyson, I need your cock. Please let me come. Please don't stop." Tears threaten to fall from my eyes again. He has me so worked up. One of his fingers reaches around to find my clit, and he begins rubbing small circles.

"Pretty little slut taking my dick like a good girl." His words make me want to explode. I clamp down tightly on him, squeezing the life out of his cock. With any luck, he will cave and give in to what I need. He continues to move in and out of me as another whimper leaves my throat.

He pinches my clit between his fingers, finally vocalizing the words I've been waiting for. "Come for me, baby. Show me how much I own this pussy."

Relief floods me, and I lose myself in the pleasure of doing exactly as he says. I come so hard. I cry out as the orgasm racks through my entire body. It consumes me in a way that I've never experienced before. After a few moments, I hear him groan and thrust into me one last time before stopping.

I slump hard into the sofa, letting the after-sex haze take over my thoughts as he pulls out of me. He steps away, disappearing into the bathroom. I hear him fiddle around a bit, but I don't have the energy to move. My entire body feels nothing but complete bliss, every cell relaxed. It takes me a moment to realize I'm crying. I don't know why, but I can't stop it.

A few minutes later, he reappears and leans down to lift me up. My hands are still bound, but I let my head fall onto his chest. He carries me to the bathroom and places me in the tub. Did he draw me a bath?

The water feels warm, and I melt into it. He pulls the sweatshirt that's stuck on my arms down enough to unclasp the belt and pulls both the shirt and belt off of me. One at a time, he grabs my hands and rubs my wrists, ensuring they're okay before sliding into the tub behind me. He positions me in front of him, letting my back rest on his chest. We sit like that until the water starts to get cold. He hasn't tried to talk to me, but him being here to make sure I'm okay after sex is more intimate than I'd like.

"Grey," I say quietly.

"Yeah, little shadow."

"I can't let you in again. This didn't mean anything." I feel the way his body stiffens behind me. This meant something to him.

"Can we go talk? I just have a few things to get off my chest. If you're still not interested in hearing anything after that, I'll go for now, but I'm not walking away from you this time, Ava."

He stands up to get out of the tub and wraps a towel around his waist before looking down at me, waiting for my response.

"Fine, we can go talk." I stand to get out of the tub, but my legs are still weak, and I almost fall back into the water.

He reaches out to steady me, helps me out, and places a towel around my shoulders. He's being too nice. Part of me feels like he's trying to manipulate me. It's too weird that a few days ago, he hated me, and now he's obsessed with me.

"I'm going to put some clothes on." I push past him to leave the bathroom and slam my bedroom door closed behind me.

I opt for something comfortable: navy blue sweatpants with a random college name down one leg that I got from a thrift store and an old oversized gray T-shirt. Once dressed, I leave my room to figure out where he is. He's sitting at my kitchen table with a glass in hand. The pizza has been moved to the counter, and he looks lost in thought.

"You bribed Chloe with pizza, didn't you?" His head whips over in my direction, and he smiles.

"She really doesn't like your cooking. I made sure to at least get it from the place you like." He gives me a half smile.

"I know I said we could talk, but I'm exhausted. Honestly, I would just like to go to bed."

"Give me a few minutes. You don't have to say anything. I just need you to listen."

"Fine." I make my way to the chair next to him and sit down.

He pauses for a moment and sighs. "I couldn't let you stay."

I'm already annoyed with this conversation because my choices are mine only. He didn't let me do anything. I chose to go after he pushed me away, and I would have chosen to stay for him if he gave me the chance.

"I didn't tell you about the Crimson Rose because I didn't want you to be pulled into this life. Letting you go was the hardest thing I've ever done. I got the tattoo on my chest a few

THE AFTERTHOUGHT

months after you left to remind me of what I lost. It had to be done. I couldn't leave with you because I need the crew and the outlet it provides."

I look up at him.

"You know that I've always had these urges with fire that I've struggled with. I did my best to ignore them, but it got to the point where I couldn't anymore. The gang gave me a safe place to let that piece of me shine. People fear me. I have a scorching reputation. Pun intended."

"That doesn't explain why you're here now, though."

"I fully intended to let you go. I didn't think you would ever come back to Dune Valley. You didn't come back when your mom died, and there wasn't anything here for you. When I saw you again, I tried to convince myself I didn't want you. I tried telling myself I could make you leave again, and things would return to normal. The truth is, you're the only thing I've ever wanted more than the flames."

"You lost me seven years ago," I say, determined to not let him into my heart.

His eyes narrow. "No. You're mine, Ava. I'll give you some space to accept that, but you are mine. I've had a taste of you, and I promise you, baby, I'm never letting you slip away again."

"I can't be yours."

"You don't have a choice in the matter. I know you took that job that Alec offered you. Did he tell you who he was?"

This has my curiosity. "Who is he?"

"Alec Boone is the leader of the Cobras."

I freeze. The leader? He is just as bad as the rest of the people in this town. No, he's worse because he runs the gang that rivals the Crimson Rose.

"He, what?" I whisper.

"He is their leader Ava, and you let him fuck you without a single care in the world. He did it because he knows you're mine. He's trying to start a war between our gangs."

No, there's no way he knew who I was. I need to figure out what I'm going to do with this information. The normal reaction would be to immediately cut ties, but that's not where my mind goes.

"Tell me who put those marks on your chest and stomach." He interrupts my thoughts.

"We're not talking about that tonight."

"I'm not leaving here until you tell me."

Fuck, he will literally stay here too. I use the one thing I know I can against him—his weakness for me right now. "I'll tell you. I promise. I'm just tired, and it's hard to talk about it." I give him the saddest eyes I can while looking at him. "Can we please just talk about this another day? I promise to tell you everything."

His eyes bounce back and forth between mine, clearly conflicted. "You will tell me."

I nod, and he lets it go. "I really need to get some sleep. Tonight was a lot."

He stands up and pulls me into a hug. I relax into him so that he doesn't suspect anything. I don't want to give him any reason to try and linger. I just need him to leave. Things between us won't be any different tomorrow, regardless of whatever claim he thinks he has over me. I can't allow it to be different after how badly he hurt me.

When he pulls back, I notice he's chewing on a piece of gum. He must have put it in before I came out of my bedroom. I get a whiff of cinnamon. The smell brings me back to that day. No, no, no. Not now. I feel wobbly and put my hand on the table, trying to steady myself, but it's useless. The memories pull me in.

Chapter 17
Avalynn

"You little fucking bitch. Did my wife hire you to follow me? Did she think it would be that easy to get rid of me? Sending some pathetic girl to trail me and try and catch me in a fuckup." Spit from the intensity of his words came down to coat my face. The smell of cinnamon protruded from his mouth. It was similar to the smell of the Big Red gum from the grocery store.

His grip around my throat tightened when his other hand moved to his pocket. He pulled out a knife, and my eyes widened, silently begging for him to let me go. The small breaths I was able to take quickened when I caught sight of the blade. I tried to kick out from under him, but it was useless. My body was tired from the lack of oxygen, and he was bigger than me. I couldn't breathe, but the cinnamon smell burned through my nostrils.

The blade came down across my chest first, cutting my shirt open and slicing me down the center of my body. I felt the warm blood almost instantly pooling around the cut.

I tried my best to kick around and free myself from him as he held the knife above me, watching as the blood flowed freely from me. He laughed at my attempt to speak. His hand tightened further on my neck, threatening to completely cut off my airway.

"You can't report back to my wife if you're dead, you fucking bitch," he yelled as I felt the blade slice into my stomach this time. I was too worried about trying to breathe to focus on anything else. Over and over, he cut into the skin of my stomach and chest, marking me up. The wetness of the blood was all I could feel as the tears flowed freely down my cheeks. Time seemed to go on forever, an endless loop of suffering in hell.

He stood up to spit on me. His saliva landed on my face, but I couldn't move. The mixture of the spicy scent with the wetness of the blood and spit consumed me. I'm going to die here, was all I could think. He was gone now, but I still couldn't move. I couldn't get up. I tried to yell out, but nothing came from my voice. I was too weak. My phone. I just needed to reach my phone. Everything was so blurry, but I dialed 911 before I felt my head lull to the side and let the darkness welcome me.

"Ma'am," a stranger says, waking me up. "You're going to be okay."

"You're going to be okay." I hear someone whisper in my ear while rubbing my back.

I'm on the floor now, pulled against Greyson's chest, gripping his shirt as he rubs up and down my back. Oh no. I let him see me triggered again. He isn't going to let this go now that he's seen the scars, too. I close my eyes for a moment and lose myself in the comfort of his touch, but I still smell the cinnamon on him.

"Cinnamon," I say as I try to stay centered, but the memories are pulling at the corners of my mind.

"What?" he questions as I try to pull myself away from him. He only holds me tighter, like he never wants to let me go. I want to feel safe in his hold, but the cinnamon smell is overpowering. I catch another whiff, and again, I fall into the memories.

It was supposed to be easy. All I had to do was sneak in and snap a couple of pictures to give to his wife, and I would've been fine. It's a job that I did countless times. There is never a shortage of shady men in the world that wives need followed.

David and Ashley were in the middle of a pretty dirty divorce, and she was trying to get custody of their children. David had a nasty drug addiction.

"Ava baby, what's happening?" He lifts the two of us off of the floor, bringing me back to the moment, and carries me over to the couch. After carefully setting me down, he kneels on the floor in front of me, grabbing my hands and looking up.

"It's the cinnamon smell. I can't smell it without... Never mind. Can you just go rinse with the mouthwash in the bathroom?" My words come out like a plea.

I look away from him just as his jaw tics. He can see my vulnerability, but he doesn't fight me further. He stands, and just before he turns, he grips my chin and forces me to look up at him.

"When I get back, we're talking about this." He doesn't give me a chance to answer. The next thing I know, he's in the bathroom clanking around.

I don't like the way I feel after I'm triggered into these flashbacks. I pull my knees up to my chest and wrap my arms around them. A dull ache begins to spread through my head. I'm exhausted after the events of the day. I really just want to go to bed. My head comes down to rest on top of my knees, and I let out a deep sigh.

I feel the cushion beside me sink down, and an arm wraps around me, pulling me into his warm chest. We sit like this for a few moments, and I let my mind wander to how different things could have been. I may have never ended up at the hands of David if Greyson had just manned up. Instead, he pushed me away, and the entirety of my life changed. Everything would have been different if he had chosen me back then. I let a tear fall from my cheek before putting my wall back up.

As if he could sense my change in body language, he pushes me back up to a seated position. "What was that all about?"

"I don't want to talk about it. You should go home. It's late."

"No."

"Greyson, can you just let it go? It has nothing to do with you."

He grips my chin, holding it in place. "Listen carefully, Avalynn. Anything that has to do with you has to do with me. I'm not leaving this house until you explain what just happened and who hurt you. I saw the cuts. Either you tell me who it was, or I will make it my personal mission to track them down myself."

"It's done and over with."

"No, it's not done and over with because it's still affecting you. Now tell me."

"No, Grey. It doesn't matter."

"Ava, tell me who hurt you so I can make sure they feel every bit of pain you did and then some."

"Why do you care all of a sudden? You never even tried to reach out to me until I came back to this town."

"I thought that's what was best for the both of us."

"YOU thought. You don't get to make choices for me anymore."

"See, that's where you're wrong. I thought I made it perfectly clear that you're mine. I'm done going back and forth with you about this. You can either tell me willingly, or I'll tie your stubborn ass to your bed and tease your sweet cunt until you lose every morsel of sanity."

I scowl at him, half-tempted to resist a bit more so he can follow through on his threat. I know he will. The stern look on his face tells me he isn't going to let this go. I might as well wave the white flag and give in on this one thing.

"Fine." I stand up and head towards the kitchen. "But if we're talking about this, I need a drink."

I reach up into a cabinet and grab two glasses. They're nothing special, only regular drinking glasses because my mother's choice of numbness wasn't alcohol. After setting the glasses on the table, I pull open the top cabinet and grab the bottle of amber liquid. I'm not a huge drinker, but on the days when the memories threaten to consume me, I grant myself a drink or two to make myself forget.

I give each glass a heavy pour and slide into one of the seats at the table, waiting for Greyson to take one of his own. Once he does, I take a deep breath and a heavy sip of the Whiskey, letting it numb my throat.

"I thought it was just another job. After I left here, I bounced around a bit, trying to find some sort of profession that fit what I enjoyed. I started doing Personal Investigation work. Just not the usual kind. It's all under the table and not in any sort of legal capacity. I took a few firearms training courses and some basic self-defense classes to prepare and dove right in. The jobs were slow at first. It isn't always easy to convince people women are capable of doing what men do. After a while, word spread, and business picked up." I stare down at the floor briefly before looking him in the eye. "People want answers to things, but sometimes the law doesn't want to give them those answers. They passed my name along to others. I started up my own website and had a few clients a month that paid me pretty damn well to give them the answers they couldn't find elsewhere."

"Why did you have to do it all illegally? Why not get your degree and make it official if that's what you wanted to do?"

"I was an eighteen-year-old kid who left home with nothing except a very minimal stack of cash. It didn't exactly afford me the opportunity to pay for college. Besides, my dad was a sheriff. You and I both know that the legal way of doing things isn't always the best way."

"I suppose you're right about that."

I take another large gulp of my drink. "I got pretty good at my job. I followed people around, took pictures, and found out information by any means necessary. It was all fun for me.

Every job brought forth a new challenge. I got to find proof that husbands were cheating on their wives. I found information that helped a family find the car of their son who wrecked into a lake. There was a missing girl who was sold into a trafficking ring that I was able to help locate."

"You did all of that?" he questions as if he's surprised by my abilities.

"I did, and I really loved my job. I've been able to help people regardless of the circumstances. I never had an issue with a job, except when Ashley Banks hired me."

I down the rest of my drink and point at the bottle for Greyson to pass it over to me. He slides me his glass instead and gives me the time I need to continue with the story. I stare off into the empty space beside him, trying to figure out how I'm going to talk about this without it triggering another flashback.

As if he can read my mind, he scoots his chair closer to mine and reaches out to touch my arm. I look down to the place his hand rests on me. The warmth from his touch grounds me in the moment, and I take a deep breath and continue on with my recollection of the events.

"It was supposed to be easy. I'd done jobs like this one in the past with zero issues. Stalking around in the shadows is something I'm pretty good at."

He laughs. "I don't know about that."

"You only caught me that day because I lost sight of you and then lost myself to a memory when I saw the blood on my knee." I look over at him with annoyance.

"Whatever you say, little shadow. So, what happened?"

"Ashley was trying to get photo evidence of her husband doing drugs. She wanted full custody of their kids. He was abusive and a real piece of shit. She didn't want her kids around that. When I met with her, she said she wanted to give them a real chance to grow up with a good childhood. I felt for her because I wished my mother cared enough about me to want to give me that opportunity. I took on the job because it meant getting a few kids away from growing up with an addict for a parent. They would have a shot at escaping the childhood trauma that causes."

I reach out for the glass in front of me, with the arm that Grey isn't touching, and bring it up to my lips. My hands have started to shake. I've never told anyone about what happened that day. Nobody except for the officer who took the report that ended with absolutely nothing happening. Turns out David has a friend who made it all disappear.

"All I had to do was catch him in the act. I don't know why I decided to go to his house to do it. I should have tried to catch him in a more public area, but I thought I had his routine down. I felt ready. There was a really big window that looked into the living room. I had a small collapsible stool that propped me up to the perfect height to look into the corner of the window without being seen. At least, I thought I couldn't be seen." My voice cracks a bit at that last sentence.

"Take your time," he reassures me.

"It looked like he was already high by the time I got all set up to get the photos I needed. He had a few lines on his coffee table that were portioned out and some residue next to those. I don't know how many he had done at that point or how many more he was planning to do. Blow wasn't my mom's drug of choice, so I don't know how much a person will do in one sitting. When he bent down to do another line, I took the opportunity to snap the pictures I needed. I should have left after I got them, but it was the anniversary of my dad's death. I wasn't thinking straight. I wanted to make sure this guy never got to go near his kids again. I didn't want them growing up around an addict like I had to, so I waited for him to do more."

Tears well up in my eyes, and Grey gently pushes my chin up to make me look at him. He has a fierce but kind look as my gaze bounces back and forth between each one of his eyes. "What did he do to you, baby?"

"He locked eyes with me in the window, and I froze. The look on his face was pure rage. I was frozen in fear, Grey. I couldn't move. I knew he was pissed. I knew he was coming outside, but it was like my body needed a minute to catch up with what my mind was telling it to do. It was the first time I think I've ever been genuinely terrified of someone or what they could do. He was high and saw me taking pictures of him. By the time I had enough sense to get the hell out of there, it was too late. He was outside and running at me."

The first tear falls down my cheek. This is so much more difficult to talk about than I thought it would be. I take another drink to try and calm my nerves. Greyson's finger has started tracing small circles on my arm to try to soothe me.

"I tried to run, but he caught up. He grabbed me by the throat and kicked my feet out from under me in a matter of seconds. He ended up on top of me in a straddling position with his fingers gripped so tightly around my throat that I could barely breathe."

"He signed his death warrant," I hear him whisper, but I ignore him. If I don't keep telling this story now, I don't know if I'll ever find the courage to tell it. I don't want to talk about this again.

"I tried my best to claw at him, but I couldn't breathe. He was so drugged out, and the look on his face was completely feral. He screamed at me, asking if his wife hired me. I'm sure he said other things, but I couldn't focus. I tried so hard to get him off of me and get air into my lungs. He pulled out a knife, and I lost all the will to fight. My body went limp in acceptance. I truly thought he was going to kill me."

"Son of a bitch!" Greyson yells, pushing the chair back and standing up. He starts pacing around the room, but I continue on. I stand from the chair and pull off my shirt to reveal my scars. He stops and stares at me.

"The first cut was this one." I trail my finger along the raised flesh between my breasts. "This one wasn't nearly as deep as the others."

Grey steps toward me, but I put my hand up to stop him. He wanted the details. He's going to get all of them.

"He told me I couldn't report back to his wife if I was dead. That's when he started these." I trail my fingers along the cuts on my stomach and chest. *"He had a grip on my throat, so I could barely breathe. He just kept going. I had to watch every time he pulled his hand back and sliced into me."*

I begin to sob, but I have to finish telling the story.

"I was in shock. I felt completely numb to everything that was happening. I was completely consumed with fear. After what felt like forever, he finally released his grip on my throat. All I wanted to do at that moment was take a huge gasp of air, but I couldn't. I was paralyzed with the fear that if I moved, he would know I was still alive and keep going. He stood up and wobbled a bit before leaning in and spitting on me. He kicked my leg and told me to stay out of his business."

"I promise you. I will do everything in my power to find this piece of shit and give him the death he deserves. He will feel every ounce of fear you felt and then some," Greyson states with a harsh expression.

"I laid there for a while before I got the courage to try and move. I don't know how I didn't bleed out, but I managed to get hold of my phone and call 911 before I blacked out. When they arrived, they asked me what happened, but I couldn't talk about it. My brain wouldn't let me. After I got set up in the hospital and they stitched everything up, the cops came in to take a report. I told them about David and the drugs and the camera. They did some follow-up research but said they didn't find any of that at the scene. David must have taken the camera

with him when he walked off. I don't know." I shake my head. "The cops questioned him, and he lied. He said he had never seen me before. He said that he wasn't home and had one of his friends give him a fake alibi. I tried to insist, but the cops didn't believe me. I didn't talk about it again. Not until now." I look at him. "You're the first person I've told since then."

"Ava.." he trails off.

"I found out later that David had a connection to one of the officers at the station. He lied for David and told the other officer David was with him the entire time. I'm pretty sure that officer made sure David stayed out of prison because he was on the cop's payroll somehow. I don't know. I stopped looking into it. It was too much for me. Every time I think about that day, I'm triggered into the memories."

Chapter 18
Greyson

The way she looks at me with so much vulnerability crushes me. I wasn't there for her to make sure she was okay. I hate that. I hate that she had to go through this alone and then live with it for so many years. No wonder she's so intent on keeping everyone at a distance now. I'll make sure she gets justice for that.

I take in the scars along her chest and abdomen again. Each one of them is a punch to my gut. I should have never pushed her away. I should have gone to find her.

"What was the officer's name?" I ask.

"I don't remember." She looks down at the floor, and I know she's lying. She doesn't want this to end up worse. If she thinks I'm going to let this go, she's wrong. Anyone who hurts what's mine will pay for it.

"His name, Avalynn. Give me his name. Now." I'm trying to be gentle with her after everything tonight. She's out of her mind if she thinks I'm leaving without an answer. I think she realizes it because she sighs.

"It was Officer Grant."

THE AFTERTHOUGHT

I knew my girl knew his name. I step closer to her and pull her into my embrace. She relaxes in my arms and eventually puts her arms around my waist as she sobs against my chest. I bring a hand up to rub the back of her head to reassure her.

"Nobody is ever going to hurt you like that ever again," I say.

She pulls her head up to look at me, and the sorrow in her eyes grips my heart like a vice. "You don't know that."

"Here's what I know. The next person who tries to hurt you will end up char-grilled on a skewer stick. I'll burn them to a fucking crisp and bask in every moment of it." I watch the range of emotions run through her eyes; shock, acceptance, admiration, lust.

When I glance down at the clock on her microwave, I notice that it's almost 2AM. It's been a long day for both of us, and she looks completely defeated. I grab the shirt that she took off and put it back on her before reaching out to grab her hand. She doesn't stop me, so I pull her towards her bedroom.

"We aren't having sex again. I need sleep. I have no clue what time Chloe is coming back tomorrow."

"I'm just taking you to bed." I leave out the part where I plan to get in bed with her, but she will just have to get over it. This isn't about sex right now. She needs me, whether she wants to admit it or not.

When we get into the room, I pull back the covers on her bed and motion for her to get in. She does, and I take this opportunity to strip down to my boxers. Her brows narrow, but she doesn't say anything when I slip under the covers next to her.

There was no way I was going to leave her alone after what she confessed to me tonight.

"I'll be here to keep you safe now. You don't have to worry about anyone even thinking about hurting you," I reassure her as I wrap my arm around her waist and pull her back to my chest, holding her tightly.

"You've said that to me before, Grey."

"I know I did, and I'm sorry."

She turns to face me, and I take in her beauty. Her deep brown eyes shimmer in the natural night light shining into the room. I want to kick myself for ever letting her go. My arm tugs against her waist to pull her closer to me.

"How can I trust you?" she whispers.

"You keep saying that. Just give me a chance to prove it to you. That's all I ask,"

She takes a moment to take in my request. "I'll consider it, but I'm not making any promises."

"I'll prove you wrong. One way or another, you will admit you're mine. You'll come to terms with it." I lean in to kiss her forehead softly. It's been a long time since I've felt the urge to be tender with someone, but she pulls out a different side of me.

"That's not very encouraging, Greyson."

"Maybe not, but it's true. I told you I'd mark you if I have to." A mischievous grin crosses my face, and she rolls her eyes.

"The fuck you will."

"Don't worry. I'll make sure you like it." Before she can say anything else, I pull her head into my chest, and she nuzzles in.

THE AFTERTHOUGHT

I'm not sure if it's the alcohol making her more compliant or if she is actually giving into the feelings that she's trying to ignore, but having her back in my arms feels better than I could have ever imagined. Who would have thought that after all these years, we would be right back here in the same place where I chose to walk away from her? Now, I'm making the choice to never let her go.

I let myself drift off to sleep for a few hours, holding her in my arms, before I hear my phone start to buzz from the other side of the room. I ignore it, but as soon as it stops, it starts back up again. I'm betting it's Kai. If it is, I know he won't stop calling until I answer. He's an annoying fuck like that.

I lean in and give her one last kiss on the forehead before slipping out of bed to get dressed. I glance down at my phone, and just as I thought, it's Kai. It's barely even 6AM. This fucker better have a good reason to be calling me. Once I gather all my things, I step outside and answer his seventh call.

"What could you possibly be calling me about this early in the morning?" I pull the Zippo lighter out of my pocket and flip it on and off, waiting for his response.

"You didn't come home last night. I wanted to make sure you were okay."

"Kai, that's a joke, right?" I swear if I left Ava in bed because of this, I'll stab him and then personally cauterize the wound. I play with the lit flame in front of me, waving it around in the air and turning my head from side to side following it.

"How pissed would you be if I said yes?"

"Very." I make my way to my car and decide to make a quick stop before I do anything else today.

"Okay, that's not why I called. Knox wants to get a bunch of the crew together today. Some of our supply has gone missing. He's trying to figure shit out."

"When and where?" I ask, knowing there's no way he wants us anywhere this early.

"This afternoon at the Garage."

"You're an asshole for calling me this early. You know that, right?" I flip the lighter shut and slide it back into my pocket.

"It wasn't my choice. Knox gave me a list and told me to make the calls immediately."

"That fucker never sleeps." I sigh. "It's fine. I have a stop to make, and then I'm coming home."

I hang up, annoyed that the call could have waited. I could have woken up next to Ava. I hate that I have to leave her to wake up alone after how vulnerable she was with me last night. I want to make sure she knows it meant something, so I drive to the coffee shop in town and order her go-to drink. I remember because she used to have me get the same thing for her at least once a week all those years ago. It's engraved into my brain.

I walk up to the counter and order two large caramel iced lattes with oat milk, a splash of brown sugar syrup, and an extra shot of espresso. She always used to tell me that espresso makes a difference, and she's right. Before the cashier rings me up, I have her add a blueberry muffin to the order.

Once I secure the caffeine and baked goods, I drive back to her house. She's still sleeping when I slip inside and place the coffee and muffin on her kitchen counter. I look around for a minute before I find something to write on and leave her a little note.

I scribble: One chance is all I'm asking for, little shadow. - Grey

I'm half tempted to go back into the room to lay back in bed with her until she wakes up, but there are things I have to do before meeting everyone at the garage later. Kicking Kai's ass is one of them. Reluctantly, I make my way back to my car and to my house, enjoying my very own iced latte along the way.

Chapter 19
Avalynn

The days begin to meld together as I fall into a routine with Chloe. My head has been a bit of a mess after telling Greyson about David. I hate how vulnerable it makes me feel now that he knows the truth. I also don't know how to feel about him continuing to be so sweet to me. I'm confused, so I've been trying my best to avoid him while I process everything. He managed to get my phone number, though, and has been calling and texting me nonstop.

My heart almost exploded when I woke up last week and saw the coffee and muffin on the counter. I'll give him credit. He's been trying his best to show me he cares. Since then, I've woken up to that same coffee and muffin on my kitchen counter every day. I'm going to ignore the fact that I go to bed with the door locked, and yet, somehow, he still manages to get in. I'm almost positive he had a copy of my key made for himself.

It's a thoughtful gesture, but I'm still guarded. He expects me to just crawl back to him with open arms and forget about everything that we went through. I've thought about it a lot this week, I'm not going to lie, but I'm struggling. He isn't going to ever leave the Crimson Rose, and I don't want to be a part of that life. Letting him in would just end with both of us being hurt in the end.

Part of me feels like telling him about David and my near-death experience with him was a mistake. It's not like he can go back and change anything that happened that day. The other part of me feels relieved to finally be able to tell someone about it. It's changed me a lot. I never brought it up to Wrenly because she was halfway across the country, and I didn't want to feel like a burden.

I trail my hand down the center of my chest from the outside of my shirt. Most people see the scars and ignore them. They wanted to avoid the awkward conversation, like I would have told them anyway. Greyson saw them and wanted to know about them.

Things between Chloe and I have gotten better. A few nights ago, she talked to me about her mom for the first time. It was the first sincere conversation we've had since that night after Greyson's birthday party. I know it was likely prompted by the visit back to her house to grab some more things, but I'm glad she is feeling comfortable enough to start opening up.

We decided that moving forward we are both going to make a conscious effort to get to know each other better. Graduation is only two months away, and I'm really hoping she and I are able to keep building our relationship even beyond that. Maybe at the end of it all, she will decide to leave Dune Valley with me. Do I still want to leave Dune Valley?

My phone dings and I glance down to find an email. It's someone reaching out for PI work. I open it up, intrigued, and read through the message. It's from an older lady who goes by Mrs. Myers. She wants to see if I can track down her son, whom she hasn't seen in a few weeks. The cops won't do anything about it because he's a grown man who has a history of gambling and other nefarious activities. The cops are convinced he is laying low somewhere until the sharks get off his back.

I consider whether this is really something I want to devote my time to. It could be true that her son is just a piece of garbage who got mixed up with the wrong people. I almost turn it down, but I notice how much money she's willing to offer me to do the job.

Money from PI work means fewer days at Temptations. I've been trying to be cautious about how much I've been working there because of who Alec is. He's been up my ass lately, too. Every time I go to work, he finds a reason to pull me into his office to "talk." All I wanted to do was have a meaningless fuck before coming back to Dune Valley, but of course, that's not how it went down. Somehow, I ended up sleeping with someone who is at odds with Greyson.

Greyson hates that I work there, mostly because he can't get to me while I'm inside the club. That's Cobra territory, and him walking inside would likely end up with someone getting shot or stabbed. I think the only thing that's stopped him from actually physically restraining me and keeping me from going to work there is the fact that he is still trying to win me over. I'm not sure how much longer that will last, though.

One thing is certain, I won't let him tell me what I can and can't do. I don't particularly enjoy working there, but I'm not ready to give in and admit that it's wrong—even if deep down, I know it is. I've been keeping my shifts to just weekends. The tips have been really good lately. I've been making so much that I've even been able to put a bit away in savings.

Today, I've been lounging around on the couch all day, waiting for Chloe to come home. We are going to hit up the movies tonight. It'll be the first time I've been there since I was eighteen. Thoughts of the tattoo Greyson has over his heart fill my mind. When did he do that?

Curiosity gets the best of me, so I march to my bedroom and pull open the top drawer of my desk. The stack of ticket stubs is in the corner where I left them. I grab the stack and look through them, trying to find the one with the words "I love you" on the back.

I don't even remember the movie that was playing that night because I was so wrapped up in him and the perfect moment between us. He looked into my eyes and tucked a piece of my hair behind my ear before he leaned in and kissed me on the cheek. I thought I would melt right there, but when I smiled at him, he told me he loved me.

My heart skips a beat when I finally find it. I'm not really sure what I expected to see when I pull it out, but what's noted takes me by surprise. Below the words "I love you" is another set of words. My heart aches at the sight of them—three words that mean more to me than most people.

Tears well up in my eyes as I read them: "Forever my heart." That's what he would tell me every day, and I would respond with "Forever my always." It was our own little cute saying to each other, something unique to us. Chills spread through my body, and I let a bit of my wall down. I pull out my phone and snap a picture of the ticket before sending him a text.

> Me: I need to ask you something.

> Grey: Hey, baby, ask away.

I roll my eyes at his excessive use of 'baby' when he talks to me. He's pretty much decided that we are back together even though I've told him we aren't. He just tells me that I'm being moody and will accept it eventually. I send him the picture that I just snapped.

> Me: When did you write this?

> Grey: I was wondering when you would find that.

> Grey: I stopped in to check on your mom pretty often after you left town. Part of me was secretly hoping that you would come back.

THE AFTERTHOUGHT

> Me: If you told me that back then, I probably would have.

> Grey: I found the ticket stubs one day when I was checking on her. That was always our place. I never knew you kept all of the stubs and wrote things on the back of them.

> Me: I wanted to make sure I remembered.

> Grey: I found the one that you wrote 'I love you' on, and I borrowed it so that I could get a mockup of your handwriting. I wanted you with me, always, even if I couldn't have you. I had my guy tattoo it over my chest so that you would be forever my heart, just like I used to tell you. I wrote it on there before I put it back.

> Me: Grey... what if you ended up with someone else?

> Grey: There's never been anyone else, little shadow.

> Me: But you didn't come after me. You could have come after me. You could have told me to come back.

> Grey: I know. I'm sorry for letting you go, but it's what I thought I had to do at the time. I'll prove how sorry I am.

> Me: I need to think about all of this.

> Grey: Think all you want, but I'm not giving up this time. You're mine, Avalynn.

I drop my phone on my desk, trying to figure out how to process this little conversation. I want to shut him out, but I can't. It's becoming very apparent that things between the two of us are getting more complicated than I anticipated they would when I came back to town.

I hear the front door shut, and it pulls me back to what I'm supposed to be doing—getting ready for the movies. I peek my head out of my bedroom door just in time to see Chloe. It looks like she's been crying again, so I step out into the hallway.

"Hey, what's going on? Are you okay?"

"Matt was being sus. I just lost my mom. I can't lose him too," she chokes out, sobs threatening to break free again.

"You're going to have to help me out a little bit here. What does sus mean?"

"Ughhh, you can't be serious, Ava." She lets out a little giggle between the tears.

I pull her in for a hug. Normally, she would push me away, but to my surprise, she accepts it and hugs me back.

"Do you want to cancel the movies tonight? We can stay in, go get a few tubs of ice cream, and binge the Twilight movies."

"Those movies are terrible." She wipes her eyes and looks at me. "You would really want to watch those instead of going to the drive-in?"

"I just want to spend some time with you. It doesn't matter where we go or what we watch," I tell her, and she smiles while pushing me away.

"Go get ready. We have a movie to see."

I laugh and head back into my bedroom to throw on something comfortable but cute. I decide to wear a pair of black fishnet tights and a short black skirt. This is my usual style combo, so why change things up now? I grab a long-sleeved tight black shirt and slip that on, throwing on a black and white checkered crop top over it.

Once satisfied with my clothing choice, I grab my phone off of my desk and pop across the hall to Chloe's room. Her style is the opposite of mine. She's wearing a pair of ripped jeans and a pink crop top. If she didn't resemble my dad, I would doubt whether or not we were actually related.

"Are you putting on any makeup or doing your hair?" she asks while reaching into her backpack to pull out a pink makeup bag.

"Should I?" I didn't plan to do anything special with my hair today, but I suppose I could put forth some sort of effort and curl it.

"You don't always have to make yourself look good for other people, Ava. Sometimes it's nice to just do it for yourself."

I take a moment to absorb her words, and she's right. I do feel much better about myself when I take the time to do my hair and makeup. She's so young, but she can be so wise every now and then. Shaking my head, I step into the bathroom to plug in the curling iron. Chloe comes in a few seconds later.

"Will you curl mine too?" She looks a little nervous to ask.

"Absolutely. I can show you how if you want. It's super easy." I motion for her to come over and sit on the toilet so I can start curling once the wand gets hot.

"My mom used to do it for me," she says quietly. "I really miss her."

"I'm so sorry. Do you want to tell me a bit about her while I do your hair?"

"Are you sure you want to hear about her?" She eyes me with a bit of disbelief.

"Of course I do. She raised a strong but stubborn kid. You can talk to me about her whenever you want. I wish I had a close relationship with my mom. Hearing about yours is refreshing."

"When you never know whether the day will be your last or not, you learn to let the little things go and enjoy the moment. My mom was sick my entire life. We made sure to never regret a single day we got together because we knew time wasn't on our side." She takes a deep breath. "I've had this sort of resentment towards you since finding out about you. I thought that you had things so much better than me. You got to have two parents. Even if our father died, you still were able to make those memories with him."

She's right about that, and it makes me feel guilty. I got to experience a decent childhood for the first 10 years of my life before our father died.

She settles in, telling me a story about a weekend camping trip that she and her mother went on a few years ago. They thought it was going to be a great idea to get out and unplug, but they quickly realized that neither one of them knew anything about camping. They spent a few hours trying to set up a campsite before giving up and driving to the nearest town to get a hotel. What started as camping ended as a girl's night at a hotel, doing their nails and facials.

I watch the way she smiles at the memory, and I make a mental note to try and do something like this with her. Not camping, that's her experience with her mom, but maybe a girl's day where we could go get our nails done. There is still so much that we don't know about each other, so any little bonding experience will be worth it.

She stands and looks in the mirror. "You definitely have to teach me how to do this. It's so cute! Thank you! You need to hurry and do yours so we're not late."

I laugh and throw a few curls into my hair before running my fingers through them to comb them out. My roots have grown more than I would like. I need to make a point to grab some dye this week to freshen it all up or make an appointment somewhere. I feel so much better when my hair has its bright orange hue. It makes me feel powerful. I can't explain why.

After I unplug everything and tell Chloe it's time to get going, I grab my keys, and we slip into the car. The drive isn't too long—this town isn't big enough for anywhere to be more than a 10-minute drive—but I find myself feeling a bit nervous. The last time I was at the movies was with Greyson, and I don't know what being there without him will feel like.

The theater comes into view, and I quickly pay the attendant before driving around the lot to try and find a spot. The movie Chloe picked was some kind of action thriller that I've never heard of. This theater always plays a mixture of older and newer movies. This one was released maybe fifteen years ago. I go to park in a row toward the front, but Chloe stops me.

"We should go to the back. This is too close."

"Those spots are always taken. We should have gotten here sooner if you wanted one of them." The back spots are always taken first because that's where all of the teenagers go to make out with each other, where nobody can see.

"Can you just check?" she persists.

"Sure," I concede.

When I drive through the back row, I'm shocked to find an open spot. I quickly back my car into it and look over at Chloe to find a smug look on her face. She is so much like me sometimes. I swear it's like I'm having a conversation with myself.

"Fine, you were right."

"I know," she says, laughing as she pulls open the car door.

"The movie should start soon. Did you want to run to the concession stand first?"

"No, I think we should go over here." She grabs my hand and pulls me over to the car parked next to us. I try to stop her, but she's strong for such a little thing.

When I catch sight of the people in front of us, I'm rendered speechless. I take in the setup that I haven't seen since I was eighteen. A large blanket is laid out on the ground with a massive pile of pillows towards the front of the car. They look similar to how others have theirs placed, but it's the bright orange color of these pillows that tells me these belong to Grey. There is a small cooler, which I'm sure is filled with a variety of different drinks because he always wanted to make sure I had options. On top of the cooler is a pack of blueberry muffins.

My heart wants to explode in my chest. I turn to look at Chloe, and she has a huge grin on her face. A guy is standing next to her, and I eye him up and down. He is young with a bit of blonde stubble on his face. He leans down to whisper in her ear, and she looks up at him adoringly. This must be Matt.

The sound of someone clearing their throat has me turning back around. Greyson is standing there in front of me with an iced latte in hand and a pleading look in his eyes.

"Hey, little shadow. What do you think about a date night?"

My heart slams. This might be one of the sweetest things anyone has ever done for me. I want to tell him no. I want to push him away to protect myself, but I can't, so I nod. He closes the distance between us and pulls me close enough to lean in and drop a kiss on the tip of my nose.

"Just a chance," he says, and I nod again.

"One chance," I whisper, and he bends down to give me a chaste kiss on the lips. I pull back and turn to look back at Chloe. "You worked with him to set this up?"

"Sorry, sis. He was very persuasive and a bit of an asshole, but I like you two together." She laughs, and Matt intertwines his fingers in hers, leading her over to my car where all the blankets and pillows we brought are sitting in the backseat.

I'm frozen in place for a moment, processing her words. It's the first time she's called me sis. It's just a word, but I can't help but smile back at her. Finally, she's giving me some sort of sign that we are developing a bond. Dune Valley might be growing on me.

Chapter 20

Greyson

My heart slams in my chest when I see her car pull into the drive-in. I made sure to threaten every single person who tried to park next to me to ensure the spot was open for her. I wanted her to pull in and see the setup. It's exactly how I used to do it when we were younger. I could tell she wasn't going to just fold and let me have the chance I was asking her for. She's still too guarded. I'm playing all my cards here. My initial response was to try and force her hand, but I think this gentler gesture will help her realize I'm serious when I tell her she's mine and has always been.

I feel the way my palms begin to sweat while I anticipate her reaction. I dig into my pocket to pull out the lighter, flicking it off and on to try and calm my nerves. This is ridiculous. A few weeks ago, I was a hard gangbanger that everyone feared, and now I'm acting like a lovesick fool. This girl has so much more power over me than she even realizes.

It was pretty easy to convince Chloe to get her here. All I had to do was dangle her little boyfriend in front of her as bait. I thought it would be a bit more difficult for Ava to agree to come with her, but she is trying her best to build a relationship with Chloe. She didn't even hesitate to say yes when she asked.

Every bit of this was worth it. The way she looks right now, as she stares up at me with the most beautiful face full of adoration, is something I will burn into my memory. I pass her the coffee in my hand and watch as she takes a big gulp. The tension in her shoulders instantly releases. It's honestly amazing how much a little bit of caffeine and sugar can change her perspective.

I lead her down to the blanket, and we settle into the comfort of the pillows before I pull another large blanket over us. There's a chill in the air tonight, and I need to make sure my girl isn't cold. The sun has started to set, and the movie will be starting soon.

She reaches over to the muffin container and pulls one out to eat, washing it down with another gulp of coffee. I lean over to grab water from the cooler and just watch her. I can't take my eyes off of her. Every single thing she does has me in a strange trance. I'm obsessed.

When she finishes the second muffin, she makes a satisfied sound and sinks further under the blanket. I reach an arm around her, pulling her close to me. I'm surprised when she relaxes into my hold and looks up at me.

"Thank you for all of this." Her words shock me.

"You're being strangely compliant. Should I be worried?" I know I shouldn't be pointing out the obvious, but she is usually a bit more strong-willed than this.

"I don't know. I'm still struggling, Grey, but I can appreciate a genuine gesture when I see one. Between this, your tattoo, and you knowing about my scars, I'm just in my head a bit about everything. I'm still being cautious, but I can't help but be drawn to you."

I place two fingers under her chin and tilt her head up, pulling her lips to mine. She tastes sweet but bitter, like the coffee. "I love when you're stubborn, but I love when you're open like this, too."

"I thought I had to be hard around you, but you're softening me up a bit." She giggles.

"Good. I'm glad that my irresistible charm is wearing off on you a bit."

"Don't be cocky. I'm still really concerned with where this is all going to go. If I let you back in completely, what happens? I don't want to stay in my mother's house in this town forever. There are too many hard memories. What happens when I let myself fall for you again, and our lifestyles clash? You have the Crimson Rose, and I think I've made it pretty clear that I don't want to be in that life."

"Let's just take things day by day and see what happens." I offer.

"Taking things day by day still ends with me getting hurt in the end. You have to understand that." She tries to argue, but I lean in and silence her with another kiss. When will she realize she's the only thing getting in the way of this right now?

I pull back, letting our foreheads stay connected. "I'm not letting you go, Ava. We will just have to figure something out." I lean in and kiss her again. "You're my flame. Mine. And I'll never stop flying to you. You'll never be free of me again."

I swoop in to consume her in kisses but pull back when I feel the wetness from her cheek on mine. I bring both hands up to her face, placing her cheeks in my palms and using my thumbs to wipe the tears away.

"I'm obsessed with you, Avalynn Blake," I whisper before releasing her and digging in my pocket for the gift I got her. "Hold out your hand. I have something for you."

She eyes me cautiously, but she does it anyway. I place the small cool item onto her palm, and she looks down to see what it is. Immediately, she has a confused look on her face. She pulls out her phone and shines it over the small crystal to get a better look at it. She turns it around in her hand as she inspects it. The dark gray stone is a puffed heart with deep red flecks through it. It almost looks like blood splatter.

"What is it?" she asks.

"It's a bloodstone."

"Bloodstone?" she repeats.

"Yeah, I looked it up. It's supposed to help with strength and courage or something like that. At least, I think. I could be wrong. I saw it, and it made me think of you, so I had to get it for you."

"That's really sweet of you. I haven't gotten any new crystals since you used to buy them for me. Thank you." She seems a bit hesitant to bring up the past, but I catch the way she turns the phone light off and squeezes the stone in her hand. I can tell she wants to say something else. She keeps it in though.

We sit in silence for a while, just enjoying each other's company. Chloe and Matt are on their own set of blankets in front of Ava's car next to us. It's too dark to see what they're doing, which gives me an idea. This movie is boring and predictable. I'm ready to have some fun of my own, and I doubt anyone will notice with everyone distracted.

I slide my hand up her thigh, a few inches every minute or so, to see how she responds.

"Grey," she warns while keeping her eyes on the screen.

I lean in to kiss the tender spot under her ear on her neck, running my nose up it. "How quiet can you be, baby?" I kiss her again and don't miss the way she tilts her head to the side ever so slightly to give me more access. "You can be so quiet that nobody will know, or you can scream my name for everyone to hear. I'm good with whatever you prefer."

"My sister is right over there."

"Shhhhh," I whisper in her ear. "You don't want to draw her attention."

My hand slides under her skirt, and I already know I'll be tearing yet another pair of her tights. She would be better off if she didn't wear these things. In her defense, she wasn't expecting me to be here.

My hand moves its way slowly to her center, and she lets out a low moan as I gently caress her. I lean back in to latch onto her neck, not caring if I mark her while I rub her pussy from the outside of her clothing. I take in the way her breathing picks up and can feel the way her heart pounds in her chest. I bite down softly on her neck, and she rolls her head to the side.

"You like a little pain, baby?" I bite down a little harder, and she whimpers.

"Fuck," she breathes out.

My hand picks up its pace, rubbing her while I bite and suck my way up and down her neck. I can't wait to feel how wet she is. Thinking about her sweet cunt has my cock painfully pressing against the zipper of my pants, begging to be freed. As if she can read my mind, her hand reaches over to grip me, but I pull back. A wicked grin crosses my face when I pull the blanket up and prepare myself to slide under.

"Greyson." She gasps and reaches out to grab me when my head slips under it.

I quickly position myself right where I belong between her legs. Her hands grip my shoulders under the blanket, trying to keep me from the inevitable. It's warm under here, but I only have one thing on my mind—her.

I slide my fingers up her thighs, squeezing them tight enough to leave bruises. Her hips raise in response. I'm sure she would tell me that she wants more if she could talk to me without everyone hearing. Who am I to decline my girl's needs?

My hands move to the center of her tights, and I rip a big enough hole in them to reach what I really want. I flip the top of her skirt over my head and spread her legs wide before leaning in. I pull her panties to the side and use my fingers to spread her pussy as my tongue makes its first contact.

She pulls her skirt up to her stomach and runs her fingers through my hair, gripping tightly and pulling me against her dripping pussy. I twirl my tongue around her clit, groaning at the taste of her. So fucking sweet.

I slide two fingers into her and curl them at the angle I know she loves. Slowly, I thrust my fingers in and out of her while continuing to devour her. My tongue flicks at her clit, and I hear her say my name. She starts to grind her pussy against my face more aggressively, and I grin. That's my filthy girl.

I split my fingers inside her before adding a third. She clenches around me at the intrusion, and her fingers free themselves from my hair as she grips the blanket we are lying on. I pull my face from her center and bite down on her inner thigh while my fingers plunge into her. She brings her hands back to my hair, pulling me back to her clit, telling me she must be getting close. I dive back in, lapping at her.

When I close my mouth over her clit and start sucking, her hips begin to buck wildly. She clamps down on my fingers, squeezing them. "Oh my God." I hear her say as I let her ride out her high, enjoying the feeling of her coming apart on my fingers.

I emerge from underneath the blanket and barely have a moment to react before she grabs me by the back of the neck to pull me into a deep kiss. Our tongues dance for dominance as she moans in my mouth. I slide my hand up to her throat, holding her in place so I can take the lead, but I feel her stiffen under me.

Immediately, I let go and pull back. "What's wrong?"

"Just don't touch my throat like that. Ever since.." She trails off. "It just puts me back in that moment."

She doesn't have to say anything further. I lean in and kiss her one last time before pulling her into me so we can finish the movie. I'm not going to let anything ruin our perfect date.

"I'm going to hunt him down and serve him to you on a silver platter, little shadow. You just wait and see."

"Just leave it be, Grey."

"No. He put his hands on you. He doesn't deserve the air he's currently breathing."

"It's not worth it."

"We're done discussing this, Ava. I'll get him for you, baby, and you can end his pathetic life however you want to."

She doesn't argue with my last statement. I imagine how fun it would be to watch my girl torturing this piece of shit in the torture shed. My cock twitches just thinking about it. I bet she would like the way he screams when the flames flicker against his skin. Tomorrow, I'll be letting Knox know I need to take a little vacation so I can track this fucker down.

Chapter 21

Greyson

It's been a few weeks since Ava and I went on the drive-in movie date. I've been bringing her favorite coffee and blueberry muffin every morning, and she's slowly opening up. I like to leave them on the counter for her. She never questions how I get into the house. We've gone on a few dates, and she's started texting me on her own more often now. For the most part, things seem like we are in a normal relationship, even though she still refuses to admit she's mine.

I have maybe a month left before Chloe graduates to try and convince her not to run again, not that I would actually let her go this time. She needs to decide for herself, though, for this to work. If I have to force her, I will, but I'd rather not take that route.

I've been trying to find time to skip town so I can track down the fucking asshole who hurt her, but Knox has been keeping me busy with gang business. Our shipments keep turning up missing. We have a rat somewhere, and he is determined to find out who it is.

The biggest issue with the entire situation is that the drugs aren't disappearing. They are ending up in the hands of the

Cobras, and people are starting to talk around town. People are getting scared to do business with us, and the Crimson Rose is developing a bad reputation. They want our guarantee there is no risk of their product being lifted. Right now, we can't give that to them, so they've been going to the Cobras. These fucking people don't even realize the drugs they are buying from them are the same drugs they should be getting from us.

Leave it to Alec to be a slimy motherfucker and steal from us instead of doing things on his own. It's why the Cobras will always be second-rate compared to the Crimson Rose. Ava is still working at his fucking club too. She keeps telling me she's going to stop working there, but she hasn't yet, and it's pissing me off.

Knox has been telling me I need to get my girl under control, and I've been trying, but I don't think he realizes she's not the kind of girl who likes being told what to do, at least not when we have clothes on. She is too strong-willed and will make a point of going out of her way to do the opposite of what I want her to do if I ever tell her she isn't allowed to do something.

I've considered having one of the younger kids pretend to hang with the Cobras, but that idea was knocked down real quick. Something needs to be figured out real soon, though, because I can't keep doing this in-between bullshit where I'm trying to accommodate both Ava and Knox.

I pull my car up to the garage and walk straight past it to get to my torture shed. Knox asked me to meet him here, and I hope it's to try and get some information out of someone. I'm itching to let out some of this shit I've been feeling. I've been flicking my lighter off and on all day to try and control the urges.

As I open the door, a sinister grin spreads across my face when my eyes land on the guy tied to the chair in the center of the room. Fuck yes. I spot Knox in the corner talking to Kai and make my way over to them.

"Who is he?" I waste no time asking.

"He's a Cobra." Kai smiles.

"What's the snake doing in our shed?" I ask Kai, and Knox shakes his head at us. He doesn't appreciate the playful sarcasm we share.

"Boss got him for you to play with," Kai jokes, and I look over at Knox in question.

"Yes. You can do whatever you need to do to him to make him talk. He knows something about who's been stealing from us. I want to know exactly what he knows."

Nothing else needs to be said. I crack my knuckles and walk to the shelves filled with tools, picking out a few things to have fun with. This is exactly what I was hoping for today.

I take my time lighting the fire in the wood burner near the tool shelves before I step in front of the snake and rip the tape off of his mouth. It's more fun when I can hear them scream.

"You two can stay and watch if you want, but this might get a little messy." I laugh. "Do you need him alive, boss?"

"Yes, Greyson. He needs to be alive with all his limbs attached."

"Fine, but what about his eyes? Does he need to be able to see?"

The guy starts shaking his head frantically. "FUCK, MAN. Just let me go."

Knox stands there with his arms crossed, not saying anything else. He didn't tell me no on the eyes question, but he didn't exactly say yes, either. I'm going to have to take the silence as a no. He likely just wants to scare the guy into being more willing to talk.

"I think we will start out with something easy." I walk over to the wood burner and use the fire-safe tongs to grab a hot coal before going back over to the guy.

"Care to tell me what you know?" He just stares straight ahead with a blank look.

Boring but perfect. I was hoping he would be fun to play with. I lower the hot coal over his pants on his thigh. I watch as it begins to burn through the blue jean material. He starts jerking around in the chair, but I hold it firmly in place with the tongs. When it finally burns through the jeans and starts to hit his skin, he lets out a scream. I leave it there for a moment before lifting it up and giving him another chance to talk.

"Feeling chatty yet?"

I'm met with nothing, so I go back to the wood burner to repeat the process, over and over, along the length of his legs. This continues for about five minutes, and the guy still refuses to talk. He's a tough nut to crack, but I'll get through to him. A sick idea crosses my mind, and I turn to look at Knox.

"Is his dick off limits?"

Kai laughs from the corner of the room. "What are you going to do, fuck him?"

I shoot him an annoyed look. "No, asshole. I just think it might be fun to see if it shrivels up from my blowtorch." I look back over at Knox, waiting for him to give me his decision.

"I suppose that's fine," Knox says.

I have to stop myself from running over to the shelves to grab the torch. When I stand back in front of the snake, I click the torch on for show. If this doesn't get the guy talking, we might as well just kill him now. No man, in their right mind, would ever let someone fuck with his dick.

"Last chance," I warn, but still, he says nothing.

I bring the torch down slowly to his crotch, and the guy starts to jump and shake in the chair. I hold the flame over his jeans for maybe two seconds before he breaks. It's just enough time for the fabric to burn through, but it never actually makes it to the skin.

"I'll talk! Just leave my dick alone."

"Damn. This was just starting to get fun. So, who is fucking with our shipments?"

"We don't know his name."

"Hmmm, not good enough," I say, clicking the torch back on.

"No, stop! I swear!" he cries out, scared to lose his pathetic dick.

"You know something else. Spit it the fuck out. I'm losing patience." I bring the heat close to his groin again.

"The guy wears a mask. I don't know who he is!" he yells, and I pull back. "We meet at Temptations in the VIP rooms."

"And?" He's being short. He knows what I want to hear. I shouldn't have to keep asking him questions.

"He's been telling us all the drop spots. He wants us to be there when the drugs are being delivered. The first few grabs were to see if we could handle it on a larger scale. Alec has it all planned out and is just waiting for the right time to pull the trigger. We show up and steal the drugs by any means necessary. The guy who has been telling us about the drop spots has some information that Alec needs. I don't know anything else. I'm too low on the totem pole. I only hear about things that filter through the other Cobras."

I pause for a moment, waiting for him to continue, but he doesn't, so I bring the torch to his arm and watch as it sears his skin.

"I swear that's all I know!" he yells.

I turn and look over to Knox. He seems satisfied with his answer, and while I would love to sit here and torture this fuck all day, the little bit I've done has calmed my urge. I'm able to think clearly again. There is something way more important I should have my thoughts on. Finding David.

Even thinking about that guy and what he did to Ava has me ready to go on a murderous rage. I pull my knife from my pocket and stab it directly into the Cobra's thigh. He screams out in pain, tears streaming down his face, like the pathetic piece of shit he is.

"Next time someone asks you a question, you should tell them the truth from the start. It's a real inconvenience to have to ask the same thing over and over just to get an answer," I say before ripping the knife from his thigh and dropping it on the ground next to me.

I pull my ring off and click on the blowtorch, bringing it near the metal before searing it on his skin. Satisfaction runs through me as his cries fill the room. Another pathetic scumbag who wears my mark to show everyone in this town not to fuck with me. This one tried to hold out, I'll give him that, but he still folded way too fast. I barely even got to have any time with him. I'm actually a bit disappointed by the lack of loyalty the members of the Cobras seem to have.

I head over to the wash sink Knox conveniently had installed to quickly wash my hands before tossing the towel on the floor. One of the younger guys can pop in to clean all of this up. It will be a nice lesson for them on what happens when you're not loyal to your crew. I make my way back over to where Knox and Kai are standing, determined to use this moment to my advantage.

"One more thing before you go." I catch Knox's attention.

"What is it?" he asks.

"I'm heading out of town to track a few people down. When I get back, I'll be bringing them here. I need someone to keep an eye on Ava while I'm gone."

"I need you here. You know how unstable things have been. I can't afford to have one of my best guys leaving right now. We have our own shit to handle."

"I respect you, Knox, but I'm not asking for your permission. I'm simply giving you the courtesy of telling you before I go."

He stays quiet for a moment. I don't give a fuck if he likes it or not. I need to do this for my girl. He is just going to have to deal with it.

"Fine. Do what you need to do, but make it quick. The Cobras are planning something big. I can feel it."

"I'll only be a few days." I turn to Kai. "I need you to grab Ava her coffee and muffin in the mornings while I'm gone. And can you check in on her? Or have Wrenly do it? I know she's been missing her lately."

"What the hell do I look like? Your little bitch?"

I glare at him. "You look exactly like my little bitch. Don't make me shave your head while you're sleeping. I know you're getting close to winning that bet. How about I make it all for nothing?"

"Hey man, don't threaten these gorgeous locks. I've got you."

Knox shakes his head at the banter between the two of us before we leave the shed and walk back up to the garage to meet with a few of the others. Some new protocols need to be implemented to weed out the rat we apparently have in our midst.

Chapter 22

Avalynn

While I drive to work, I let my mind wander. Things between Greyson and I have been feeling kind of normal. It's odd. I find myself missing him when he isn't around, but I still can't let myself fully commit to him. I still have so many questions. How will we make this work if he intends to stay with the Crimson Rose?

I've been feeling increasingly awkward with working at Temptations and have considered quitting a bunch of times. Most of the guys who frequent the place know I've been seeing Greyson. Alec has been keeping them at bay for now because I've been insisting that Grey and I are nothing official, which is technically true. I just don't know how much longer I can stretch that half-truth.

There are other bars I can work at. In a way, quitting means I am choosing Greyson. Am I ready for that? I've already chosen him in certain ways over the last few weeks. I know I can't keep working for his enemy. It's too dangerous, and it's only a matter of time before there is some sort of incident.

Me and Grey are complicated. He says that I'm his, but he is also mine, even if I'm not ready to admit it to him. I know if I ever saw another woman hanging around him, I would punch that bitch square in the face.

Mrs. Myers also sent another email inquiry. She's determined to figure out what happened to her son. She's now offering double the initial amount she was willing to pay. It's too good to pass up at this point. I can take this job, quit Temptations, and take my time finding something else. I guess I'll be talking to Alec after I finish my shift.

It's the weekend, so I'll have plenty of time to do a deep dive into Mrs. Myers' son. It'll be the perfect thing to keep myself busy while Greyson's out of town. He dropped by this morning with my coffee and muffin and told me that he would be gone for a few days but refused to tell me why he was leaving. I suppose it has something to do with the Crimson Rose, and he doesn't want to involve me in it.

I tell myself it's okay to miss him as I park my car and mentally prepare myself to work my last shift with his enemy. The club is already popping when I walk into Temptations. The music is loud, and one of the more popular girls is on the far stage. A large crowd of men gather around her, tossing bills in her direction. Men really are simple-minded creatures sometimes.

I step behind the bar, waving at Bruce. I wasn't expecting him to be working with me tonight. There must be some kind of special client here. He's only ever here when there is someone important in the VIP rooms.

"Hey sexy, over here," a man yells from the far end of the bar.

THE AFTERTHOUGHT

I roll my eyes and make my way to him so I can take his drink order. If Grey knew people were talking to me like this when I worked here, I have no doubt he would kill every single one of them. It makes me smile thinking about how protective he's gotten of me.

"Yeah, that's right, sway those hips right on over here," the guy yells out again.

I'm not wearing anything too revealing. I never do. Tonight, it's a simple black skirt and crop top combo with my fishnet tights under them. My hair is down and curled. I find it pulls more tips when it's down instead of when it's pulled back. Some people are just disgusting and have no issue sexualizing you after a few drinks, regardless of what you're wearing.

"What can I get you?" I ask, playing nice even though I want to smash his face on the bar.

"If I can't have you, I'll have to settle for a Miller Lite." His head falls down a bit. I can tell he's had several drinks already.

"Coming right up." I turn away, trying my best to remind myself to just get him his drink and move on to the next person.

The next hour or so flies right along. The asshole from earlier went back to the main stage and hasn't bothered me again, thankfully. I've made a decent amount of tips tonight, and I feel good about talking to Alec after my shift.

"Ava?" One of the girls from the VIP rooms calls out as she steps towards the bar.

"Hey, Candy. What did you need?"

"Can you get these orders to the guys in VIP? I really need to use the bathroom," she begs.

"Alec made it pretty clear that I'm not supposed to go back there. Can you have Bruce do it?" I ask.

"Bruce is a bit busy." She points over to one of the tables by the small stage where he is currently sitting while one of the girls gives him a lap dance.

"Fine. Just tell me what they need."

She hands me a piece of paper, and I get to work making the three drinks. Once I have them made up, I wait on the few people who are at the bar, hoping she will come back from the bathroom. She hasn't, so I grab the tray and make my way to the back rooms with the drinks.

It's a lot quieter back here than it is in the main room. The music has a softer hue to it since it's more sectioned off. I'm surprised when I walk through and find all the rooms completely empty, save the last one, which seems to be where our special guests are occupied.

"I need you to be sure you're there on time. They're already getting suspicious," I hear someone say as I get closer. The voice sounds familiar, but I can't figure out why. I freeze and wait to see if they are going to say anything else. Maybe I can figure out who this is if I hear them talk again.

"The Crimson Rose will be nothing but a pile of ash when we are done with them. They will be left with nothing. The drugs will belong to Alec, and the Cobras will have whatever funds

THE AFTERTHOUGHT

you need to get the girls you're after and move them. I think this is the best direction for all of us to go in."

"They've already gotten their hands on Freddy. Greyson almost burned his dick off yesterday. You're sure if we do this, there's no chance they will be able to retaliate?"

"You let me handle Greyson Hayes. He's got a weakness now."

"Greyson doesn't have a weakness," one of the voices says.

"That's where you're wrong," the familiar voice says. I already know they are referring to me. "Greyson will find his way to a nice prison cell soon enough. I've already got something in mind to get him in control."

Fury courses through me at the mention of Grey's name. What the fuck are they trying to set him up for? The Cobras plan to steal drugs from the Crimson Rose to finance some sort of trafficking ring. I can't let this happen. Grey needs to know exactly what's going on if he doesn't already.

I bring the tray of drinks to the small table in front of the couch the three men are sitting on. One of the men is wearing a weird mask that covers the entirety of his face. I try not to look at him too long because I can tell by his body language that he's uncomfortable with me being back here. I'm uncomfortable too, considering he was just implying I'm Greyson's weakness.

"Is there anything else I can get for you?" I question, but nobody answers.

The men simply take their drinks off the tray and place their empty glasses on it. My eyes catch sight of a familiar birthmark on the masked man's hand, and immediately, I know why one of the voices sounded familiar. The masked man is Sheriff Wolfe.

I lean in to grab the tray, pretending I don't have any knowledge of who he is or the things that were said just before I walked into the room. All I want to do is finish my shift without drawing attention to myself and let the Crimson Rose know what I've learned tonight. I only have an hour left until the club closes, and I can safely relay the information.

I never thought I would be willingly helping out a gang, but when it comes down to it in this town, you are either on one side or another. I've tried my best to stay out of it, but this is important.

The guy who was bothering me earlier is back at the bar again, but this time, he brought a few of his friends with him. I was hoping Bruce would deal with them, but he has been less than helpful tonight. He hasn't said a single word to me and has been doing the bare minimum when it comes to serving drinks.

"Does the carpet match the drapes?" one of the guys calls out.

"I'd like to put my face under that skirt and find out for myself." The guys sitting next to the perv all laugh at this statement.

I march right over to them, grabbing a bottle of beer on the way and smashing it on the counter in front of him. They all freeze, eyes widening as I hold the half-broken bottle in his face. His eyes narrow, but I don't back down.

"Say that fucking shit to me again and find the fuck out what happens."

"Ava!" Bruce yells, pulling at my wrist to get the bottle out of the customer's face.

I spin around to face him. "You're going to let them disrespect me like that?"

"You work at a bar in a strip club. What do you expect the customers to say to you?" he spits.

Fuck this, I've had enough. I toss the broken bottle on the floor and pull my wrist from Bruce's grip. "I don't need any of this," I say before marching straight to Alec's office.

I knock a few times, but nobody answers. The door is unlocked, so I take it upon myself to push it open and immediately regret my choice. Alec has a woman bent over his desk, slamming into her hard. He pulls on her hair, making her cry out, and slaps her ass, similar to what he did to me.

"I'm busy," he says while looking over his shoulder. His eyes darken when he notices it was me who walked in. He doesn't stop fucking her though. He only picks up his pace. "Feel free to take a seat and watch. I'll be done shortly."

"I'll pass. I was just stopping in to let you know I quit."

"You'll wait," he states firmly, and part of me is concerned that he knows I overheard something I shouldn't have earlier. I want to leave, but I decide to play the fool and make my way to the couch to sit and wait for him to finish fucking someone right in front of me.

"That's right, whore. Squeeze my cock," he tells the girl, slapping her ass again. His head turns to look at me. "You can always join if you want."

I scoff, ignoring him to stare off at the wall. I can't even believe I let him touch me. What the hell was I thinking? A few weeks ago, I might have let him do it again. He's not bad looking, but he's so full of himself. A realization crosses my mind. I'm disgusted by the idea of any man besides Greyson putting his hands on me.

When did this happen? When did I let him tear down my walls? I thought I was being careful, but in reality, he has owned every single piece of me for as long as I can remember. When did I let my love for Greyson take over my rational thinking? Most importantly, why am I realizing this while watching his enemy fuck a girl on his desk?

Alec lets out a deep grunt, signaling his completion, and pulls himself free from the girl. I watch with disgust as he pulls the condom free from his cock and drops it in his trash can. When the girl stands, I realize it's Candy, and a part of me feels bad for her. She doesn't look like she enjoyed that at all.

"Go clean yourself up and get back to work," he tells her. She uses the towel he hands her to wipe herself before leaving the room.

"I'm not staying. I just wanted to let you know—"

"That you quit, yeah, I heard." He laughs and comes over to sit on the other side of the couch. "Tell me, why is that? Does your little boyfriend not want you working here?"

"We've been over this. Greyson is not my boyfriend. I'm quitting because I don't enjoy being asked if the carpet matches the drapes. I don't want men making comments to me about putting their face up my skirt, and I certainly don't want to be made to feel like a cheap whore when I try to defend my self-respect."

"Ava, you can't be serious. You're quitting because some drunk fuck at the bar made dirty comments to you?" Alec chuckles.

"I'm quitting because I should have never been working here in the first place." I eye him carefully, not wanting him to know that there is more to this. If he finds out I was in the VIP rooms and connects the dots, I'm fucked.

"There's no way I can change your mind?" He scoots closer to me, and I immediately stand. I know this pig did not just fuck Candy and then try to flirt with me. It's gross.

"I'm leaving. I wish you nothing but the best. Oh, and by the way, I broke a bottle. Feel free to take it out of my check."

I can read the look on his face, and he's questioning whether or not he wants to let me leave. I move quickly before he can try to stop me and shuffle out of his office. I practically run to grab the rest of my things. I don't take a full breath until I've made it out of the club and to my car. I put the car into gear to get home as fast as possible and pull out my phone to call Grey to tell him what I know.

Chapter 23
Greyson

I couldn't exactly ask Ava where to find David because I want it to be a surprise for her—a nice little romantic gesture, if you will. I snooped around in her room a bit while she was working one night and found exactly what I needed. Ava is the sentimental type. She likes to keep things for memories. Usually, it's for good memories, but I figured it was worth checking. If there was a chance that she kept it, that would be the easiest route for me.

I found the hospital bracelet I was looking for in the top drawer of her desk, mixed in with a few other miscellaneous things that she's added since coming back to town. When I googled the hospital's name, I was able to get the location and phone number. I quickly called them to confirm that she was there during that time. They advised that she was there; however, they could not release personal details regarding her stay. I don't need the details. I already have them.

It's a small hospital just outside of Orlando, Florida. Of course, the crazy fucker lives in Florida. It was pretty simple at this point. Ava told me Ashley Banks hired her, so I searched for

David Banks within a 25-mile radius of the hospital and ended up with two options.

When I drove to the first one, the house was nothing like what Ava described, so I moved on to the second. This house matches her description perfectly. I've been sitting in my car across the street watching it for a bit now. My eyes occasionally land on the lawn, and I wonder where she crawled through that grass to fight for her life. Nothing but sheer anger courses through me as I picture her helpless and alone. My poor girl had to be so scared. I'll ensure his fear is double what hers was.

This guy will probably think me kidnapping him is the worst thing to ever happen to him. I can't wait to see how he reacts to waking up in my little torture shed with my queen standing right next to me and my blowtorch. The thought alone makes my cock strain in my pants. She is going to look fucking stunning getting her revenge.

My phone rings, and it pulls my attention away from the house. It's Ava, so I swiftly answer. "Hey, little shadow."

"Grey, some stuff happened tonight at Temptations. I need to talk to you. Do you have a minute?" She sounds on edge, and I don't like it one bit.

"Did someone hurt you?" I immediately regret leaving her there. I should have brought her with me.

"I'm fine, but I overheard something tonight that I think you should know about."

"Okay, I'm listening." My heart is racing in my chest as I wait for whatever she is about to say.

"For starters, I quit my job."

"Little shadow, that's the best news I've heard all week. I thought you were going to tell me bad news." Thank fuck she quit. I thought I was going to have to burn that place down and start a war.

"I am, at least I think it will be. I just wanted to start with something that would break the ice a bit."

"Why did you quit? I swear, if someone put their hands on you, I'll cut them off, cook them, and then force feed them to the piece of shit."

"Nobody touched me," she reassures me.

"What was it then?" I've been trying to get her to quit for weeks. Her being there around all those Cobras was always a disaster waiting to happen. I'm surprised they left her alone, considering Alec knows very well who she belongs to.

"There was some creep at the bar making lewd comments to me. I tried to brush it off for a while, but he ended up pushing me to the point where I couldn't take it anymore."

"What did he say to you?"

"He brought up being between my legs, so I held a broken bottle to his face and told him to say it again." I'm met with a mixture of emotions when she tells me this. I want to skin the fucker alive for talking to her like that, but I'm proud of her for not sitting back and taking it.

"Listen, baby, I'm so proud of you for sticking up for yourself. Nobody should be talking to you like that. I will take care of that place, don't you worry. I'll find him and make sure he realizes who he spoke to. Nobody disrespects my girl and lives to speak about it."

"Don't be crazy. I handled it. I don't need you sticking your nose in. That's not why I wanted to talk to you anyway."

"I swear, if Alec did something, I'll come home right now and slit his throat."

"No. Would you stop being so murdery and let me say what I need to say?"

"I'm sorry. I don't like being so far away from you."

"I overheard something that I shouldn't have. The usual girl who works in the VIP rooms needed to use the bathroom, so I had to take a few drinks back there. I heard someone talking about stealing drugs from the Crimson Rose. I didn't hear the entire conversation, so I can't be sure where they are planning to hit you all, but I know it's soon."

This confirms our suspicions. We knew something big was coming soon, just not exactly when. "Okay," I tell her, waiting to see if there's anything else.

"There's something else. I'm 99% sure Sheriff Wolfe was one of the guys there. He had a mask on, so I could be wrong, but I saw the birthmark on his hand, and it definitely sounded like him. He said something about making sure you ended up in prison."

The sheriff? FUCK! That would make sense, considering a lot of our problems started when Knox took him on as a new client. He was supposed to help us spread our reach, but that fucker has been working with the Cobras all along. I'm going to have to talk with Knox about how he wants to handle this. We will definitely need to look further into it. I sure as fuck will not be ending up in prison.

"Everything will be okay. Don't tell anyone else about what you heard. I don't want anyone using it as an excuse to come after you while I'm out of town."

"When are you coming home?" she whines.

Home. She called Dune Valley home. My heart aches a bit when I hear those words. She misses me and wants me home. I'll have to make sure to reward her nicely when I get back.

"Soon, baby. I just need to find something first, and then I'll be back. You'll be the first person I come to see; don't worry."

"Okay. I have to go inside. Chloe and I are going to watch Dirty Dancing. Can you believe she's never seen it before?"

I laugh at the annoyance in her tone. It's always been her favorite movie. I'm sure she will have Chloe addicted, too. "Enjoy your movie night, little shadow."

The phone clicks, and I already miss her voice. I need to hurry up and get these two pieces of shit in the trunk, so I can get back home to my girl. I hate her being in that town alone.

I quickly dial Knox to fill him in on the situation while flicking my lighter on and off. He is just as surprised as I was to find out the little bit of information about Sheriff Wolfe. Ava doesn't know that the sheriff works for us. He was the contact I was meeting the day I saw her again for the first time.

Knox tells me he will figure out how to use this to our advantage. The Cobras don't know we have this bit of information.

We have a few days until our next scheduled drop. I should be back in Dune Valley before then.

It's time to speed things up here. As soon as it gets dark, I'll be slipping right into David's house, grabbing him, and throwing his useless ass in the trunk. I still have to get my hands on Officer Grant tonight, but I lucked out, and he is on call.

I drive away from David's house and find myself a nice coffee shop, ordering myself the same drink that Ava likes. It's not the same as being there with her, but it brings me a small level of comfort. Right now, I wish I was back in Dune Valley with her watching her as I fuck her mercilessly. She makes the most beautiful face when she falls apart.

Time goes by fairly quickly, and the sun is beginning to set. It's time to go back to David's house. I changed my mind about how I want to go about this. It needs to be set up perfectly. I park my car right across the street from his house. It's pretty secluded here, so I'm not worried about anyone seeing me. I grab my bag from the passenger seat and slip on my black balaclava that I haven't worn since I killed Gary Myers.

It takes every ounce of restraint in me to keep my shit together as I walk across the lawn to get to this spot where I can peer into the large window that Ava described. I want this to feel as familiar as possible to him. I want him to think about how the last time he saw someone outside this window, it was my girl.

I look inside the window and find him sitting on the couch with his feet propped up on a coffee table. There are empty food and beer containers piled up around him, but he doesn't care.

He just sits there clicking through the channels on his TV. What a pathetic piece of scum.

I stand in his yard, peering into the corner of the window, simply waiting for him to notice me. Luckily, it only takes a few minutes for his eyes to lift and meet mine through the window. He quickly jumps before standing up, yelling something, and pointing in my direction. I narrow my eyes and tilt my head to the side, not moving from my position.

I see him toss the remote on the couch and move out of view. Perfect. He's on his way to me, just like I wanted. I imagine Ava standing here frozen in place like she explained to me. A pang of guilt fills my chest. I never should have pushed her away.

"HEY! Who are you?" the guy yells over to me.

I turn to face him, a sinister smile crossing my face under my mask. It's too bad he can't see it. I'm sure I would look completely manic and unhinged. He doesn't deserve to see me. He pulls a knife out of his pocket, charging at me. Is it the same knife he used on Ava? I step to the side, letting him run straight past me. He stumbles a bit, most likely high.

When he charges at me again, I push him down to the ground. He falls hard, and a groan leaves his throat as he tries to roll over on his side. I step towards him and kick him hard in the ribs, over and over. He curls himself into the fetal position, yelling for me to stop. I can't stop picturing Ava helpless and at his mercy.

I step back from him for long enough to grab my bag off the ground and pull out what I need. Quickly, I secure his feet and hands, then throw some tape over his mouth. He's too drugged out and worried about the pain to even fight me as I do it. I slip a large strap under him and drag him to the edge of the road before popping the trunk and hoisting him in. He's not small, but the drugs he's on give me the advantage. I'll have to wait to give him the drugs I brought to keep him unconscious. I don't know how they will interact with whatever he's taken, and I can't have him dying before I get him back to Ava.

Now that he's secured, I get to have fun with his house. This place doesn't deserve to exist. I open the back door of my car to pull out one of my favorite toys, my flamethrower. It's already gassed up and ready to go, and my body is buzzing from the anticipation. Quickly, I check the house. David lives alone and has no pets. Perfect.

I stomp across the lawn and stand in front of the house, practically jumping for joy. My finger presses the trigger, and the dancing flames shoot from it, immediately lighting up some of the shrubbery around the front of the house.

I focus the flames on the front porch, watching as the fire begins to engulf the wood. Slowly, it overtakes everything, and I have to take a few steps back as the heat becomes too hot for me to withstand.

One final thing. I walk around to the side of the house with the window and light up the patch of grass outside it. I burn the entirety of the yard as I walk backward until I'm safely on the street, watching the flames engulf this shit hole.

There is something so fucking satisfying about burning down a house. Seeing the fire at this scale and knowing it's because of me gives me chills. The only thing that could make me happier in this moment is having my cock buried in Ava's sweet cunt. I would burn down the world for her if it meant she never had to live with a single painful memory ever again.

I wish I could stay and watch the destruction, but unfortunately, I have one more person to secure before I can go home to my baby girl. I was smart and grabbed David's phone from his pocket before I locked him in the trunk. Scrolling through the contacts, I land on the one that I was searching for and press the call button.

It rings twice before a man with a deep voice picks up. "David, I thought I told you not to call me unless it's important."

"Officer Grant?" I question.

"Who is this, and why do you have David's phone?"

"David gave me the phone and told me to call you. He said there was some sort of issue with the last deal. He needs you to meet him." I'm banking on the fact that this cop is also involved in David's drug dealings. Ava knew he was doing something shady for the officer, but she wasn't sure what exactly that was. I took a lucky guess.

"Fuck," he mutters. "I told him this might be a problem. Where does he want to meet? I'm on call tonight, so I can make it look like a regular call."

This was too fucking easy. "They burned his house down," I say, trying my best to sound panicked. "Can you meet at the

THE AFTERTHOUGHT

abandoned gas station down the road from David's as soon as possible?"

"Yeah, I'll be there in ten minutes. Tell him this is the last time I stick my neck out for him. He's caused me enough trouble over the years already."

"Got it. See you in a few," I say before hanging up. If only this guy knew the trouble that awaits him when he pulls up to the gas station.

Like clockwork, within just a few minutes, I see the police car pull into the abandoned station. I stay in my spot, comfortably behind the wheel of my car, with my mask on, because I know their cars tend to have cameras. Once the officer gets out, I roll my window down to wave him over to the car and roll it most of the way back up.

My windows are tinted, so he can't see inside, but I have it rolled down just enough so that he can hear me from the outside. "Get in," I say.

He seems a bit cautious, turning his head from left to right to make sure there is nobody else around. Ultimately, he pulls open the back door and slides in, signing his death warrant.

"Where is David? I thought I was meeting him."

"He's a bit tied up right now, so you get me instead."

"What's the big issue that you had to pull me out here for?"

I turn in my seat, pulling the syringe from the center console but making sure it's hidden so he can't see it. "You see, Officer, it seems you hurt my girl, and I can't let that stand."

I turn so that I'm fully in view, but before he can register the fact that I have a mask on and am holding a syringe, I plunge it into his leg and empty the contents. For being a police officer, he really sucks at having any kind of situational awareness.

"Take a nap, Officer Grant. We have a really important meeting we must see to once you wake up," I say as his head slumps down.

I put the car in drive and pull away from the station, making sure to avoid any possible camera angle from his patrol car that would catch my plate. Once we are a few miles outside of town, I pull over, tie him up, and secure the tape over his mouth. I should throw him in the trunk with his buddy, but I'm not sure if there will be room. That bastard better be alive. I haven't heard a peep from him since tossing him in there.

Now that all this is taken care of, I throw a blanket over the officer so I can be on my way back to Ava. I can't wait to see the look on her face when she finds out I got them for her. She will never have to worry about these men, or any others, hurting her ever again. She has me to protect her now.

Chapter 24
Avalynn

Not having Greyson here feels strange. Until he left, I didn't realize exactly how much I let him back in. He found a way to not only latch onto me but also have me swooning for him, regardless of how many times I told him no along the way.

Kai has been leaving my coffee and muffin at my front door in Greyson's absence. It's sweet that he thought of me enough to have someone do that. He was romantic when we were younger, but I didn't expect it this time around. I thought life would have hardened him along the way. A gangbanger who has an affinity for fire doesn't exactly scream romance. He always seems to consider me, though. I laugh and wonder what he had to threaten Kai with to get him to run his errands.

I've been hard on Grey for good reason, but I've never felt more at home since being back here in this town and around him. In a way, it feels like I've never left. He has this obsession for me, and I can't help but fold to my feelings for him as well. I've been struggling to imagine what it would be like without him, which is a problem because he is still a very active member of the Crimson Rose.

I pick up the heart-shaped crystal he gave me at the drive-in and turn it around in my fingers a few times. Every time I turn it, the light catches it a different way, revealing a multitude of colors. There are greens, grays, and deep red specks all throughout. It's incredibly beautiful. I haven't let it out of my grasp since the day he gave it to me. It's been a nice trinket to fiddle with when I'm feeling stressed or anxious.

I need to keep my mind busy today. I'm going to devote my time to researching for Mrs. Myers so I can email her with an update. I was able to track down her son's last known location and a few other things over the last few days.

I've made connections to the criminal underground while doing my PI work. Some are people I've helped over the years, and others are people who were hired to work alongside me for specific jobs. It's been helpful to have those resources, although I seldom take advantage of them. Today, though, I'm going to. I send a quick email to one of my contacts, Barrett Monroe, asking him for all the camera footage within a five-mile radius of a specific address, and move on to my next task.

Thanks to Gary Myers' mother, I've gained access to his email. From what I've seen, the guy was pretty shady. I understand why the cops have no desire to search for him. There are countless back-and-forth coded emails. I can't tell exactly what they are about, but I know enough to be able to read between the lines. He was involved in something suspicious, for sure.

I scroll through all the emails again to see if anything pops out, and I land on one that talks about placing an order for blood-red flowers. Could he be referring to the Crimson Rose? Did he owe them money, or was he buying from them? I wonder if Greyson would have any info on Gary. If he does, would he be willing to give it to me?

I'm not sure where he would stand regarding me researching something that could potentially involve the Crimson Rose. I know he said that he's all in with me and that he doesn't plan to let me go, but again, I'm circling back to his gang presence. Do I come before the Crimson Rose now?

Just when I'm starting to feel like I'm at a standstill with this, my phone pings with a message from Barrett regarding the video footage. There's a reason he is the best at what he does. He's so fucking quick. Several files are attached, so I find my laptop to view them more clearly.

The first video I pull up shocks me to my core. It's the outside of Gary's workplace. The tall building has cameras in the main lobby area that show a tiny glimpse of the front of the building. A vehicle pulls up. To anyone else, it would look like a normal car service, but when the person comes into view, my heart stops.

He's disguised well enough that he wouldn't look suspicious, but I know Greyson when I see him. This is definitely Greyson opening the door for Gary Myers and then driving him away. I don't bother watching the rest of the videos. They don't matter. I already know Grey is involved. I'm going to ask him what he knows. If he wants a future with me, he better be honest about it. I'm not sure what I'm going to say to Mrs. Myers. That is all going to depend on what Grey tells me.

I sigh, slamming my laptop closed. The one job that I take while being back in this town has to be connected to my boyfriend. I pause. Did I just refer to him as my boyfriend? Shit. That's what he is, though. Greyson Hayes is my boyfriend. Fuck.

I check the time on my phone and notice that it's getting close to when Chloe comes home from school. How did I manage to waste the entire morning away? She only had a half day today because she's a senior, and all of her finals are already complete. It's hard to believe she graduates next week. I'm so damn proud of her.

I've been trying to spend as much time with her as possible lately, and we've really gotten to know each other. I knew she liked 80s music, but I didn't realize how much. It's a lot. I mean a lot. It's so strange for someone her age to like that kind of music, but it connects her to her mom. I admire that she's found a bit of peace from listening to it. My only request was for her to not play that song. I didn't tell her why, and she never asked, but she agreed.

I've caught her crying a time or two. She's started letting me sit with her in her room to talk through what upsets her. It's almost always triggered by seeing something that reminds her of her mom. It's been a little rough for her with graduation getting so close and her mom not being there for it.

THE AFTERTHOUGHT

Tonight, we are going to do something a bit different. She asked if I would take her to a small field outside of town to plant a tree with her in memory of her mom. They used to go there together to star gaze. She told me that a few months before her mom passed away, she told her that anytime she felt like she was sad or alone, she should look up to the stars because that's where she would be. A bright star shining down on her.

Even the thought of that conversation makes tears well up in my eyes. Her mom gave her the comfort of that memory. I'll do whatever I can to help Chloe honor it. We went out yesterday and got a tree to plant. Nothing special, just a small oak tree that will grow to be big and strong. It will be a place for her to go back to any time she wants to connect with her mom. I think it's special, and I'm honored to be able to do this with her.

I pull out my phone to send a quick text to Grey because if I've learned anything from Chloe, it's that I need to be better at living in the moment and appreciating the people I have.

> Me: Hey

> Grey: Hey baby, everything okay?

> Me: I just miss you a little and wanted you to know.

> Grey: Yeah?

> Me: Don't let it go to your head.

> Grey: Too late for that. It's gone to my now inflated head.

> Grey: Both of them.

> Me: You're insufferable.

> Grey: Only the best for you, little shadow.

I can already picture the stupid grin I know is spread across his face. It makes me smile. The front door opens, and Chloe flips off her shoes. She makes a show of tossing her backpack on the couch before flopping down next to it.

"You okay?" I ask.

"I'm fine. Let's just go get this over with." Her eyes are red and puffy like she has been crying. I'm fairly sure she's being defensive and irritable because she's emotional about this. I get it.

I walk over and sit next to her on the couch. "We don't have to do this today if you aren't comfortable. This is completely up to you." Her head sags, and she fiddles with her fingers. "Just know that I will be here for you, whatever you decide."

"I haven't been back there since she died. What if going there without her doesn't feel the same?"

My heart breaks for her. I reach out to touch her hand, and she looks up at me. "That place the two of you shared, it's a gift,

Chloe. I know you're scared, and I will be right by your side, but I really think when you go, you will feel more connected with your mom than you have in weeks."

"You're right. This is dumb. I'm sorry, I just don't know what's going on with my head."

"It's not dumb. You're still grieving. It's completely normal." I reassure her.

She takes a deep breath, closes her eyes, and nods her head. "Okay, let me go change, and then we can go." She eyes up my outfit. "You're not wearing that, are you?"

It makes me chuckle. "I was going to, but I don't have to."

"A skirt in the middle of a field? Maybe jeans instead." She states plainly. This is all for her. If that's what she wants me to wear, that's what I'll wear.

"I'll put some jeans on." I laugh.

Not too long later, we are in the car, and she's showing me the way to our destination. It's on a hill just outside of town. I pull up, realizing that from here, you can see the entirety of Dune Valley. How did I live here my entire life without knowing about this place?

To the right of the parking lot is the field that we came here for. I park, and we both step out of the car and walk towards the edge of it. I have the tree in one hand and a backpack filled with a blanket and some food over my shoulder. Chloe stares out into the field with teary eyes.

"Are you ready?" I ask.

She turns her head to look at me and nods, so I reach down to grab her hand reassuringly.

"Lead the way."

We walk across the well-maintained grass path down the middle of the field. I wasn't exactly sure what to expect when coming here, but it's not this. There aren't any other people around. Part of me wonders if this is someone's private property, but it's not noted anywhere, and there's a public parking lot. When we get to about the midpoint, she pulls me into the grass and reaches out for my backpack. She lays out the blanket, flopping down on it, and urges me to sit next to her.

"It's different being here in the daytime." She smiles while looking out across the field. "When we came here, it was dark. This is the best place in the area to see all the stars."

"Maybe one day we can come back at night, and you can show me," I prompt.

"Yeah, I think I'd like that."

We sit there in silence for a while, enjoying the fresh air and overall peaceful feeling the place brings. I give her the space that she needs to process being here and the support she needs to know she isn't alone.

She looks over at me. "You know, when I found out about you, I thought there was no way that we would form any kind of relationship. I mean, how could we? I spent the first seventeen years of my life knowing nothing about you. I was sure that you had to know about me and just didn't want anything to do with me. I was wrong."

"I swear if I knew about you, I would have tried to connect with you."

"I've been trying to figure out why my mom didn't tell me about you. I wondered why she would keep you a secret from me when we never kept any secrets from each other. I get it now though."

I look at her curiously, my brow creasing.

"I think that my mom wanted to keep me to herself while she could because she knew she didn't have much time left. She had this weird sixth sense about things. I think she knew that you and I would be okay. She knew we would find our own way to forming a real sisterly relationship."

"I think you're right," I admit. "It may have started off a little rocky, but all sisters fight, at least a little."

"We grew up so differently, and yet we ended up in the same exact place." She sighs.

"You're not wrong about that. I'm thankful we ended up here. It's been a long time since I've been able to call someone family," I tell her, and she smiles.

"Family," she repeats. After another moment, she finally makes eye contact with me again. "Come on, let's go plant the tree for my mom."

We walk to the corner of the field where there is a small bench with a big empty space behind it. It looks out of place. I can't help but wonder why there aren't any trees around it.

It's like she can read my thoughts because she says, "There used to be a really big tree here when I was younger. A pretty bad storm blew through and knocked it down. Whoever manages the property had the entire thing removed. My mom and I always said that we wanted to plant another one here in its place." She steps forward and bends down to touch the empty grass. "I don't think she planned for me to be doing it alone."

"You're not alone, Chloe."

"Yeah, maybe, but it's not the same." She wipes the tears from her face and sniffles a bit before looking up at the sky. "I miss you, mom."

I pull her in for a hug and hold her tightly as she sobs against my shoulder. Her arms finally wrap around me, and she gives in to all of her emotions. "I couldn't do this without you. Thank you so much for being here with me."

"I'll always be here for you. I'm not going anywhere," I tell her, and in this moment, I know it's the complete truth.

We spend some time pulling ourselves back together before I pull the small shovel out of the backpack we brought and start digging the hole. Chloe didn't want to get dirty, so it was on me to complete the task. I should have brought a bigger shovel, but at least the ground was soft. Eventually, I dug a hole deep enough, and she dropped the tree into it.

"Do you want to say a few words?" I question, and her eyes light up at the suggestion.

"I think that might be nice, actually."

I go to take a step back to give her some privacy, but she reaches down to grab my hand to stop me. "Thank you."

I nod at her, and she releases my hand, letting me step away. I gather up everything we brought and make my way back to the car. She'll come back when she is ready. If she needs me, she knows I'm not far.

Chapter 25
Avalynn

When we got back from the field yesterday, emotions were still high, so Chloe went straight to her room. A few hours later, she finally came out to the living room and insisted we watch the newest season of some reality dating show. It was trash TV at its best and exactly what we both needed after the heaviness of the day.

I heard from Greyson this morning. He's coming home tomorrow. I'm going to use today to my advantage and have a girl's day. It's Saturday, so Chloe doesn't have school, and it's not like it would matter if she did. With her graduating so soon, I would let her stay home if she wanted to.

The two of us have really formed such a close little bond in such a small amount of time. I think the fact that we have both experienced loss has helped.

In true sister fashion, she keeps bugging me about my relationship with Grey. She was so proud of being able to set up the drive-in date night and has been excited that we are back together. I couldn't tell her that we never officially got back together. Greyson just said I belonged to him, and I stopped fighting somewhere between the iced coffees and orgasms.

My phone vibrates, so I pull it out and see it's another email from Mrs. Myers. I've been trying to avoid contacting her until I have time to talk with Grey about what I found out. I swipe the email notification away and pull up my texts. She can wait a few more days.

> Me: What's your ETA

> Wrenly: Be there in a few. I had to get your coffee so your psycho boyfriend doesn't murder mine.

> Me: That was not necessary.

> Wrenly: I'm not taking any chances. You know they call him Coal on the streets, right?

> Me: He's harmless.

> Wrenly: To you, maybe. The rest of us are all fair game.

I laugh. Even Wrenly is calling Grey my boyfriend at this point. I don't think he would kill Kai over something so silly, but then again, I never really know what to expect with him. He is always full of surprises. It seems like Wrenly and Kai are officially a couple now, though. I can't wait to get the details about that today.

We have a busy day planned. First, we are going to get our nails done, then we are all getting our hair done, and we are ending the day with a nice meal at one of the restaurants in town. It's nothing fancy, but it will be nice to have girl time.

"Chloe, are you almost ready?" I yell out. She hasn't come out of her room yet, so I'm not sure what she's doing in there. She doesn't answer, so I try again. "Chloe!"

She finally pops her head out of the door, "Chill. I'll be out in a minute."

She quickly shuts the door again, and I'm confused. I saunter over to the door and knock, but she yells at me.

"I said I'll be out."

"Why are you being weird? What are you doing in there?" I twist the handle and crack the door open, my eyes immediately widening at what I see.

"OH MY GOD! I told you I'll be out."

A mixture of amusement and horror overtakes my face. "Uh-hhh, hi Matt." He pulls the covers up over his body to hide himself. I pull the door open a little further and look over at Chloe, who is wearing nothing but his shirt and a pair of underwear. "I trust that you two were safe?"

"AVA! That's seriously so embarrassing!"

"If you're old enough to have sex, then you should be old enough to talk about sex." I shrug and cross my arms over my chest, waiting for her answer.

"If you have to know, yes, we are always safe. I have an implant, and we use condoms." Her face is a deep shade of red, and I am loving every moment of this.

"Good. I don't need to know anything else. You're almost eighteen. Just be safe please," I say to her before turning back to Matt and pointing a finger at him. "And you better not hurt her."

"I would never," he says.

I look between the two of them again and laugh. "Wrenly will be here soon. You two better get dressed. We're having a girl's day. You're not skipping out on us, Chloe."

With that, I turn and leave the room, remembering what it was like to be seventeen and in love. Specifically, I remember what it was like to be in love with Greyson. I remember some of the good memories instead of the painful ones. It's a nice reprieve.

I hear a commotion outside, pulling me from my thoughts. Someone is kicking the front door and yelling something. It doesn't sound aggressive, just loud, so I walk over to pull it open.

"It's about time. I told you I was close." Wrenly says as she pushes her way past me to get to the table. Not only did she get me a coffee, but she also got one for herself and a smoothie for Chloe since she's not a super fan of coffee.

"Hello to you, too." I laugh, making my way to grab the drink from the table.

"You're lucky I've known you half of my life, and I don't want to be murdered by your boyfriend."

"He is kind of murdery, isn't he?" Chloe says as she walks into the room and straight to the smoothie on the table. "Thank you for this, by the way."

"He is not murdery." I roll my eyes at both of them. "If we're going to sit here and talk about our love lives, maybe we should talk about you and Kai," I say to Wrenly. "Or how Matt is currently in Chloe's bedroom naked."

"No, he's not!" Wrenly exclaims before practically running towards Chloe's room.

"Leave him be!" She yells after her, but before she can make it to her room, the door opens, and Matt steps out.

He cautiously eyes Wrenly in the hallway before locking eyes with Chloe. "I'm going to head out if that's okay?"

"Yes, please get out of here before they start asking you for details." She looks nervously at Wrenly and then at me, and I shrug.

He walks over to her and pulls her in by the waist before leaning down and giving her a big kiss. It's actually super sweet and earns him some bonus points, in my mind. He is willing to make sure she knows he cares for her, regardless of us teasing him. After a moment, he frees her and makes a hasty exit.

"That was some kiss," Wrenly jokes as the two of them walk back towards the kitchen.

"Enough from both of you." She looks between me and Wrenly, who is now drinking her coffee beside me.

"We're just getting started, little sis," I tease while she rolls her eyes. This entire moment feels... normal.

"Okay, so, nails first?" I ask Wrenly. She's the one who threw this entire day together.

"Yes, and you're driving," she casually tells me.

The nail salon isn't my favorite place to go, but Chloe loves it, so we added it to our list of things for the day when deciding to make a whole girl's day. It doesn't end up being terrible. I didn't get fake nails. I just had them paint this really pretty orange color to match my hair. I think Grey will appreciate it when he sees it.

Chloe got hers painted in her school colors, black and red. It almost broke my heart when she talked about how she and her mom used to do this. They weren't able to get them done for the few months before I came to town because she got super sick. It was the beginning of the end for her.

I'm glad that we were able to do something together that reminded her of her mom. I like the fact that I can be there for her. Those memories are hard to process at first. I remember what it felt like when I was trying to grieve the loss of my dad.

Wrenly got her nails painted black and had a green clover painted on them. Something about how Kai likes lucky charms. It's odd but a sweet gesture for her to think of him.

We came to the hair salon after finishing our nails. It was perfect because I needed a refresher. My roots are out of control. Chloe is getting some blonde highlights and a trim to prep for graduation. Wrenly is getting a quick cut to keep her sharp edges. It's grown to her shoulders, and she likes it to be at that perfect middle ground between her ears and shoulders.

We settle in while waiting for our hair to process, and I decide it's time for Wrenly to spill the beans on her and Kai. I turn to face her. "You and Kai?"

She blushes. "I was wondering when you were going to bring this up."

"I want to know everything," I say, and she glances over at Chloe.

"I want to know everything, too. I'm almost eighteen; stop treating me like a kid."

"Fine," Wrenly gives in.

"Chloe, don't take it personally. Wrenly was just trying to find a way not to talk about it," I tell her.

"You just wait, Ava. Your time is coming, too." She laughs, and I have no clue what I'm going to tell them when they finally start asking questions about Grey and me.

"How did this whole thing start?" I inquire.

"It just happened. I don't know. We've been running in the same circles for a while. This town isn't that big. When you know the same people and go to the same parties, sometimes people just connect," she says while smiling. "He is this tall guy with long hair and tattoos, who on the outside appears to be a crazed psycho, but that's not him at all. He is funny, and sweet, and so romantic it makes me sick sometimes. I'm happier than I've been in a really long time."

I look over at my best friend and the way that she talks about her partner. I'm happy for her. She deserves someone who makes her feel amazing, and it sounds like Kai is doing exactly that. Regardless of the violence this town can bring about, she found safety in him.

"He better not hurt you, or I will have to kill him," I tell her.

"If he hurt me, I think I would kill him first," she confesses. I wouldn't put it past her. She has a wild side, for sure.

We spend the next hour or so talking about everything between the two of them, from their first real date to the night at Greyson's party to how she's been staying with him here and there. It feels good to finally be able to catch up with my friend and have Chloe here, too.

Once we finish at the salon, we do a little bit of shopping before it's time for an early dinner. The restaurant we chose has a variety of everything. Wrenly is a vegetarian, so we needed something that would provide her with options, too.

The hostess seats us close to the door in a four-person booth. Chloe and I sit on one side, facing the door, and Wrenly sits alone on the other. There aren't very many people here, and nobody is sitting anywhere near us. It's kind of like we have the entire half of the restaurant to ourselves.

We are about halfway through our meals when the door opens, and I see a familiar face. A face that I was really hoping to avoid.

Alec walks in with two other guys. Based on the snake tattoos on each of their arms, I can tell they are part of the Cobras. Alec must sense me looking at him because he turns to look in our direction and immediately smiles when we lock eyes.

I say a silent prayer that he will just go on with his day and leave us alone, but I'm not that lucky. I see him lean in and whisper something to one of the guys next to him before he casually slips away from them to saunter over to our table.

He slides into the seat of the booth next to Wrenly and just stares at me. This is a bold fucking move, considering it's well-known around town that every single female sitting at this table is in one way or another connected to the Crimson Rose.

"I don't remember anyone inviting you to our dinner," I state plainly.

Wrenly pushes herself as far away from him as possible as Chloe sits in silence. Her eyes have gone wide. She is seemingly stunned that the leader of the Cobras would have the audacity to sit at our table with us.

"That's not a very nice way to say hello to an old friend," he says, not taking his eyes off of me.

"We are not, and never have been, friends."

A soft chuckle leaves his throat. "I seem to remember you like to play hard to get. I've always been a willing participant though. You don't have to be so abrasive, Ava."

My eyes narrow. "You were a stranger in a coffee shop. Nothing more."

"Clearly. That's why you came to work in my club, because I was just a stranger." He slides out of the seat but still stands at the end of our table. "Tell your little boyfriends they need to watch their fucking backs and stop threatening my men. They shouldn't be letting their bitches out of sight; it's a dangerous town."

"What, Alec? You're too afraid of the Crimson Rose, so you had to threaten a group of women trying to have dinner?" I raise a brow, not backing down in the face of his threat.

"I'm not afraid of anyone. Least of all a man whose woman I've had my cock inside."

Chloe whips her head around to look at me, and I can feel Wrenly's gaze burning into me, too. My cheeks flush with embarrassment. The slimy fuck would make a point to bring that up. We didn't even know each other when it happened. I stand and shove him away from the table, making him laugh.

"If you ever want to be with a real man again, you know where to find me. I can bend you right over my desk and make sure you're properly taken care of," he says as he turns and disappears to the other side of the restaurant.

"What the fuck was that about?" Wrenly immediately asks.

"It's a long story," I say with a sigh. I'm not hungry anymore, and I have no desire to be here. Glancing between Wrenly and Chloe, it seems like they may be feeling the exact same way.

"Let's settle our bill and get out of here. There's wine at the house. I'm suddenly craving a big fucking glass."

They both nod, and within a few minutes, we have excused ourselves from the restaurant and are back in the car, driving to my house. Alec thinks he got a nice dig today, but he should be terrified about the recourse. Once I tell Greyson all about our little run-in, I can guarantee he will want to do something about it. I'm not even going to stop him. That fucker is lucky I didn't punch him square in the throat. I definitely should have.

Chapter 26
Greyson

I get the two fucks secured in my torture shed and take a step back to glance at them. I'm not sure how Ava is going to react to this. With any luck, she will be thankful. I know she told me to stay out of it, but these two signed their death warrants the moment they wronged my girl. I'll do anything I have to in order to make sure she knows I'll always be here to take care of her. I have a lot to make up for, after all.

The officer starts to yell from his chair, shaking it to try and free himself. It's pointless. This isn't my first rodeo. I know the proper way to secure someone to ensure they don't escape.

"As much as I'd love to jump in and start this whole process now, there is someone who needs to be here first. I've been away from her long enough." I shake my head at them. "You two stay put. I'll be back soon, and we can have some fun."

I turn to leave, making sure to secure the shed doors first. A few crew members are at the garage, as usual. I pop my head in when I walk past just long enough to let them know to keep an eye out. I want to make sure nothing happens to my new toys while I'm gone. I might have to talk to Knox about installing exterior cameras.

THE AFTERTHOUGHT

Once I'm finally in my car and on my way to Ava's house, I realize I don't want to be away from her for this long ever again. Her sister's graduation is right around the corner, and with any luck, this one final gesture will be enough for her to admit we belong together. She's close. I just know it.

I stop at the coffee shop quickly to pick up her coffee and muffin. A few minutes later, her house comes into view, and I can't help the smile that forms on my face. I haven't even seen her yet, but I can feel the tension releasing from my body. My little shadow has become the fire that fuels me.

Before I can get fully inside the door, she runs up to me, latching her arms around my neck. "You're going to spill your coffee, baby."

She giggles, and it just might be the sweetest sound I've ever heard. I lean in to give her a kiss, and she deepens it, not wanting to let me go. I'm not sure what happened to her stubborn attitude, but it seems like me being gone for a few days must have made her realize how perfect we are together.

When she pulls back, her cheeks flush with that gorgeous pink color I love. "I missed you, little shadow."

"I missed you too."

That's enough for me to lose all self-control. I step inside and place everything on the table before marching back over to my girl and sweeping her up in my arms, bridal style. She laughs and buries her head in my chest. I walk her right to her bedroom. She deserves a proper hello from her man.

Once inside her room, I kick the door shut, toss her on the bed, and tilt my head toward the hallway. "Chloe?"

"She's at Andrea's. I guess Andrea and her boyfriend broke up. She didn't like that all he wanted to do was hang out with her dad. Plus, I wanted to make sure I had the house to myself when you got here." A mischievous smile crosses her face as she props herself up on her elbows.

"Did my dirty little slut miss me?" I grip her legs and pull them to the edge of the bed before sinking down to my knees in front of her.

"Yes," she breathes out. I pull her leggings off in one swoop, along with her panties, and pepper kisses along her inner thighs.

"Tell me you're mine."

She stays quiet, so I bite down, causing her hips to buck up. She likes a little pain here and there, but she will tell me that she's mine today. I'll make sure of it.

"Little shadow, be a good girl for me, and I'll let you come." My tongue runs along her center, and she moans, her head falling back onto the bed. I pull away from her. "Tell me."

She reaches down to grab at my hair to guide me back toward her, but I swat her away. I'll get the words I want out of her one way or another. I stand up to quickly flip her onto her stomach with her bottom half hanging off of the bed. Her feet reach the floor, and she tries to push herself up, but I push down on her back with one hand between her shoulder blades and pull my belt free from my pants with the other.

"Hey!" she cries out as I pull one of her hands behind her back and then the other, securing them with the belt. I'm going to have to invest in a nice pair of handcuffs for her. I pull my clothes off and toss them in the corner.

"I gave you a chance to be a good slut for me, but you want to be bad, don't you? Do you want me to punish you, baby? All you had to do was ask."

My hand slams down on her right cheek, making her cry out.

"Greyson!"

"I fucking love when you scream my name."

I smack her other cheek, watching as a faint red outline of my hand appears on her skin. My cock strains for attention at the sight of it. I smack each side two more times, listening as she cries out softly each time. With the last smack, her cry transforms into a moan. I almost have her where I want her.

"I bet your pussy is dripping. Should I check?"

"Yes," she whines.

"Such a greedy girl." I lightly slide my finger along her center to find that she is, in fact, soaking wet. I dip a finger inside and pull it back out, spreading the wetness up to her ass.

"Greyson," she warns with a stern tone.

"Has anyone fucked you here, baby?" I tease at her back hole, holding her in place when she tries to pull away. She doesn't answer me, so I smack her cheek again, prompting her to respond.

"No," she cries out.

Good, I'll be the first to take that, just as I was the one to take her virginity all those years ago. My finger plays with her back entrance, and slowly, I slip one in. She complains a little, so I bring my other hand down to run it along her pussy. When I find her clit, I begin to rub small circles while pushing and pulling my finger from her ass. She caves into the pleasure and starts to moan.

"Grey, please, more," she begs.

I spit on her ass and slowly press a second finger in, watching as she stretches around them. She takes it so well. After a few minutes, I add a third, and her breathing begins to pick up as my fingers move in and out of her while I rub her clit. Just as she gets up to that edge, I pull them from her, and she whines in protest.

"Tell me you're mine," I say again.

"Just fuck me, please."

"So greedy. Fine. Let me show you who you belong to." Immediately, I line myself up with her pussy. I could go easy on her, but I don't. With one thrust, I seat myself fully inside her perfect cunt.

"Grey, a condom," she cries out, trying to pull away from me.

"No," I state, slamming into her. "You're mine, Ava. Admit it for me, baby, and I promise I'll come in your ass instead of your pussy."

"That's supposed to be better?" she says between the panting.

"Yes, because if I'm coming in your ass, I'll make sure you come first. How badly do you want to come, little shadow?"

"Please," she begs.

"You know what to say." Over and over, I thrust into her, picking up the pace as I go. Her hips begin to move with mine as she silently begs me for more.

"I'm yours," she says, barely audible.

"Louder." I smack her ass with another forceful thrust.

"I'M YOURS!" she cries out.

"Good fucking girl."

I spit on her ass again and shove my fingers back in, keeping my movements at the same pace as my cock.

"More," she moans when I scissor my fingers inside her.

I smack her ass with my free hand, and she clenches around me. "That's it. Grip my cock like a needy slut."

She clenches again, and I know she's so close. I keep up a steady pace pushing my cock in and out of her pussy while my fingers continue to plunge into her ass. It's taking everything in me to not blow my load into her right now, but I promised her she would get to come first.

As if she can read my mind, her pussy clamps down on my cock, and she cries out as she finds her high. She makes the sweetest fucking sounds as she loses all control, spasming around me a few times until her orgasm recedes.

I pull out and lean down to whisper in her ear, "Make sure you stay relaxed, baby."

Slowly, I guide my cock into her ass, inch by inch, letting her adjust to the intrusion until I'm fully seated. I worked her pretty well with my fingers, but I still give her a moment before I begin to move inside of her.

She feels so fucking tight. I'm not going to last very long at all, so I bring a hand back down to her clit to show it some attention. With any luck, my girl will come with me while I rail her from behind.

"How does it feel to have me buried in your ass?"

"G—good," she replies. "So fu—fucking good."

"I figured a filthy slut like you would love it. Be a good girl for me, baby, and come for me again."

I pick up my pace, and thankfully, it doesn't take long for her to get right back to the edge. She moans loudly, telling me she's close and that it's too much for her. "Fuck," I grunt as I empty myself into her. Chills spread through her body, and as she rides out her very own high.

After a moment, I pull out of her and unfasten my belt to release her arms before falling onto the bed next to her. I pull her into me so that her head rests on my chest. We stay like this for a few minutes, just basking in one another. Nothing else matters. Her fingers trace over the tattoo on my chest. She's transfixed by the small words I had added before I left town. I look down at her and grip her chin, pulling her gaze to meet mine.

"Forever my heart," I whisper. It's been a long time since I've said those words to her, but the meaning is the same today as they always have been. Her eyes close as she takes in my words.

"Sometimes, I feel like I was nothing more than an afterthought to you?"

"You are more than just an afterthought. You are everything. My past. My present. My future. The reason my heart beats in my chest. You are my biggest regret and my greatest gift, all at the same time. I would do anything for you if you let me."

"Do you mean that?"

"I do. I love you, Avalynn Blake. Forever my heart."

"Forever my always," she whispers back.

She doesn't say that she loves me, but she doesn't have to. The three words she just said mean so much more than I love you ever could. She snuggles back into me for a few minutes, and while I wish I could stay here with her like this forever, I have to show her the surprise waiting in my torture shed.

"Let's go take a shower. I have something I want to show you."

We shower quickly, and I have her dress in clothes that she wouldn't mind throwing away before we load ourselves in the car for the short drive. We pull up to the garage, and she immediately looks nervous. She's made it clear several times now that she doesn't want anything to do with gang life, yet I've brought her to one of our main hangouts.

"It's not what you think," I blurt out before she can say anything. "Do you trust me?"

She eyes me wearily but nods. "Yes."

I step out of the car and walk around to her side, opening the door and reaching out my hand to her. "Come with me. I have a gift for you."

She doesn't say a word as I lead her from the car to behind the garage, where the shed sits in the trees. I pull open the door, and just before stepping inside, I grab her by her shoulders and force her to look up at me.

"I'm right here with you, baby. There's nothing you need to be afraid of. If it's too much, just let me know." Her brow furrows, but she nods her head.

I grab her hand to lead her inside, and we only make it a few steps before her entire body goes rigid. I look over to her to find her eyes locked with David's and nothing but pure terror on her face. She goes to take a step back, but I place my arm behind her, preventing her from retreating.

"He's tied up. He's not going to hurt you. He's never going touch you ever again," I assure her. She looks over at me with tears in her eyes. When a tear drips down her cheek, I bring my thumb up to wipe it away and cup her face.

"Grey," she says with a shaky voice. She's not sure what's happening, but that's okay. I'll help her.

"I brought them here for you, Ava. They don't get to leave."

She looks over at both David and Officer Grant and then back to me. She pauses for a moment as if she is trying to decide what to do, but she simply loops her arms around my neck and pulls me in for a kiss. I melt into her, feeling the way the warmth of her mouth ignites mine. She is absolute perfection. She pulls back and looks at me with nothing but intrigue on her face this time.

"What are we going to do with them?" Her brow raises in question.

Fuck yes! She is into this. I grab her by the waist and lead her to the shelves filled with various tools. "We are going to make them pay for hurting you."

"You did this for me?" she asks, not believing me even though I just told her I did.

"Yes."

"You may have just won over my heart again." She smiles as she reaches out to grab something off the shelf.

I don't notice what she grabs. I'm too transfixed by her words. I won her heart. She admitted earlier that she's mine, and now she is telling me I have her heart. This is exactly what I was hoping for.

"Let me show you why some people call me Coal." I reach out to grab my favorite blowtorch and then grab her hand to lead her back toward the two soon-to-be-dead-assholes in the center of the room.

Chapter 27
Avalynn

When I saw the knife on the shelf, I knew that it was what I needed to grab. I'm not a violent person, and in any other situation, I would have told Grey that he was out of his mind. This is different. This is the man who almost killed me. This man is the reason I haven't been able to feel safe for years. I've had to live with the memories of that day on repeat in my mind over and over again.

David has a stone face to him, but I'll do my best to make sure that changes. He still believes he's getting out of here alive. He's not. Directly next to him is Officer Grant. He looks a little more disheveled than David. He keeps trying to murmur something under the tape that covers his mouth.

I don't care what he has to say or what happens to him. He knowingly played his part, and now he can pay the price. David was the one who hurt me; I'll handle him. Greyson can take out his anger on Officer Grant. I know I'm going to see a much more brutal side of him today, but I'm not afraid. I know that Greyson would never physically harm me. He has proven that no matter what, he will protect me.

I never thought I would be the kind of person to willingly want to take another person's life. My father is most likely rolling in his grave right now, but you know what? My father had his secrets. Why can't I have some of my own? Today, I'm taking back my power. I'll never be able to thank Grey enough for this gift.

Greyson watches me carefully, not saying a word, as I step in front of David and tilt my head to the side. I take a moment to absorb how pathetic he looks right now. This man, who I allowed to make me feel so weak and vulnerable for so long. I don't bother taking the tape off of his mouth. There's nothing he can say to me that would take back everything I've felt since he attacked me.

"Grey, do you have scissors?" I ask, without taking my eyes off of David. I want him to be afraid of what I'm going to do and know I'm not going to back down.

"Anything for you, baby," he calls out. Moments later, scissors are placed in my hand.

I take a step forward and cut off David's shirt, leaving him bare from the waist up. His hands are conveniently tied behind the back of the chair, so I have full range to do to him exactly what he did to me.

The first cut I make is down the center of his chest. I trail the knife along his skin, watching as a faint red trail of blood is left in its wake. He screams something from behind the tape, and I look up to see his eyes widen. He's afraid now. Good. He tries to shake and pull himself free, but there's no point. I take a step back and keep my eyes on him.

"How about rope? Is there rope around here?" I call out to Greyson.

A moment later, a rope is dangling in front of my face. I finally pull my eyes from David to glance at my boyfriend, who is beaming down at me. I take the rope from him and lean up on my tiptoes to give him a peck on the lips before pulling back.

"Do you mind if I get to work on Officer Grant while you handle him?" he asks sweetly.

"Not one bit." I smile and turn away, bringing my attention back to David.

Quickly, I make a slip knot on one end of the rope and step forward to slip it over David's head. I keep the other end in my hand and pull roughly. His eyes practically bulge out of his skull when the rope tightens around his neck, cutting off his airflow. I keep it tight enough for him to struggle to breathe but not too tight to where he would pass out. I want him to be awake for this part.

I hear a scream from Officer Grant and look over to see that Greyson has cut off several of his toes and is using a hot iron to cauterize the wounds. I shudder, focusing back on my own tasks.

One by one, I go to work cutting lines onto David's stomach and chest. I shut out everything around me and hone in on the exact spots where my scars stain my skin. I want to make sure I match exactly what he did to me. One line across the abdomen, another across the chest. I don't even realize how much time has passed. I just let the rage take over.

When I finally take a step back, he is covered in blood. Deep red lines drip from each of the cuts. My chest is heaving. I didn't realize I was breathing so hard, but the satisfaction I felt from inflicting each one of those cuts caused a massive surge in dopamine.

It's hard to explain how free I feel right now. The best way to describe it is similar to being buried in the sand and having someone dig you out one scoop at a time. Each cut was a scoop of sand, freeing me from the weight of being buried for so long.

David stopped fighting at some point. His head now hangs down at his chest. I'm fairly certain he's passed out. Pathetic. He can dole it out, but he can't take it. I stayed awake the entire time he assaulted me.

I will grant him one reprieve. I won't kill him. I also won't stop Greyson from doing it if he wants to. I know he wants to. He made it pretty clear that neither of them will be leaving here.

Another loud scream tears me from my thoughts, and I look over at Officer Grant. Grey has his lighter out and is burning a patch on the guy's arm. I should be focused on the fact that Grey is burning him, but all I can focus on is the lighter.

I walk over to Grey and grip the hand that holds the lighter. His blue eyes shoot up at me, and I see pure rage in them for a brief moment before they soften. Almost as if seeing me instantly calms something in him.

"You kept that all this time?" I whisper.

His brow furrowed in confusion. "Kept what?"

"That lighter?"

A soft smile crosses his face, and he steps away from Officer Grant to step into me. He raises his hand to gently caress my cheek, and I lean into it. A moment later, his lips meet mine with the most gentle kiss he's ever given me. I melt into the vulnerability oozing from his every move.

He pulls back too soon and whispers, "It came from you. There's no way I would ever get rid of it."

"Grey," I whisper.

His hand reaches around my waist, and he pulls my pelvis into him, the hard outline of his erect cock pressing into my lower stomach.

"I've carried you with me every single day. Here." He points to his chest. "And Here." He holds up the lighter. "This lighter was my comfort for a long time. I like to fiddle with it, flipping it on and off. Most people assume it's the fire that calms me, but they are only partially correct. You've been my calming fire since the day I met you, Avalynn Blake."

"I wish you hadn't pushed me away before." I sigh. "Everything could have been so different. Would you ever walk away?" My heart races in my chest in anticipation of his answer.

"From what?"

"The Crimson Rose."

"It's complicated. They're family, and I'm not a good man. I enjoy burning people alive, lighting fires, and watching the way the flames reduce things to nothing but ash. The Crimson Rose is how I've been able to manage that side of me," he admits, but when his eyes meet mine, I see nothing but determination. "But, if you think I would ever let you leave again, you're mistaken. We are going to figure this out together."

My eyes bounce back and forth between his, and I nod. "Okay."

"Okay?" he questions.

"Yes. I'm sorry for being so hard on you this whole time." I believe him fully. I just needed to take some time for his actions to support his words. He's gone out of his way to show me that he cares over and over again. I have to trust that this time, he won't hurt me again.

"You did what you had to do, baby. With a woman as strong as you, I expected it."

The compliment melts my heart. I don't feel strong. I didn't for a long time, but after dealing with David, I finally found some of the strength that I lost.

"I told you I'd make you admit you're mine," he states confidently.

A groan from David brings me back to reality, and I turn to look over at him. His head is still slumped, but he's starting to stir a bit. "What are we going to do about them?"

"I just have to do one more thing before I kill them. Normally, I'd burn them alive, but I don't want you to have to see that."

I watch as he picks up a few things and pulls the ring off his hand. He heats it on one end and then sticks it onto Officer Grant's neck. The skin sizzles, and he screams out in pain for a few seconds before Grey steps behind him and snaps his neck. My eyebrows raise in shock.

I watch as he moves towards David next. He doesn't burn David because he didn't torture him. When he steps behind him to prepare to snap his neck, I step forward, stopping him.

"Wait," I call out.

He looks up at me, and I grab the rope that's still attached to his neck. I pull it tighter, cutting off David's airway. I never thought I would kill someone, but I can't let Grey do this. This is something I need to do for myself. I pull the rope until I can't physically pull it any tighter and watch as he struggles for air.

I should feel bad, but I don't. I keep the rope tightly in place, not allowing him a single breath of air. Time doesn't exist at this moment. I have no clue how long I stand there, but when I finally drop the rope and look over at my boyfriend, he is beaming with pride.

"That was the hottest fucking thing I've ever seen," he says with darkened eyes.

He walks over, pulls me in, and immediately devours my lips. I wrap my arms around his neck as his hands reach down to grip my ass briefly. Then they slide down a bit further, towards the back of my thighs, so he can lift me up. My legs wrap around his waist, and I lean into his hold, craving more.

Our kisses deepen as he carries me over to one of the tables that sit next to the tool shelves. He sets me down on the edge and swipes everything behind me onto the floor in one quick motion. Before I can say anything, he flips my skirt up and tears open my tights.

"Greyson!" I yell, causing him to stop.

"What's wrong?" he questions.

"You have got to stop tearing into all of my tights like a savage."

He chuckles and positions himself between my legs. "Don't interrupt my meal, Little Shadow."

"I'm serious!" I protest.

"I'll buy you a new pair of tights every day if it means I get to rip them open and devour you."

Without another word, he dives right in. His warm tongue reaches my center, and my head falls back as the pleasure overtakes me. I moan loudly when his tongue starts to circle my clit. He slowly focuses on all of the places that he knows will ignite my body, and I lose myself in the feeling of him.

My heart pounds in my chest as he slides two fingers into me, moving them in and out at the same slow and tortuous pace his tongue currently has on my clit. Pleasure builds in my core, and I feel that gentle ache for more. He curls his fingers inside me, which is enough to bring me right to the edge. I reach down to grip his hair, willing him to pick up his speed, but he pulls back.

"Please, Grey," I breathe out between my now short, quick breaths.

"You know I love it when you beg," he says, and it's almost enough to make me come right here and now. I love it when he makes me beg. "My perfect little slut, so greedy. Tell me what you need, and I might give it to you."

"Please make me come."

"That's my girl. So needy and desperate."

He dives back in, but this time, his pace quickens. It's all I need to be thrown over the edge as his tongue flicks over my clit. Pleasure courses through my entire body while I explode, clamping down on his fingers. He hums against me in approval, waiting for me to ride out the shock waves currently pulsing through my body.

The next thing I know, my back is flat on the table, and my legs hang over the edge. His pants are at his ankles, and he moves to step into me. I stop him, pulling myself up.

"Let me," I say as I slide off of the table and onto my knees in front of him.

I reach out to grip his cock and look up at him for a moment before running my tongue along the length of it.

"Fuckkk," he groans, making me smile.

I lick him from base to tip before taking him into my mouth. My tongue wraps around his hard cock, and I do my best to swirl it around, letting him feel the desperation of being teased.

After pulling back, I repeat the process a few times before I take him into my mouth one final time, watching as his head tilts back in pleasure. I pick up my pace, choking every time I reach his base while bobbing my head up and down. Drool runs from the corners of my mouth.

His fingers tangle into my hair, and he pulls me off of him. Saliva drips down my chin. "I'm going to fuck your throat, and then I'm going to fuck that pretty cunt. You're going to take what I give you like a good little whore."

I shift on the floor in front of him, rubbing my thighs together. His words send nothing but sheer anticipation through me. I nod and open my mouth, sticking my tongue out and peering up at him.

He leans down and spits on my tongue before shoving his cock back into my mouth. My throat grips around him, and he rubs the sides of my cheeks. "Relax your throat, and let me use you, baby."

I do exactly that, letting him slam into my throat over and over again. Tears well up in my eyes and eventually fall down my cheeks. He lets up enough for me to move my tongue around him a bit with each and every thrust.

"You're taking me so well," he says before pulling his cock from my mouth. "Up on the table, little shadow. I want to feel your pussy gripping my cock when I come inside you." I doubt he has a condom, but I don't care anymore. I started birth control last week, and I want to feel him bare.

I stand up and hoist myself up onto the table, lifting up my skirt and spreading my legs so he can see his prize. He grips my knees and pulls me to the edge before lining his cock up and shoving it inside me with one powerful thrust.

I fall back onto my elbows, the pleasure consuming me as he grips one of my hips and moves at a quick pace. His other hand slides up and down my stomach and chest. He pushes up my shirt and firmly grips my breast through my bra. There may be bruises there tomorrow, but it sends a current of shock waves straight to my pussy. I tighten around him when he finds my nipple through my bra and pinches it between his fingers.

"Does my dirty girl like that? So fucking perfect."

"Fuck me harder, Grey."

He pulls his hand out from under my shirt and shoves two fingers into my mouth. I choke around them, and he groans in approval, thrusting harder. I arch my back off of the table and let the heavenly sensation from each punishing thrust overwhelm me. He feels so fucking good. His fingers leave my mouth and find my clit, which sends me directly over the edge. I cry out, clamping down hard around his cock.

"That's it, come on my cock," he says, and I do.

Moments later, he groans, and I feel his warm come filling me up. His head falls back in satisfaction before he stills inside of me and pulls me up to a seated position. His mouth finds mine again. He kisses me deeply, like I am the only thing that matters. When he finally slides out of me, he pulls up his pants and heads over to the sink to grab a few things to wipe me with. As soon as the contents hit the trash, I'm lifted off the table and pulled into his chest tightly.

"Let's go home. I'll have someone come in and deal with these two."

With that, he leads me out of the shed and away from my past, which will never be able to torment me ever again.

Chapter 28

Avalynn

After we got back to the house, we spent the rest of the night in various positions of undress. Chloe was at an all-night party with Andrea and the rest of their senior class. We used that to our full advantage. I'm amazed I'm even able to walk right now.

When I make my way out to the dining room, I smile at the coffee and blueberry muffin waiting for me on the table. Today, there's something extra. A small bouquet of wildflowers sits with them. I pick them up and find a note attached to the bottom, "The wild ones are always the most beautiful." I smile, knowing he's talking about me.

I need to inquire about a new job today. The goal is to find something more permanent now that I'm no longer working at Temptations. After finishing my coffee and muffin, I grab my keys and head out the door to drive into town. Before realizing what I'm doing, I find myself parked outside the Dune Valley Police Department. Maybe I can be the change and make my dad proud after all. I nervously head inside, hoping I won't run into Sheriff Wolfe.

An older officer sees me and walks over to me, offering his hand for me to shake. "Hi there. I'm Officer Collins. What can I do for you today?"

"I was wondering if you needed any help around here."

"Actually, we could use a new office assistant. Mary is about to go on maternity leave, and we haven't hired anyone else yet. Do you have experience?"

"Not directly, but I'm a fast learner."

He eyes me for a moment in contemplation before nodding. "I'll have to check with Sheriff Wolfe, but I'm sure we can work something out. I appreciate a younger person like you being so passionate about their job search. It's not every day that someone comes in and personally asks for one."

"I prefer face-to-face interactions. It lets people get a real judge of my character, rather than just being another piece of paper," I lie.

"You're a smart girl. Stop by sometime next week, and we will get everything in order for you."

"Thank you so much, Officer. I look forward to working with you."

I walk out of the station, immediately questioning my sanity. Am I really going to work alongside Sheriff Wolfe? After what I found out, I should stay away from that crooked asshole. I suppose sometimes it's best to keep your enemies close. That's what I'm going with in this scenario. All I have to do is pretend I don't know anything while I'm there. He doesn't know that I know he was at the club. I may even have access to learning more about him or any other cops the Cobras have in their pocket by working there.

I caught Greyson up on everything he missed while he was out of town between our sex sessions last night. I had to tell him about how Alec threatened us at the restaurant. He didn't take that very well.

I'm nervous he's going to do something that he shouldn't. Once he sets his mind to something, there is no changing it. He is persistent as fuck. It's one of the qualities that I've grown to love about him.

My phone rings, and I glance down to see it's a random number I don't have saved. I shouldn't answer it. It could be a PI job. Maybe it's Mrs. Myers trying to get an update on her son's disappearance. Reluctantly, I press the answer button.

"Hello?" I question.

"I missed the sound of your voice."

"Who the hell is this?"

"You hurt my feelings," he says, and immediately it clicks.

"Alec. I blocked your number." I roll my eyes.

"Yes, I'm aware. It's a minor inconvenience, but I was able to find a way around it." He chuckles before continuing. "I've heard through the grapevine that you've gone and forgiven your little boyfriend for everything. It's unfortunate. I thought we had something special."

"Is there a reason you're bothering me?" I'm close to hanging up when he catches my attention.

"I know what you did. I didn't think you were stupid, but apparently, I was wrong," he states plainly.

"What are you talking about?"

"I know you were in the VIP room at Temptations the day I had a special guest. Candy was supposed to be working, but she sent you back there."

"How do you know about that? Did you hurt her?"

"Candy will be fine. She's learned her lesson. I think what you should know is that nothing happens in my club without me knowing about it. I have cameras, Avalynn." His tone sounds short. I was worried about this exact scenario.

"I delivered drinks and left, that's it." I keep my tone flat, trying to sound convincing.

"You and I both know that's not true. I saw you stop to listen in on the conversation my guys and their special guest were having before you delivered their drinks. I don't know exactly what you heard, but I highly suggest that if you value your precious boyfriend's life, you will keep it all to yourself."

"If you think Greyson is afraid of you, you're out of your mind," I spit.

"Greyson Hayes never had any sort of weakness—until now. Green is a good color on you, by the way. It's different from your usual black style. I like it."

I freeze, knowing what he is implying. He has eyes on me right now. My heart slams in my chest. I look up and down the street to see if anyone is watching me.

"Don't fuck up my plans, Avalynn. I would hate for you to end up in an unfortunate situation because of your boyfriend. He would do anything for you, including turning himself over to a group of men ready to do their worst to him."

I grit my teeth, refusing to give him any sort of reaction. Does he think that I'm not going to tell Greyson about this call? He's out of his fucking mind. Maybe he's expecting me to tell him so that it will distract him away from whatever business he has going on with the Crimson Rose. I know things have been out of sorts with them lately. He's been making comments about how more things have been going wrong than usual.

"Do you hear me?" he yells. "Keep your useless mouth shut, and nobody has to get hurt."

"Yeah, sure Alec. Whatever you say," is all I respond with before hanging up on him and blocking the phone number he called me on. I won't be answering any more calls from numbers that I don't have saved on my phone. Fuck the PI work.

I start my car to drive home, checking my mirrors at every turn to ensure nobody is following me. Maybe I'm being paranoid, but you can never be too careful. When I park the car in my spot across the street from my house, I notice the front door is wide open. I should drive away, but panic floods through me. What if Chloe is in there?

I rip open my glove box and pull out my pistol before running across the street and into the house. "CHLOE!" I call out, but there is no response. I sprint through the house, checking everything around me cautiously to ensure that nobody else is in here.

When I get to her room, I throw open her door and instantly feel relieved when she isn't there. A piece of me relaxes, but I'm still on edge. I clear the rest of the rooms and make my way back to the living room when a figure appears in the doorway.

"Uh, Ava?" Chloe questions. I turn to face her, relief instantly spreading through every part of my body. "What the hell are you doing?"

I put the safety back on the gun and place it on the table before running over to her and pulling her into a hug. "I'm so glad you're okay."

She lets me hug her for another moment before asking, "Why are you wandering the house with the door wide open and a gun? When did you even get a gun?"

I ignore her question about the gun. She doesn't need to know I've had it since everything happened with David and that it's not entirely legal. "The door was open when I came home. I was worried something had happened to you. I was trying to make sure that you were okay."

"Aweee, you worry about me?"

"Yes, I worry about you," I confess. She's so ridiculous sometimes.

She starts laughing and walks away. When I turn to go toward the living room to follow her to her bedroom, something catches my eye. A piece of paper with a handwritten note sits on the kitchen table.

Watch your back.

I grab the note immediately and put it in my pocket so Chloe can't see it. I take the gun and put it on my desk before making my way over to her room. When I open her door, she is sitting on her bed with her phone in her hand and a huge smile on her face.

"You miss him already, don't you?"

"You could have knocked." She drops her phone, looking guilty, and glares at me.

"Who are you talking to?" I ask.

"It's Matt, obviously. Who else would I be talking to? Is there something you need?"

"What's going on? Why are you being so short with me? I thought we were past that." I walk over and sit at the edge of the bed.

She sighs. "I'm sorry. I'm just a little stressed out with graduation. I didn't mean to be so short with you."

"You don't have to apologize. I get it. There's a lot going on at once. Just know I'm on your side."

"Yeah." She pauses for a moment before continuing. "Do you think you'll stay then?"

"What do you mean?"

"After I graduate. You were going to leave town. It hasn't exactly been a secret. I mean, I'll be fine. I can move back into my old house, and Matt can move in with me."

It breaks my heart that she's been thinking about this. How could I not realize that it would affect her? She just lost her mom. She never knew our dad. Now, her sister, whom she just found out about, is leaving her too. It's a wonder she trusts Matt so much.

"Did you want to leave Dune Valley?" I ask. "If that's what you wanted, we could sell the two houses and relocate somewhere."

She looks down at her phone and then at me. "If Matt came, I would consider it, but I don't think I want to. I'm okay with going to the local university."

There it is, the stark reminder that I was in the exact same position as her when I was her age. Things turned out to be so chaotic for me, basing my future on a boy. I can't tell her she's wrong because that would make me a hypocrite. I just smile. If she wants my advice, I will gladly give it to her, but I remember being seventeen and hopelessly in love. If she thinks the two of them will rule the world together, then that's what they'll do.

"It would take something big to make me leave again," I admit.

"You mean Greyson being an asshole again?"

"I don't know Chloe. It's more complicated than that. I have you now, too."

I didn't expect this town to feel so much like home when I came back, but I think it's less about the town and more about the people in it. I was so guarded before. I never let anyone in. Now, I have Chloe, Greyson, and even Wrenly, who I had kept at a distance, regardless of our continuous friendship throughout the years. I have people that I have let back past my walls.

For the first time in a long time, I feel like I have people who love me, and I love in return. Not out of obligation but purely because they want the best for me. A family. I didn't think I would be able to say that again. I was okay with being alone forever if it meant I wouldn't end up hurt again, but I'm willing to risk being hurt now for a chance at happiness.

"I need to tell you something," Chloe interrupts my thoughts.

"You're not pregnant, are you?"

"Oh my god, no! I told you I was being safe, but it is serious."

"You can tell me anything, Chloe."

"Matt and I are going on a road trip after graduation. I was nervous about telling you because I didn't want you to leave after I left. We have a month-long trip planned, full of driving around and tent camping all over."

"When are you two leaving?"

She hesitates. "The morning after graduation."

"And you'll be gone for a month?" She nods, and I take a deep breath. "Okay, you will call and text me every single day so I know exactly where you are."

"If that's what you want."

"In that case, I'm really excited for you. I hope the two of you have the best time. It's going to be amazing, seeing all of the things out there." I reach out to grab her hand reassuringly. "I will be here when you get back, with whatever snacks your little heart desires and enough movies to stay up and binge all night."

She smiles and leans across the bed to hug me. "Thank you. I was really worried that you were going to leave when I told you I wasn't going to be here for a while."

"Chloe, we spent seventeen years not knowing each other. We have a lot of time to catch up on. You can't get rid of me that easily."

"You'll be okay here without me?" she asks.

It's a question I wasn't sure I was going to have to consider, but I think I will be just fine. I have a job lined up, and Greyson promised me that he would always be there for me, no matter what.

I stand up to make my way to the door, but before I leave, I turn to look at her. "Come on. We need to have ourselves a girl's night. Tell your boyfriend he gets you for a month; he can handle a few hours without talking to you."

"Fine, but I'm not eating your food. We're ordering pizza from that place that Greyson got it from before."

I laugh, and we spend the next few hours watching a combination of movies and the most ridiculous reality TV shows. I ordered the pizza that she very kindly requested, and we had the best time. When the night comes to an end, I send Grey a quick text to let him know I'm heading to bed and slip under the covers to dream the night away.

I'm startled awake a few hours later when I feel the bed shift. An arm wraps around my waist, pulling me in close. The smell of burnt leather and mint consumes the air around me, and I sink into his hold. There is a faint smell of something else on him though. It almost smells like lighter fluid.

"What are you doing here?"

"I missed you. Go back to sleep." He leans in to kiss my shoulder.

"How did you even get in here? It's the middle of the night," I question.

"Shhhh, that's not important. Go to sleep, little shadow."

I wiggle my butt against his pelvis, and he pulls me in closer, nipping the corner of my ear.

"As much as I would love to bury my cock in your sweet pussy, it's been a really long day. Just let me hold you."

"Okay," I concede.

He kisses the back of my shoulder again and says, "Forever my heart."

"Forever my always," I say back before sleep pulls me under.

Chapter 29
Greyson

All I wanted to do was stay in bed with my girl, but I couldn't. Everything in this damn town is going to shit. We've been stressing over today's drop ever since Ava told us what she overheard at Temptations. I was fuming when she filled me in on everything that happened regarding Alec the other day. He's lucky I've been busy.

I can't believe that son of a bitch had the nerve to not only disrupt her while eating but also call and threaten her. What did he expect? For her to not tell me anything? There has always been an unspoken rule between our gangs to never involve women or children, but he crossed that line. I won't stand for it. I don't care what Knox has to say. I'm taking matters into my own hands on this one. First, I have to deal with gang business.

I make my way to Adam's Garage to meet with some of the guys before we go over to the warehouse to do the drop. Everyone is on edge because we know something big is going to go down. We don't know exactly what to expect, but we will be ready.

"Let's get right down to business," Knox says after I walk up to the bay filled with other crew members. I give him a slight nod, and he continues. "We go in as planned. Greyson and Kai will take the duffle bags with the new product. We should expect them to come at us, guns blazing. Once all the gunfire has calmed down, we will signal Greyson and Kai to complete the job. We can't let the Cobras get the jump on this. This is one of the biggest exchanges we've ever done, which is why we anticipate them targeting this one. If the Cobras get their hands on the drugs and the cash, they will have everything they need to finance whatever they want. We're talking potentially half a million dollars on the line here."

Some of the guys around the garage begin to whisper amongst themselves. I push past everyone to the front of the room to stand next to Knox. "Keep your shit together. We're perfectly capable of handling this. They don't know we are expecting them." This seems to calm a lot of people down.

"We will have a group of men on each corner waiting for them. Kill who you need to kill in order to protect what's ours," he states plainly.

He finishes his speech, and we wait out the next few hours as we prepare for the exchange. Once we deal with the Cobras, we have to handle Sheriff Wolfe and find the snake in our midst. That's a problem for tomorrow, though. Today, we focus on this.

There's a weird anticipation in the air as we pull up to the warehouse. I check my surroundings carefully, knowing that the Cobras are on their way even if I can't see them right now.

"Are you ready for this?" Kai asks.

"I'm ready to get it fucking over with so I can get back to my girl," I confess.

"She's it for you, isn't she?"

"Yeah. I was an idiot for ever letting her go."

"Look at the two of us. A few months ago, we were both bachelors, and now we're practically wifed-up."

"The problem now is that people have started to associate my love for Ava as a weakness. They will realize real soon how wrong they are. She may have my heart, but I'm that much more unpredictable when it comes to protecting her." I look him straight in the eye. "If a person even looked at her wrong, I wouldn't even think twice about reducing them to a pile of ash. I mean it, Kai. You know I wouldn't even feel any remorse when doing it either."

He holds his hands up in defense. "Woah, killer. You know, I was going to say it was nice that you found someone to mellow out some of that psycho energy, but clearly, I was wrong."

"Let's go, asshole." I shove the door open and head straight to the trunk to grab the small dolly and load the bags onto it.

Once we have all eight duffle bags loaded, I push them into the warehouse. I can practically feel the eyes on me, waiting for everything to go down. I'm not normally a gun kind of person, mainly because I prefer to burn my victims, but today, I have two strapped along my waist. One in the front and one in the back.

We get inside the abandoned warehouse a few minutes earlier than planned, so our buyer hasn't arrived just yet. I pull out my lighter and flip it on and off a few times to try and alleviate some of the anxiety over what's about to happen. It doesn't work, so I pocket the lighter and pull out my phone to send Ava a quick text.

> Me: Forever my heart.

> Ava: Forever my always.

> Ava: Is everything okay?

> Me: I'll see you when I get home tonight, baby.

I pocket my phone again before reading whatever she sends next. She has to know something is up. I want her to know how much she means to me, just in case. The garage doors on the warehouse are open, and we see another car pull up to park next to ours. It's showtime. The Cobras won't be hitting us until the money and the drugs are in the same place. That's the smartest way to ensure they don't lose the product or the cash. We still have a few minutes left before the main event.

My heart beats rapidly in my chest, and I harden my face. Three people approach us in masks with duffle bags on a dolly of their own. We don't need to see who they are in order to do business with them. Money talks, and as long as they are willing to spend their money, we are willing to sell them the new drugs. Sheriff Wolfe put us in contact with them and had it all planned out. His intention the whole time was for the Cobras to look good in the end. Jokes on him. Whatever's left of the Cobras after today will look more pathetic than ever.

I step forward to shake the hand of one of them and quietly whisper, "We got word this exchange has been compromised. Act normal, but prepare."

The person takes a step back and then looks from left to right, giving each of their fellow associates some sort of signal to be on the defensive. Not even thirty seconds later, I hear gunshots erupt from outside of the warehouse.

"Stay in here, and let us handle it!" I yell at them while running to the garage doors.

Within seconds, Kai and I are sliding both doors down, preventing anyone from entering through them. If they want to come in, they will have to come in the main door where Kai and I are standing guard. Knox wanted the two people he trusted the most on the inside to protect these buyers, so here we are.

I resist the urge to peek my head outside, listening as guns pop off from every direction. A shadow casts on the door, and I look over to Kai, who is ready with his gun pointing toward the door. The buyers are huddled up in the opposing corner of the warehouse, waiting out our gunfight.

The door opens, and I hear a bang. Immediately, the body that just entered falls to the ground from Kai's shot to the center of his forehead. Three more men try to push their way through the door, and all three of them end up with the same fate as the first. The sounds of the gunfire begin to fade, but we stay on edge, waiting for the signal. We won't let our guard down a second sooner. You never know when a stray snake might come out and bite you.

My phone buzzes in my pocket, the signal. It's Knox. I click the answer button and put him on speaker. "Petunia," he says, and I hang up. We don't need to have a conversation. I heard what I was supposed to in order to finish up the exchange.

"All clear," I call out to the buyers in the far corner.

They holster their guns and cautiously walk back to the center of the room, where I meet them at the bags.

"That was a bit dramatic," one of them says.

"As you can see, the Crimson Rose is perfectly capable of handling any scenario. This may have been a rare incident, but even at that, we are always one step ahead of our enemies."

"Yes, I see. You've handled yourselves quite well. Our boss will be pleased."

"Pleasure doing business with you," I say as they grab the dolly with the drugs and stop in front of the closed doors. Once we open them, the buyers silently load the bags into their trunk and slip into their car. It's all very anticlimactic. I was hoping to get in on a little more of the action. Being inside the warehouse was so fucking dull.

Kai and I push the dolly with the bags of cash to our car and pack them away safely. We stand there for a few moments while some of the crew make their way over to us, talking about how the Cobras never saw them coming. Knox appears and instructs them to fan out and drag all the bodies from the surrounding area into the warehouse. It'll be easier to dispose of them when they're in one place.

"Did we have any losses?" I ask him.

"Five." He sounds tired. This is only the beginning of his night. He is going to have to pay his respects to each of the five families of the members we lost today. "We decimated them. They came full force and weren't expecting us to be ready for their attack. We hit them from all sides, just like we planned. It was over way faster than expected. I don't think we will have to worry about them again for a long time. There isn't much left."

"Fuck, I'm jealous I missed all the action."

"I needed to make sure you were with the buyers. I couldn't risk someone being in there that I don't trust. This was a big deal for us. We're set for a while now. With the Sheriff going against us, it was imperative that this went off without a hitch."

"You don't have to explain anything to me. This is your crew, Knox." I take a moment to look him over before deciding there is a way that he can let me have at least some of the action. "Actually, there is something that I need to do."

"Whatever you need."

"I'm burning down Temptations. Alec threatened Ava. Not once, but twice. If I let it go, then I look weak. I won't allow that. You know as well as I do that we've always left the women and children out of this. He took it too far. It can't go unanswered."

"If you're going to do it, today is the best time."

"It'll be done tonight."

"Do what you need to, but Greyson," he pauses before continuing, "whoever lived through today will likely end up at that club tonight trying to regroup. You know there will be casualties."

"When has that ever bothered me before?" I ask.

"Have at it, then."

"Thanks. I'll see you back at the garage so we can secure the cash, and then I'll be on my way."

"Sounds good."

I spend the next few hours with the crew securing the money from the exchange and going over how we want to move forward in terms of the Sheriff and whoever was helping him. We still have to find out who that is.

I'm bouncing with excitement as I head out to Alec's little club. It's time to make that son of a bitch pay for fucking with my girl. The club comes into view, and I park directly in the parking lot, not worrying about whether or not their cameras catch what I'm about to do. The cameras will burn along with any evidence they record. It will go unsaid that I burned this shithole down. It is my signature, after all.

I've taken a back seat for way too long while that slimy motherfucker involved himself in my girl's life. He thinks he can touch what's mine. Talk to what's mine. He thinks he can threaten her and not expect me to retaliate. He's as good as dead. I'm going to take his precious club from him first.

This is personal now. I don't care what comes from it. I will never allow someone to treat Ava the way he did. People think she makes me weak. A mischievous grin crosses my face. I can't have people thinking I'm weak. That just won't do.

I rip open the back door of my car and grab the chain, heading straight to the front door first. Once I chain it shut, I go around back and do the exact thing to the back door. Whoever is inside won't be getting out now. I don't give a fuck about a single one of them. The club is closed, so I know the dancers are home and safe, at least.

I grab the cans of gasoline from my car and waste no time, splashing it along the entire side of the building. I make sure to get as much of the flammable liquid on the structure as possible. This needs to be a complete loss before the fire department shows up.

Adrenaline pumps through my veins as I finally run out of gasoline. I grab my flamethrower from my car. I can set the blaze with this but still keep a relative distance. I stare at the building for a moment, cursing every single bad memory that my girl had to endure here and press the trigger.

Within seconds, the outer wall of the building is ablaze. I gather all my belongings and return to my car to distance myself from the flames. I watch as the fire grows from one wall to another, slowly overtaking the entirety of the club and lighting up the night sky. Time passes quickly, and I lose myself in the sight of the flames.

It takes about 15 minutes for the fire department to finally show up. It's already too late for them to do anything, which is exactly what I hoped for. The flames have overtaken the entire building. Their sole purpose now is to contain the fire and prevent it from spreading.

I smile to myself, feeling the rush from burning the fucking place to the ground. I wish I could stay and watch it all reduce to nothing but complete ash, but I have something else on my mind. My little shadow and her perfect cunt. I put my car in drive and step on the gas to get to her house as quickly as possible.

Chapter 30
Avalynn

It's later in the evening when Grey practically runs through my front door. He catches me off guard and waltzes right up to where I'm sitting on the couch, bends down, and throws me over his shoulder like a savage.

"Greyson, what the hell?!" I yell.

He marches us straight to my bedroom, ripping the door open. Chloe and Matt pop their heads out of her bedroom but quickly shut the door. Moments later, I hear music from her room. Fucking hell. My sister knows my boyfriend is about to dick me down.

"Grey!" I yell again as he tosses me onto the bed. He smells like gasoline and smoke. He immediately looks down at me with darkened eyes. The corner of his mouth tips up in a menacing grin. "It's all over. I burned it down."

"What are you talking about?" I squirm to slip off of the bed and stand next to it.

He ignores me, goes straight to my desk, pulls open the drawer, and looks at the new toys we recently invested in. He grabs a few items and then turns back to look at me. A sinister look crosses his face. He's about to fuck me like a god, and my pussy is screaming in anticipation.

He takes a step toward me, closing the distance. His hand lightly pushes on my shoulder, and I sink to my knees in front of him like an obedient little slut.

"Such a greedy whore for my cock, aren't you, little shadow?"

I nod, and he steps forward to tie a blindfold over my eyes. He reaches down to guide me back to a standing position and then strips me bare. He leads me over to the bed and lays me down on my back before securing my arms above my head. My legs end up tied to each end of the bed. I'm spread wide for him, vulnerable and completely at his whim.

"Grey," I whine.

Soft lips meet mine in a sensual kiss. I try to arch my chest up to him, begging for more, but he ignores it. He just keeps kissing me. He peppers them up and down my neck and then back to my lips. Not being able to see where the next kiss will land intensifies the anticipation tenfold.

A hand lands on my stomach, and he slowly moves it higher until he cups one of my breasts. His fingers find my nipple, and he tugs slightly on it as he kisses my neck. A moan falls from my lips as I let the sensation consume me.

Loud music still fills the house, drowning out the noises that I can't help but let fall from my lips as he continues to tease me. Over and over, he slides his hand from my breast to the crease right where my thigh meets my center. So fucking close. I just want him to touch me.

"Please," I try.

"Baby, you beg so nicely." He leans in to say in my ear before continuing with his torture.

He steps away for a moment, and I hear the faint sound of his belt buckle clanking on the desk. It's hard to hear the small sounds he's making because of the music, but I'm fairly certain he's stripping. Finally, a finger grazes over my center, and I buck my hips up, needing more. Pleasure courses through me at even the slightest touch.

"My greedy girl." He runs his fingers through me again. "Look at you, soaking wet, and I've barely touched you. What a dirty, desperate slut."

Two fingers slide into me with ease and curl up to hit the perfect spot. "Oh my God!" I cry out.

"God's not here, little shadow, but I promise, what I plan to do to you will be just as heavenly."

He pulls his fingers from me and shoves them in my mouth. Without instruction, I close my lips and swirl my tongue around them to lick them clean. I can't see him through the blindfold, but I know he approves. He pulls his fingers out and steps away again, and disappointment hits momentarily before I feel my legs being untied.

He settles between them and leans over the top of my body to whisper in my ear; the feeling of his bare chest on mine sends electricity to my core. "The blindfold stays on until I say so, or I tie you back up, understand?"

"Yes," I tell him, and I feel him unbind my hands. I instantly grab his neck to pull him in for an all-consuming kiss. Our tongues dance with one another for control as he groans in my mouth. He pulls the blindfold off of my eyes and looks down at me adoringly.

"You don't even understand what you do to me. Just one tiny taste of you is so fucking addicting." He leans in to bite and suck up the length of my neck again. There will be marks there tomorrow, but I don't care. "Tell me you're mine."

"I'm yours, Greyson."

"My perfect, greedy girl." He pushes my legs back towards my head and slams into me. It's hard and rough, but it's exactly what I need.

His thrusts are ruthless, and at this angle, he is able to get so much deeper. It doesn't take long before I'm teetering on the edge. He lets go of my legs, letting them fall to either side of him, and grips my hips tightly to keep up his brutal pace. My arms reach around to pull his chest down to mine and run my nails down the length of his back.

"Fuckkkk," he groans.

This is more primal than we have ever experienced together. We have a pure animalistic need for one another, so I do what my instincts tell me and take control. I attempt to roll the two of us over and am pleasantly surprised when he aids me in the process.

"Ride me, baby. Show me what that cunt can do to my cock."

He makes me feel like I'm the only thing that matters, a goddess. I lean back and start to grind on him, moving my hips in a circular motion. My head falls back, and his hands land on my hips.

I lean forward to hold myself up with my hands on his chest as I ride him harder than I ever have before. Bouncing up and down on his cock has pleasure building and a familiar ache beginning to take over. He pulls me close to his chest and takes over, thrusting up into me hard and fast. I clamp down on him as I cry out his name, "Greyson!" Shock waves of pleasure radiate from my center, spreading to the tips of my fingers and toes.

His fingers tangle in my hair, gripping hard and pulling my head back. I ride out my high as he continues to thrust into me from his place below me. He jerks inside me with a grunt, and I feel the warmth from his come fill me. When he finally slows, he wraps his arms around me, holding me in place with his softening cock still inside me.

"You're it for me, baby. You know that, right?"

"We're really doing this, aren't we? After all these years," I breathe out.

He rolls me to the side and tilts my head up to kiss me. I feel truly at peace in his arms. We stay this way for a little bit before I finally stand up, throw my robe on, and head to the bathroom to clean up. I take a moment for myself, eyeing the marks he left on my neck after being practically ravaged, and remember there's something I need to talk to him about.

I stalk to my room to find him fully dressed and sitting on the edge of the bed.

"Grey, I need to talk to you about something."

"What's going on?" He pulls me down to sit on his lap.

"I was hired to do a job for someone named Mrs. Myers. Does that name mean anything to you?"

"Should it?" he questions. His finger trails small circles along my thigh where the robe has pulled open.

"Her son's name is Gary Myers," I state plainly, waiting to see how he will respond. He better not fucking lie to me.

"I see what you're getting at, little shadow, and if you're asking me about it, then I assume you already know more than you should."

"I know you were involved somehow."

"Yes," he admits.

"Do you know where he is? I don't think she's going to let this go. If she doesn't get answers from me, she will hire someone else."

"I know where he is, or at least what's left of him. It's not much, most likely just whatever stray bones that weren't taken by animals."

"I have an idea that might handle both your problem with Sheriff Wolfe and Gary Myers," I tell him.

"I'm all ears."

I go on to tell him the details of everything I was able to find regarding his involvement with Gary. It's not a lot, and unless someone knows him directly, they would never be able to connect him to the case. I suggest recovering whatever's left of him and planting it at Sheriff Wolfe's house. I can easily get access, with Chloe being Andrea's best friend.

We would just need a distraction. I could throw a nice dinner party for the sheriff, his wife, and Andrea to get them out of the house long enough for Grey to plant the remnants on his property and get out unseen. We could call in an anonymous tip to the station. Easy-peasy.

The sheriff goes away for murder, and the Crimson Rose never has to worry about him messing with their drops or the gang in any way ever again. On top of that, Mrs. Myers gets the answers that she is looking for, and I get paid.

"I think it needs a few tweaks here and there, but it's definitely a workable plan," he tells me just as I hear a pounding on my bedroom door. I didn't even notice the music being turned off.

I rush over to pull it open to find Chloe with wide eyes. "What's going on?" I ask her.

"I have to go to Andrea's house. Her dad." She hesitates. "Her dad is missing."

I turn to look at Grey, but he looks just as shocked as I do. "What do you mean missing?"

"The club across town, Temptations, caught on fire tonight. They think her dad was there. His car was parked nearby." Tears well up in her eyes. "I have to go be there for her, Ava. You know how hard it is to lose a parent."

"Go get whatever you need ready. I'll take you over there."

She leaves the doorway, and I walk back over to Grey. He looks up at me, and I know without question that he is the reason the club burned down. He doesn't have an ounce of remorse on his face.

"Looks like we will have to find another way to handle Mrs. Myers," he tells me, standing up to pull me into a hug.

"That's what you burned down! How many people were inside, Grey?"

"I don't know, and I honestly don't care. They were closed. Every single person inside that building was associated with the Cobras in one way or another. Alec threatened you twice, Ava. That couldn't go without some sort of repercussions."

"I didn't ask you to burn down a building for me." A tear slips down my cheek. I'm not sure if I'm upset or happy that he did this for me.

"I would burn down the world for you. Anyone who gets in your way. Anyone who threatens you, touches you, or upsets you. I would burn it all."

I step back from him to create some distance. I need to process this. "I have to take Chloe to her friend's house. I'll most likely stay there with her."

"I'm just a call away if you need me," he tells me, standing up to gather the rest of his things so that he can leave when we do.

Chloe comes out of her room again, with Matt trailing close behind. He tells her goodbye, and we rush to the car to drive to her best friend's house. She's been surprisingly strong through all of this so far, and a part of me is relieved. However, I'm worried this may trigger her grief from losing her mom. When we get to Andrea's house, I grab her arm before she is able to get out of the car.

"I know you need to be there for your friend right now, but if at any point it gets overwhelming, just send me a text, and I'll be the bad guy. I'll tell them I'm making you leave."

She nods with a reassuring smile. "I'll be okay."

With that, the two of us head into the Wolfe household to spend the rest of the evening supporting her best friend and consoling the likely widowed Mrs. Wolfe.

Chapter 31

Greyson

The sheriff being inside Temptations when I burned it down was a lucky accident. They were able to confirm that he was, in fact, inside the club. A funeral for him and some of the others they suspect were inside is set for later this week.

Satisfaction courses through me, knowing that I'm the reason he won't be able to mess with our crew anymore. We secured the connections he set us up with. He knew too much and was always a means to an end. Now that he's handled, I need to have a talk with Knox so we can try to piece together who was working with the sheriff. This won't be completely over until we flush out the rat. I also need to talk with him about how I plan to move forward with the Crimson Rose.

Things between Ava and I are endgame. I know she never wanted to be a part of this life. The best thing I can do for her is to step away from it, at least as much as I can. I still owe Knox a favor, so that will need to be discussed, but it's time for my girl and I to begin our future together. I'm not going to let anything stand between us this time.

I'm sure we can all come up with some type of arrangement where I can accommodate both Knox and Ava. He may be the family I was born into, but Ava is the future I choose.

Today is Chloe's graduation, so this will all have to wait until later this week. I glance at my phone, notice the time, and realize I'm about to be late. Shit. My phone pings, pulling my attention back to it.

> Knox: I need you at the garage. Now.

> Me: What's going on?

> Knox: Now, Greyson.

> Me: Can this wait? I have prior commitments.

> Knox: Crew always comes first. I don't care about your commitments.

> Me: How long is this going to take? I promised Ava I wouldn't miss Chloe's graduation.

> Knox: I don't care. Just get here.

Anger courses through me. How am I supposed to tell her that I have to drop the ball on this? She wanted me to be there with her, sitting there and holding her hand to give Chloe a good memory. She wanted people in the crowd to support her sister, and now I can't be one of them.

I can't bring myself to tell her that I won't be there, so I say nothing. I made a promise that I'm about to break. With her trust in me being so fresh again, I really hope that she will hear me out when I get back. I will have to explain how I chose the Crimson Rose over her... again.

Fuck. This is stupid. I should just text her and let her know what's going on. I'll deal with her being upset with me. I'm not a pussy. I can handle my girl. At least this way, she won't be waiting for me to show up. I pull my phone up to send her a message, but Kai's name crosses the screen instead.

"Hey?" I say, answering the phone.

"Did you hear from Knox?"

"Yeah, I'm on my way to the garage now."

"He texted me too. Apparently, we are to meet him in your torture shed. It must be something big because he sent everyone away from the garage. I got a text from Noah, one of the newer crew members. He said that Knox doesn't want anyone going anywhere near the property."

"Why would he do that? He's never kept anything hidden from the rest of the crew before."

"That's why I called you to make sure you were going in too. Something big must have gone down with the new buyers or something. I thought everything went smoothly, but maybe they had an issue with the product."

"That doesn't make any sense. I talked with Knox about it, and they were extremely impressed with how we handled things. They wanted to do another exchange sooner than we originally planned."

"I don't know, man. I can't think of anything else that would prompt this kind of reaction." He sighs.

"I guess we will find out when we get there."

"Can you swing by the house and pick me up? I let Wrenly use my car today."

"Yeah, be waiting outside. I'll be there in a few minutes. We need to get there as soon as possible to try and figure out what's going on," I tell him with a weary undertone. He hangs up before I can say another word.

I pull up to his house less than five minutes later. Just like I asked, he's waiting outside. His hair is pulled up into a high ponytail with a bow clipped on it. When he gets into the car, he looks over at me, trying to figure out why I'm staring at him.

"Did you forget something?" I try my best to keep a straight face.

"What the fuck are you talking about?"

"Have you not looked in a mirror today?" The urge to laugh in his face is too much. I feel bad, but the fact that he has no clue makes this even better.

He pulls the mirror down, and his hand immediately goes to his hair to pull the bow off. He doesn't say a word as he pushes open the door and disappears into the house for a minute. When he comes back out, he just looks at me.

"Are we going or not?" he questions.

"I mean, yeah. What was that about?"

"Wrenly thinks it's so damn cute to fuck with me when I sleep." He rolls his eyes as I put the car in drive. "To be fair, we've been in the middle of a prank war."

"Sometimes, I really wonder about you," I tell him.

When we pull up, it's completely empty, just like Kai said it would be. It's an odd sight. I don't ever remember a time when everyone was told to stay away before. Whatever is going on has to be serious.

We step out of the car and make our way around the back of the garage to where the shed sits in the trees. A strange feeling of danger settles in my gut. Something about this isn't right, but I ignore that feeling and pull open the door. Kai and I step inside and freeze in our tracks at the sight in front of us.

Directly in the center of the room is Knox, the head of the Crimson Rose, tied to a chair at gunpoint with tape over his mouth and a half-swollen face. Before we can even react, I look to my left and find a gun to my head. I glance to my right at Kai and notice there is a guy on his side with a gun to his head in the same manner. He can't be more than nineteen. It's Andrea's now ex-boyfriend. It all makes sense now. He was running with us and feeding the sheriff and Cobras information.

This little fucking snake has been with us for months. I do my best to recall when the drugs started going missing, and when our drops started getting hit. The timelines match up perfectly. He just signed his fucking death warrant.

I calmly survey the room, surprised that there aren't any other men here besides the three of them. I could probably take them all myself, but the gun Alec is holding to Knox's head gives me pause. A stupid fucking grin is spread wide across his face.

"The fuck do you think you're doing?" I say to him, narrowing my eyes.

"I'm doing what I should have done a long ass time ago." Alec gestures to one of the two chairs set up next to Knox. "Sit down, brother. It's time for a little family reunion."

I cringe at his words. Alec is not, and will never be, my brother. "You don't have a right to call me that."

"The whore of a mother we both shared says differently. Now, sit the fuck down before I blow out his brains." The barrel of his gun pushes against Knox's temple.

"Don't fucking talk about her like that. You didn't even know her!" Anger wells up in me.

His father is the reason our mother is dead. She had an affair with his father, got pregnant with Alec, and then begged our father to take her back. Alec's father took him from her and raised him alone. He made sure he was raised to be cruel, cold, and calculated.

When our father got sick, our mother stopped in to see Alec and his father and magically had an overdose. The police ruled it accidental. No shock there, but we all know the truth.

Alec, Knox, and I may share a bloodline, but we will never fucking be family. Thankfully, in a twist of fate, Alec's father had his own overdose, which led to Alec taking over the Cobras.

"Sit down, Greyson," he states firmly, pushing the barrel further into Knox's head. "I won't say it again."

My jaw clenches, and I ball my fist at my side. The only thing I can do in this moment is start walking toward the stupid fucking chair. I hate that I fell into this trap. I should have trusted my gut when I felt like something was off.

I mentally catalog what I currently have at my disposal. The lighter Ava gave me years ago is in my right pocket. I have my keys. I could probably stab someone in the throat with one of my keys. I think they're sharp enough. That's all I have on me, keys, and a fucking lighter. I planned on going to Chloe's graduation. I wasn't prepared to walk into an ambush.

The seat I'm pushed into is in the middle of the three. Knox is on my right, and Kai is on my left. The two men who waited for us at the doorstep are behind us, keeping the cold metal of their barrels on our skulls. A stark reminder of their presence. Alec steps to the side and stands next to Knox in a position where he can see all of us.

"Care to share what all the theatrics are for? We all know you aren't killing anyone," I spit in his direction.

"See, that's where you're wrong, brother." He narrows his eyes. "If you asked me a week ago, I might have let you go. After everything the two of you have done, the only way out of this is in a fucking body bag."

"You don't have the balls."

"I don't need to have anything. If you think you can find a way out of this, by all means, have at it. You're supposed to be some sort of unbeatable criminal that everyone in town fears, aren't you?"

I don't say anything. I keep my calm so he doesn't see how deeply I know we fucked up. We should have never walked right into this trap so willingly. I need to keep him talking until I can come up with a plan. Talking buys us time, so for now, that's the only goal.

"What's the plan here, Alec?"

"You burned down my club. You killed most of my crew. In a matter of a few days, you destroyed everything I've built."

"That's how it goes. You know this as well as I do. Sometimes you get ahead, and sometimes you don't. The Cobras fell short this time."

"You went too far!"

"You and your pathetic fucking club threatened my girl. I couldn't let that go without retribution."

"You burned down my club for some used-up pussy?"

"Shut your fucking mouth before I cut out your tongue myself. You won't talk about her like that." Fury courses through my veins. He will not disrespect Ava.

"She was a pretty good fuck. I'll give her that much. Your little bitch fell right into my lap in Massachusetts. I mean, what are the chances of running into my half-brother's ex-girlfriend on a business trip. I had no clue who she was when I first saw her. I thought she was just some random fuck, but it turned out so much better than that. Her new hair tricked me, I'll admit, but when I saw your reaction to us at the coffee shop, it all clicked.

It'll be fun to take her and make her mine once you're cold and six feet in the ground. I wonder if I should fuck her next to your rotting corpse first. Do you think she would be into that?"

I go to stand up, but a hand pushes down on my shoulder, holding me in place. I grip his finger and twist it backward, making the weak bastard cry out. Instead of him pulling back, he simply knocks me in the back of the head with his gun. I feel the warmth from the blood rushing from the cut immediately.

"What's your next move? You really think you will get everything so easily?"

"I'm so glad you asked. It's really quite simple. I kill you three and take over your gang. Anyone who doesn't comply will also die."

"If you think the Crimson Rose will follow you, you're delusional."

"I think people will do whatever they have to in order to avoid death, kind of like what you're doing right now. You think you're going to find a way out of here by making me talk. I know how your brain works. I hate to break it to you, but you won't be making it out of here alive. Once I take your gang, I'll take your girl. It'll all be mine, and there's nothing you can do about it."

He takes a step away from Knox and toward me. I know that my time is up. My only regret is that I won't be here to protect Ava from him. I hope she flees town because I missed the graduation. I hope she gets as far away from Dune Valley and Alec as she possibly can.

The man behind me pulls the cold metal barrel away from my head but continues to stand behind me as Alec steps in front of me. He points the gun directly towards the middle of my forehead and cracks a half smile.

"Any last words, Greyson?"

I stare directly at him, refusing to show any kind of weakness whatsoever. He won't get that out of me. Nobody will. He shakes his head at my stubbornness, and I see his finger curl around the trigger. A loud bang echoes through the room, and time stands still.

Chapter 32
Avalynn

It's graduation day for Chloe. She woke up this morning in a panic and has been rambling about how she can't get her hair right all morning. The ceremony is set to start in a few hours, so I let her fiddle with it for a bit longer before offering to help.

"Are you ready for today?" I ask her.

"I wish my mom was here. It's weird doing this without her." Her eyes drop, with a hint of sadness in them.

"Is there something of hers that we can go grab so she can be part of your day with you?" She perks up with this suggestion.

"Maybe. You wouldn't mind driving me over there quickly before the ceremony?"

"It would be an honor. Now, let's get this hair curled."

We spend the next little bit curling her hair, and when I'm finished, she applies her makeup. We went shopping the other day to find the perfect dress to wear. I'm not made of money, but this is an important day. I wanted to make sure she never forgets it. She's leaving tomorrow morning for her trip with Matt. Until then, I am soaking up every minute we get to spend together until then.

We separate to get dressed in our bedrooms. I throw on my black A-line dress with tights underneath and finish off the outfit with my Doc Martens. I picked this dress because it has pockets, which make life so much easier. I glance down at my phone curiously when I realize I haven't heard from Greyson yet today. I send him a quick text to make sure that he is still going to meet us at the graduation and focus back on Chloe.

I walk across the hall to her room, knocking on the door before it opens up, and she stands in front of me. The dress we got her is baby pink with black floral detail that falls just above her knees. The sleeves go to her elbow, and the neckline follows right along her collarbone. It fits her like a glove and is incredibly tasteful. She looks beautiful. I'm so damn proud of her for persevering through everything she endured to get to this day.

"Are you ready?" I ask, and she smiles over at me.

"Ready as I can be. We're still stopping at my mom's house, right?"

"Of course."

"Okay, good. I think I know what I want to grab of hers." Tears well up in her eyes.

"Hey, she's right here with you. From what you've told me about her, she must always be right at your side."

"Yeah. I'm just glad that you're here." She pulls me in for a hug, and I wrap my arms around her.

"I'll always be here for you. That's what sisters are for." I pull back and give her one last glance over. "Do you have everything you need before we go?"

"I think so."

I lock up the house and cross the street to the car with her trailing behind. I remember what this day felt like. There was so much excitement but also so much fear of the unknown. Chloe is so much more prepared than I was. Her trip with Matt. Going to the local college in the fall. She never ceases to amaze me.

We pull up to her mom's house, and she stares out the window for a few minutes. I give her whatever time she needs to process her thoughts before she turns to face me with tears in her eyes.

"Will you go in with me? I don't think I can do it alone today."

"Absolutely." I grip her hand in support before stepping out of the car and over to her door to pull it open.

I hold my hand out, and she latches on tightly. We walk hand in hand inside and straight to her mother's bedroom. Chloe knows exactly what she's looking for. She releases my hand, steps over to the dresser on the opposite side of the room, and pulls open the top drawer. She reaches in to grab a small wooden jewelry box and places it on top of the dresser. I can't see the contents, but Chloe studies them for a moment before reaching in. She sets a necklace on top of the dresser and places the jewelry box back in the drawer. She gives herself a minute to breathe before turning to me.

"Can you help me put this on? My nails are too long right now to work the clasp."

I close the distance between us and get my first look at the necklace. It's beautiful. It appears to be a heart, but one side is larger than the other. The two sides meet at the bottom, but the top is open just a tiny bit. Tucked into the curve of each heart is a small stone that looks like a birthstone. I pick it up and place it around her neck, securing it in place.

Chloe steps in front of the mirror in the corner of the room and places her hand over the necklace. She closes her eyes briefly, standing there in silence before it and nodding a few times.

"We can go now. I don't need anything else," she states plainly, and I don't question it.

I drive her to the school and park in the lot before we go our separate ways. She has to meet with the rest of her class, and I have to find a seat. If I'm going to save seats for Wrenly and Grey, I should probably grab them soon before they start to fill in.

I end up somewhat close to the front but not directly in the front row in case Wrenly shows up late. She's been known to do that. I try calling Grey to see where he is, but the phone goes to voicemail. Time is running out, and the ceremony should be starting soon. I anxiously look around the crowd as people fill in to see if he is around somewhere. He's not.

Reality finally hits me; he's not showing up. He doesn't text, call, or bother to say anything to me at all. I've sent him a few messages now to see where he is, but there has been no response.

I try to call him one last time before the ceremony starts, but he doesn't answer, so I text Wrenly.

> Me: Have you heard from Kai? Do you know where Greyson is by chance?

> Wrenly: They're together. Kai texted me. Knox told them to meet him at the garage.

> Me: When?

> Wrenly: They left right after I did. Not sure when they will be back.

> Wrenly: Where are you sitting? I'm here.

> Me: Third row. I saved you a seat. Hurry up. It's about to start.

I slam my phone down onto my lap. Anger and hurt battle one another inside me. He promised that he'd be here for this. All he had to do was call or text to tell me that he couldn't make it. I don't understand. After everything we've been through, I thought it was going to be different this time. I thought I meant more to him than anything else. He is still putting the Crimson Rose first.

I'm right back in the same headspace I was in seven years ago. I was ready to take on the world with him, but he let me down.

Here we are, my sister getting ready to graduate and another broken promise. Will I always come second? I can't do this feeling. This town. Him. I can't do it.

I shake the feelings away for now and focus on making sure Chloe has the best possible day. Today is about her, I remind myself. She's leaving tomorrow. Maybe I should, too. I promised her I wouldn't leave forever, but I don't need to be if she's not here. I'll just come back when she does. I'm not going to let him treat me like I'm not good enough for a simple phone call.

Wrenly finally fills the seat next to me a few minutes after the ceremony starts. She's wearing the most obnoxious pink dress. I swear she and Chloe are so alike sometimes.

My attention goes back to the group of people sitting in front of the stage. Chloe turns to look at me, giving me a quick smile and wave before turning her attention back to the principal. He is currently giving a speech about reaching greatness.

The ceremony is pretty quick. Once we make it through the last of the speeches, names start being called. One by one, each of them walks across the stage to get their diplomas. I pull my phone out to start recording when they get close to the "M's."

"Chloe Marshall." I hear called out, and I jump up and yell for her. "GO CHLOE!!" I watch as she makes her way across the stage to shake the hand of the principal and then turn to pose for a picture. When she gets back to her seat, her eyes find me again. She holds up the diploma, and I can't help the way pride fills me. I had no clue that a few months ago, I'd be back here, in this town, with a sister graduating high school. I'm so thankful we have each other now.

The whole ceremony finishes after maybe twenty minutes, and I find myself bouncing my foot to try and rid myself of the anxiety building up in me. I pull the bloodstone heart from my pocket and fiddle with it for a few moments before slipping it back into my pocket. How could I ever let myself trust him again? I should have seen this coming from a mile away.

I take a few pictures with Chloe, smiling and celebrating her for a bit before it all becomes too much. I've got to get out of here.

"Where's Greyson?" Wrenly finally asks.

"That's the question of the day, isn't it?" I mutter under my breath.

My sister is smiling around her friends and holding hands with Matt. She looks so happy, and I don't want to bring her down with my issues. I need to make a silent exit. I turn to face Wrenly.

"I have to go meet up with him, actually," I lie.

She eyes me carefully before deciding that I'm telling the truth. "Okay. You're leaving now?"

"Yeah. I'm going to tell Chloe goodbye."

"I'll see you tomorrow. We can go get lunch since she's leaving town. I'm sure you'll need a drink or something."

"Yeah, that sounds good." I hate having to lie to my best friend, but she would try to stop me.

I interrupt Chloe and her friends, saying hi to each one before leaning in and asking her if I can talk to her for a moment in private. She hugs someone that I've never seen, and we step away from the crowd.

"Chloe, I'm so proud of you. You're such an amazing young woman."

A grin crosses her face. "You could have said this in front of everyone." She giggles but composes herself. "Thank you. That really means a lot. It's been a good day despite everything."

"I'm not sure if I'm supposed to say this, but I love you so much. I'm so lucky to call you my sister." I pull her in for another hug when I see the tears begin to well up in her eyes.

"I love you too, Ava. Thank you for always showing up for me, even if it's only been a few months. It means more than you know," she says as I pull back and give her a nod.

"I have to go, and I might not be back before you two leave tomorrow." She looks over me with concern. I try my best to keep it together. She doesn't need her day ruined with my shit.

"Is everything okay?" She raises a brow.

"Everything's fine. There is just something I need to do."

"Okay." She leans in for a hug and hesitates a moment too long. She knows something else is going on, and it breaks my heart. I can't tell her what's going through my mind right now.

"If I don't see you before you leave, call me when you get to your first location tomorrow."

"Of course," she says as I begin to pull away. "Ava," she calls out, and I stop to turn back and look at her. "I'll see you in a month, right?"

"You'll see me in a month," I repeat firmly, and she will. With that, I make my way to the car. She can ride home with Matt. I truly hope that he will take care of her while they're away.

Chapter 33
Avalynn

A realization hit me after Chloe's graduation wrapped up. Something's not right. Greyson wouldn't ghost me like this after he tried so hard to get me to fall for him again. I may have my doubts about things, but Greyson Hayes loves me. I have to get to Adam's Garage and see what I can find out. I put my car in drive, slam on the gas, and my tires squeal as I burn out.

When I arrive, the garage is eerily vacant. It makes me uneasy, and alarm bells ring in my mind. Where is everyone? I open the glove compartment of my car and pull out my pistol—45 calibers of don't fuck with me. The last time I needed this thing was when Alec called to threaten me, and I found the front door of my house open. Thankfully, I had enough sense to put it back in here the next day.

I check the clip and see I only have seven bullets. It's not ideal, but I'll work with what I have. Lucky number seven. Right? Hopefully, I won't need them. I've never shot someone before, but I will if I need to. Between my father's training when I was young and the classes I took before starting my PI work, I'm well-versed in how to handle a gun. I shut the glove box and take a deep breath, pulling out my phone to call Chloe. She answers on the second ring.

"Hello?"

"Chloe, I don't have time to talk or explain, but I need you to put Matt on the phone. Now."

"Okay." She sounds nervous, but I hear her call for him. Moments later, his voice fills the phone.

"Hello?"

"Matt, why is there nobody at the garage?"

"Knox said something important was going down, and he needed everyone to clear out." He doesn't see any issue with this at all.

"No. You need to call some of the guys and get here NOW," I urge.

"Boss makes the rules, Ava. He said to steer clear, we steer clear."

"You realize how fucking stupid that sounds, right? Get the crew here, Matt, or I swear to god, I'll cut your balls off in your sleep."

"Fuck, fine. I'll call them and tell them to meet you at the garage."

"If anyone has something to say about it, you tell them I will personally take the blame. The fucking idiots should be thanking me. A whole gang of criminals, and you all thought it was a good idea to leave the garage unattended?"

"Well, I-"

"I don't have time for this. I have to go. Call them now," I say before hanging up the phone.

I pocket my phone and very carefully walk toward the garage, peering in to find that it is indeed vacant. I decide to go around back to check Grey's torture shed. For a moment, I consider waiting for the crew to get here, but I need to know that Grey is okay. My gut is telling me something is seriously wrong.

When the shed comes into view, I can't stop my heart from slamming inside my chest. Fuck. I have no clue what's waiting for me inside. With any luck, it will be empty, or Greyson will be torturing someone. The door is open, but I can't see inside from this angle. I need to get closer.

I take a quick look at my surroundings. There's nobody around. I grip the handle of my pistol, just in case, pointing it in front of me as I slowly make my way closer to the shed. I walk along the side of the wall and begin to hear voices inside. My blood runs cold when I hear Greyson talking to Alec.

"What's the plan here, Alec?"

"You burned down my club. You killed most of my crew. In a matter of a few days, you destroyed everything I've built."

This is bad. I take a risk and peer into the doorway to see what might be the worst possible thing I've ever imagined. Knox, Greyson, and Kai are all in chairs in the middle of the room with guns to the backs of their heads. From what I can see, Knox is the only one tied up. That's one positive.

I'm so glad I trusted my instincts and came here instead of leaving town. I shudder at the thought of what could have happened if I actually left. I knew he wouldn't hurt me again unless it was out of his control. My only regret is doubting him at first. I glance towards the garage, willing the crew to show up. We're running out of time. I can tell by Knox's body language.

The crew will be here in a few minutes. I remind myself. I just need things to stay calm until then. Keep him talking, Grey, please. I try not to panic over the sight of the love of my life sitting there with a gun to his head.

Alec steps in front of Greyson, blocking him from my view, and lifts his right arm. I'm assuming he now has his gun to Grey's forehead. "Any last words, Greyson?" I hear him say, and I see red.

I don't wait a second longer. I pull the trigger and watch as my bullet pierces through the back of Alec's skull, and he drops to the ground. Half a second later, the man standing behind Greyson also falls to the ground. The sheer force of the bullet must have gone directly through Alec's skull and into the other man's. Perfect. Two for one, I love it.

Kai twists around and tries to take down the man who had the gun to his head. He appears young, and the shock from his boss lying dead on the floor is enough for Kai to get the upper hand on him. Kai seizes the gun from the guy's hand and knocks him down to the floor. He kicks him a few times, making him cry out.

Greyson quickly unties Knox and takes the tape from his mouth before locking eyes with me. His nostrils flare, and he seems more tense than I've ever seen him. I flip the safety of the gun back on and shove it in the pocket of my dress before running over to him. He grips the sides of my face and stares down at me, letting his body relax into my hold.

"You came for me, baby?" Grey whispers, and I see tears well up in his eyes. I'm too stunned by his vulnerability at this moment to say anything back to him. I've never seen Greyson cry before. As quickly as they appear, he blinks them away.

His hand finds the back of my neck, and he pulls me into him. Soft lips land on mine, demanding I surrender to him. I lose myself in his arms, knowing that he is safe. He nips and bites at my lip, forcing a moan to escape. I can't believe I almost lost him today.

Someone next to us clears their throat, and I pull back enough to look over and see Knox standing there staring at Grey and me while we make out.

"Ava, I owe you my life. I don't know how I'll ever thank you for what you did here today," Knox says sincerely.

Kai finds his way next to Knox, dragging the younger man along with him. He leaves him on the floor and places the gun in Knox's hand. For a second, I wonder if they will let him live. My thoughts are wrong. Knox doesn't hesitate to point the gun and pull the trigger. Blood splatters around us from the close proximity of the shot. He doesn't react to the murder he just committed. He simply places the gun in the waistband of his pants before looking over at me and Grey.

Grey squeezes my hand, reassuring me, as members of the crew finally appear in the doorway. They are stunned at what they see in front of them. One by one, they filter in and glance around the room to see Alec lying dead on the floor not far from us.

Knox finally speaks to the crew members who have stepped inside. "This will need to be addressed. I'm calling a full meeting. Every member's presence is required. Send out your emergency messages and have everyone meet at the garage immediately. No exceptions."

They all pull out their phones and get to work sending messages. Everyone is still too stunned to speak. They want to know how Alec, out of all people, got the upper hand on Knox. This shouldn't have happened.

Knox clears his throat again, and everyone in the room looks away from their phones and back up at him. "You all have Ava to thank for being the only one to use her fucking brain and know that something was wrong. She is the only reason Greyson, Kai, and I are alive. She will be treated with nothing but respect going forward. This is your only notice of this. Should I find out that anyone disrespects her in any sort of way, they will pay with their lives."

"And I'll be the one to personally see it happen," Greyson adds. Knox nods, and all eyes in the room move to me. I flush from being the center of their attention.

"Now that we have that matter settled, we should wait for everyone else to arrive before going over some things. We need new protocols to ensure something like this never happens again," Knox says.

Grey leans over to whisper in my ear. "Do you even realize how fucking hot it was to see you kill Alec? You know guns aren't my thing, but fuck, Ava, the sight of you holding that thing will be enough to get me hard for a lifetime."

I giggle, but he's not joking one bit. I glance down and see the outline of his cock pressed firmly against his pants. He catches where my eyes have gone, and immediately, I know he is up to no good.

He gets Knox's attention and whispers something in his ear. I see Knox nod and then move toward the door.

"I'm going to need you fuckers to take your useless asses up to the garage with Knox. My girl and I have something we need to take care of," Grey calls out, and chills course through my body.

Nobody objects. They all just filter out, following behind Knox and leaving us in the shed by ourselves. The last person to step out even gives us the courtesy of closing the door behind them.

The last time I was in here alone with Grey, he saved me from my past by bringing David and Officer Grant here. Today, I saved him. I'll never let anyone hurt him. If I have the ability to stop them, I will. This man is my entire future. I don't care where we are or what we are doing with our lives. The only thing that matters is that we get to do it together.

Chapter 34

Greyson

"First, I'm going to fuck you senseless. Then, we're going to talk about how you showed up here to save the day." My eyes darken as I take in every single inch of her. The only problem right now is that she's wearing too much clothing.

"Shouldn't we talk first? If you're fucking me senseless, how am I supposed to be able to talk after?" She tries hitting me with a smart-ass response.

"Does it look like I want to talk right now, little shadow?" I tell her.

I watch her chest rise and fall with rapid breaths. I bet if I stripped her bare and dove right into her pussy, she would already be soaking wet for me.

"Strip, now."

She obeys, not wasting a single moment. I watch the way she takes her dress off, carefully placing it on the floor before shimmying out of her tights and shoes. My eyes memorize every single part of her body. She's perfect.

Without giving her a chance to say anything, I pick her up and wrap her legs around my waist. Her arms land on either side of my head as she holds herself up. I walk her to the other side of the shed. We don't need to be around these dead fucks. I doubt she wants to catch a glimpse of them while I'm balls deep inside her. When we are far enough away, I slam her back against the wall, losing myself in her.

She pushes against my chest, causing confusion, so I pull away and look at her. "I think you're bleeding."

"I don't care."

My lips smash against hers, making her moan. I kiss her like I've never kissed her before, completely consuming myself in her taste. I pull back from her lips to move to her neck, biting and sucking up the length of it. She smells so fucking good. It's like the adrenaline from the events enhanced her usual citrus smell. I must be a little rough on her because I feel her tug on my hair to get my attention.

I carry her from the wall to the familiar table I fucked her on the last time we were here. I place her ass on the edge and quickly strip free from all of my clothes. Leaning forward, I take her breast in my mouth, rolling her nipple between my teeth and placing myself between her legs.

I sink to my knees in front of her, the only person that I would ever willingly get on my knees for, and grip her thighs. Before she can object, I bury my face in her pussy, savoring the tiny sounds of pleasure that emit from her.

My tongue trails along her center, and I notice how her hips tweak with even the slightest movement as I flick it against her clit. It's something I know she loves. I slide two fingers inside her, pumping in and out. I know exactly what her body needs and how to make it respond exactly how I want. My tongue swirls all around. She tastes so fucking good. I could spend all day feasting on her perfect cunt, and it will still never be enough.

When I come up for air, she stares down at me with those deep brown eyes that I love, filled with nothing but pure desire. She looks feral, and I fucking love it. I pick up speed with my fingers, watching as her mouth pops open and a silent moan leaves her lips. I can already feel her clamping down on me.

"Please," she begs.

"Such a perfect slut. Always so eager for more."

She's getting too close to finding her release, so I pull my fingers out of her. When she comes, it will be on my cock. A slight protest falls from her lips when I make a show of licking both fingers clean. The protest quickly morphs into gratitude when I slide my cock into her tight pussy. I pull her legs up into my elbows and slam into her, making her cry out. It's like music to my ears.

My pace quickens, and I lean forward to slap one of her breasts before rolling her nipple between my fingers. She clamps down hard on my cock. "I know my dirty slut likes a little pain. I wonder what these would look like pierced?" I feel her pussy pulse at the mere suggestion.

"Grey, please." She's so close to falling apart.

"Be my good little whore and get my dick nice and wet, little shadow," I tell her while reaching down to rub her clit.

She spasms around me, again, right on the precipice of falling over the ledge I know she's teetering on. Just one more little push should get her to where she needs to be. I shove two fingers into her mouth, and her eyes widen at the intrusion. Instead of pushing down on her throat, I hook them into her cheek. Drool begins to drip down her chin. My beautiful, dirty girl.

"You look so fucking beautiful when you let me use you as my own personal fuck toy."

She moans around my fingers, and I lean down to spit next to them. It lands right in her open mouth. The degradation is all she needs to completely lose herself. Her eyes roll back, and she clenches around my cock, crying out in pleasure as the orgasm ripples through her.

"That's it, baby, come all over my cock," I tell her, and she does.

I pull my fingers from her mouth and wipe them along the side of her chest before pulling out of her. I haven't finished, but that's because I'm not done with her. I point to the floor next to the table, and like a good little pet, she obeys without me even needing to use words.

She positions herself on her hands and knees in front of me on the floor. I kneel behind her, pushing between her shoulder blades and forcing her face to the floor with her ass in the air. I run my hand down the length of her back, watching the goosebumps I leave in its wake until I land on her ass.

I give her a firm slap, and she whimpers while arching her back. I mimic the movement on her other cheek and take notice of the bright red handprint already appearing from the first slap. She whines from the feeling of me rubbing over the handprint.

THE AFTERTHOUGHT

"You want more, don't you? My desperate slut. Tell me what I want to hear, and I'll make you come again."

"I'm yours," she says, just like I wanted her to.

I slap both cheeks again to make sure she is nice and needy before trailing my fingers along her pussy. "So, fucking wet for me."

I reach down with my free hand to tangle my fingers in her hair, appreciating the way the curls she put in today make it look like fire. Roughly, I pull it back, forcing her back to my chest. My fingers fiddle with her clit for a few moments, and she groans at the teasing pleasure.

Slowly, I sink my cock back inside her. She's so fucking wet, and I know it's all for me. My perfect dirty little slut. Just feeling her around me is enough to make me want to explode inside her.

"Who do you belong to?" I ask as I begin to move inside, thrusting in and out.

"Nobody," she tries.

I push her back down to all fours and crack my hand against her ass. "Try again, slut. Who does this pussy belong to?"

"Me," she says this time.

Again, my hand lands on her ass, making her pussy clench around my cock. I pick up my pace, thrusting in and out of her while she struggles to keep herself on all fours.

"Want to try again, little shadow? Who does this pussy belong to? Who do you belong to?"

I reach around and pinch her clit, making her sing. "Youuuu."

"That's my good whore." I pick up my pace, rubbing small circles around her clit while slamming into her from behind.

"Grey, I'm going to come again," she cries out.

"Good. Come with me, baby. Come on my cock while I fill you up."

A pleasurable scream leaves her when she tumbles over the cliff. I jump with her, grunting and releasing every single drop of myself inside her while her walls clench around me. I pull out and fall to the floor next to her, pulling her in close to me as the two of us try to catch our breath.

I turn to face her. "I thought you would be upset with me when I didn't show up to Chloe's graduation, but instead, you turned up here and saved the day."

"I was upset," she confesses.

"But you didn't run. You sought me out to give me the chance to explain things."

"I'm not going to lie. I considered leaving, but I couldn't," she admits. I can't fault her for having that moment of doubt after everything we've been through.

"What changed your mind?"

"You did." She glances up at me. "Over the last few weeks, you've proven over and over that you would always be there for me. You made a promise that you would never hurt me again, and I chose to believe in you."

I sigh and pull her closer. "I should have texted you immediately when I got the texts from Knox's phone. I hesitated, and I shouldn't have. When I convinced myself I was being fucking stupid, Kai called, and my mind was on getting him and getting here."

"What would you have done if I did leave?"

"Ava, if you left, I would likely be dead." If she would not have shown up when she did, we would all be dead.

"Say, by chance, someone else intervened. One of the crew saved the day," she tosses out.

"If I was alive, I would track you down and drag you back here by any means necessary."

"Is that right?" She raises a brow at me.

"Fuck yeah, it is. You're mine. I'd have my way with you and then put my mark on you so you never have questioning thoughts ever again. Then, I'd have to punish you for trying to get away from me."

A grin crosses her face. "Careful, you know I like being punished. I might just have to go for a little run and see what happens."

"I'll always find you, Avalynn." I lean in and kiss her. "You are the very air I breathe. The oxygen that fuels the raging inferno inside me."

She leans in to kiss me softly. I brush a stray piece of hair behind her ear and pull back. "I could sink my cock back inside you right now and get lost in you for days."

"Actually, I should get back to the house. Chloe is leaving in the morning, and she probably thinks I'm insane. When I realized something was off, I called her to have Matt reach out to the crew. I kind of yelled at him and called him an idiot."

"We were all idiots for not realizing something was up." I stand and pull her up next to me, leaning in to kiss the tip of her nose. "Let's get you home to your sister."

As we are putting our clothes back on, something catches my eye. On the floor, next to where her dress was, is the bloodstone crystal heart I got for her. I walk over, lean down, and pick it up.

"You carry it with you?" I tilt my head in question.

"You've been carrying around that stupid lighter for how many years now? Don't even start with me." She snatches the crystal from my hand to slip it back into her pocket.

I smile and grab her hand to lead her out of the shed and towards the garage. Her orange hair catches the light in the most perfect way, and I've never been so damn proud to call someone mine. I'm never letting her go.

Chapter 35

Avalynn

Greyson stayed back at the garage yesterday for the mandatory meeting with the Crimson Rose, which was perfect because Chloe and I were able to spend the evening together. Both Grey and Matt came home a few hours before we went to bed, looking tense. I'm sad they are leaving today but also excited for her to embark on their adventure. I know Matt is a good guy and will take care of her.

I roll over to find Greyson awake and staring at me. He slept here with me again last night. Now that I think about it, he's been sleeping here a lot. I look at the closet across the room and see he has a whole section of clothing in there. When the hell did that happen? It's like we've come full circle.

"You realize you took it upon yourself to move into my house," I say with a chuckle because up until this moment, I truly did not notice.

"I wasn't about to sleep without you next to me. If I had asked you to move in, you would have said no." He wraps an arm around me and pulls me closer to him. "Are you saying you don't want me here, little shadow?"

"Of course, I want you here," I say, snuggling further into his hold. "I love you. You know that, right? I love every bit of you and your crazy self," I confess to him. I don't believe I've told him those three exact words up to this point.

"I love you too, baby." He kisses my forehead. "Forever my heart."

"Forever my always," I tell him.

A pounding on the front door startles me. I eye Grey to see him grinning from ear to ear.

"What's so funny? I'm still half naked, and someone is pounding on the freaking door."

"It's just DoorDash."

I look at him in confusion because we most certainly do not have DoorDash in our town. "It's entirely too early for this. Can you just tell me what the hell you're talking about?"

"You're a hero. They're here to deliver your morning coffee and muffin."

I look at him with a mixture of annoyance and gratitude. I'm not sure which one to feel more of at the moment. I just want to be in bed with my boyfriend.

"You do not need to have your crew bring me coffee every morning."

"Don't be silly. You know I do. It's tradition now. They will be leaving it on the porch. I instructed them to get the goods, drop them at the door, and knock a few times before leaving. I'll have to talk to them about how loudly they knock. That was a bit excessive."

"You're fucking with me, right?"

"If I were fucking with you, it wouldn't be with your coffee intake. I know how you are when you don't have it. Why do you think I always make sure you're caffeinated and well-fed?"

My eyes go wide, and I playfully slap him on the arm. "Greyson!"

He places a finger under my chin to tilt my head up, and a moment later, his lips land on mine. I melt into him. We are genuinely happy, and I'm just over the moon that everything has worked out. When he pulls back, I protest. Maybe I want to stay in bed with him all day.

"We've got a busy day. You have to see Chloe and Matt off, and then we have to meet with Knox."

"I have one more thing I need to do later in the evening, too," I tell him, and he raises a brow at me.

"Calm yourself down. I wasn't talking about sex. It's a surprise for you, but I think you're going to love it. I'm guessing you're sleeping here again tonight?"

"I'm sleeping wherever you are, little shadow. How else will I get to slide myself inside that sweet cunt of yours? Besides, I live here, remember?" He smirks.

I roll my eyes. "Can you go five minutes without being sexual?"

"I could, but we have a few years of missed time to make up for." He kisses me again and then slips out of the bed.

I lay here for a moment, grateful that everything between us has finally worked itself out. The only thing left for us to tackle is where he stands with the Crimson Rose. When Grey came back last night, he said that Knox wanted to meet with me today about how he could repay me for saving his life. Grey and I talked about our situation pretty extensively and came up with a solution that I hope works for everyone.

The goal is to see if Knox will grant him permission to remain involved in some things but be fully removed from other parts. Mainly the drug drops, deals, exchanges with buyers, or anything that would involve matters outside of him physically torturing or killing someone for information.

It's a win-win, really. Grey gets to have an outlet for his fiery urges, and I get to have him away from the direct danger of something happening to him. My initial feelings toward the crew have softened. I like how everyone looks out for one another. They are almost like family.

I throw on some clothes and make my way out to the dining room. Grey has already grabbed the coffee and muffins from the porch and placed them on the table. There is enough for everyone today. Matt and Chloe are both sitting around the table, whispering, and laughing with each other. Young love. It's so cute and innocent.

"How long until you leave?" I question as I reach to grab my coffee.

"We were waiting for you two to finally get your lazy asses out of bed. Couldn't leave without saying goodbye."

"It's not goodbye; it's just see you next month," I assure her before flopping down in one of the chairs and grabbing a muffin.

"See, I told you to wait until after she had a bite or two before you try talking to her," Greyson says while trying to hold back a laugh. I shoot him a glare sharp enough that if it were a dagger, it would pierce his skin. He thinks he's so funny today.

I shift my attention back to Chloe. "Where are you off to first?"

She practically bounces out of her seat. "The first stop is somewhere in upstate California. Then, we're going to make our way down to Sequoia National Park. I'm so excited to see the trees. I hear they're massive!"

"Remember what I said. I want a call every day and updates with every spot you two end up in."

She smiles at me, nodding.

We spend some time chatting at the table before the two of them decide they need to be on their way. When Chloe steps over to hug me and tell me goodbye, I can't stop the tears from falling. She pulls back and looks at me.

"I'll see you in a month," she confirms, and I pull her in for one last hug.

"Please, be safe," I say before they walk out the door.

I turn to look at Grey and find him staring at me, studying me. I feel like I have to defend how I'm feeling. "A few months ago, I didn't even know she existed, but somehow, we have grown so close in such a short time. I'm really going to miss her."

He walks over to me, places his hands on my waist, and pulls me into him. "Don't worry. I'll keep you busy."

I roll my eyes again. "You're feeling all kinds of ridiculous today, aren't you?"

"I'm just happy. You chose to stay. You chose me. It's the best feeling in the entire world. I would have made you stay. You're mine, but it's better knowing that you want to be here with me."

"Come on. We have to go meet your brother," I tell him, and within a few minutes, we are out the door and on our way to Adam's Garage.

When we arrive, I stare out of the car window for just a moment thinking about what could have happened if I hadn't shown up yesterday when I did. If I was just a few minutes later, everything would be completely different right now. I reach into my pocket and fiddle with the crystal that Grey gave me while closing my eyes and taking a deep breath.

"Let's get this over with," I tell him, pushing the door open to head inside.

A group of crew members are working on a car in one of the bays but pause when they catch sight of us. Each one of them nods at me and then to Greyson as a sign of respect before we slip past them and into the office.

Knox is sitting there on the phone, holding up his pointer finger, indicating he needs a moment. He points toward the seats in front of him so Grey and I can sit down. I watch as Grey pulls out his phone to power it down and places it on the desk in front of him, so I follow suit.

"I'm honored to tell you the news. This could open up a ton of new opportunities for our area since the Cobras are decimated. The few of them that are left will be struggling to organize themselves. I predict we have nothing to worry about at all for quite some time."

He's quiet for a moment. I'm guessing whoever is on the other end of the call is speaking.

"I promised you the best of the best. I never break a promise." He pauses again. "Yes, I hope to speak with you again soon."

He hangs up and then pauses to look between me and Grey. His face is swollen on one side, and he has a wild-looking black eye that is starting to form. A mixture of deep red and purples covers his face, but it doesn't seem to affect any of his abilities. "Ava, I wanted to extend another personal thank you for what you did yesterday."

"Greyson was in trouble." I shrug. "I will do whatever I have to in order to make sure he is safe, just as he would do for me."

"I want you to know that if there is anything that you need from either myself or the Crimson Rose, you should ask for it. I will do everything I can to guarantee you and your sister are always looked out for going forward. I know you have Greyson to ensure your safety, but a few extra people having your back also never hurts."

"I appreciate that, Knox. There is something that I would like to ask of you."

"You've thought this through already?" He raises a brow at me in question.

"I figured it was a possibility that you would want to grant me some sort of favor. I did save your life, after all."

He laughs. "No wonder he's so obsessed with you. You're not only fully capable of defending yourself but also smart." He turns his gaze to Grey. "Better not let this one go."

"She's not going anywhere," Greyson states plainly.

Knox turns his gaze back to me, motioning for me to move forward with whatever I need to say.

"I want to discuss Greyson's current standing with the Crimson Rose." He shoots a glance back at Greyson, and I see Grey nod out of the corner of my eye.

"Very well. What exactly are you thinking?"

"You get Coal, and I get Greyson," I state.

"Coal?" he questions.

"Yes. That's what they call him on the streets, isn't it?"

He nods, so I go on to tell him about the hybrid method Greyson and I discussed. He could call Grey to handle anything that would take place in the torture shed but essentially leave him out of the rest. He sits quietly, absorbing all of the information, not giving us any indication of whether or not he will accept or decline.

Once I finish, he takes a moment to consider what I've laid out for him. I know I'm asking for him to let his right-hand man step away from the major duties. I didn't think he would accept right away, but when he glances back at Greyson and takes in the look on his face. I see Knox nod in acceptance.

"We can try out your hybrid method. If it goes well, then it will be fine as long as Greyson is still able to be somewhat involved. He has a special set of skills that are hard to come by."

"Agreed. He needs to use those skills. I would never try to stop him from doing that. It's part of who he is."

"Excellent. Anything else?"

"Yes, actually. Gary Myers. His mother is poking around at his death. I've been investigating it for her. I think everyone in this room knows who caused his untimely demise. I want it handled."

"Done. I'll have it covered up to look like he was in the fire at Temptations. I'll send you whatever documents you need in order to wrap up your investigation. I can have it all fabricated fairly quickly. Anything else?"

"I believe Grey still owes you a favor," I state, not asking because Greyson already told me he does.

I take in the way Knox clenches his jaw at the mention of the favor. I'm sure he assumed he could use it as his wild card, should the need arise. I'm not taking any chances with our future.

"Consider the favor fulfilled. Once we leave our meeting, we will all move forward with no debts," he reluctantly says.

"Okay." I nod.

"Anything else?"

"That's all from me. This is all I will ever ask of you."

"A small set of demands in the big scheme of things," he says with a wave of his hand. I expected more pushback, but I'm beyond happy that there's none. "You two can head out. Again, Ava, I will never express enough how much I appreciate your presence last night. You were the only one with enough sense to actually consider something might be wrong. I've already laid into the crew for being a bunch of fucking morons."

Funny, I thought the exact same thing last night. "Men don't always think logically," I tease.

"Watch yourself, little shadow. You've just earned yourself a lot more time with me. I might have to punish you," Grey says, and my cheeks flush.

"Alright, I have a few other meetings that I need to address. You two can be on your way to do whatever you need to do." He gestures to the door. "Greyson, I'll be in touch when we need your expertise."

"You better. You and I both know I'll never turn down the chance to light a motherfucker up."

"Also, if you could let the crew know, I would appreciate it. I think they will receive the news better coming from you."

"Sure thing."

I shake my head and walk to the car. Greyson hangs back at the garage to talk with some of the crew and update them on how things will be going forward. He will likely be hung up for a bit explaining everything, which is perfect. This gives me the alone time I need to get a few things done.

I run my errands before heading back home. Now that I'm staying in town permanently, Grey and I are going to have to find a new place to live. There are bad memories here—memories with my mom and dad. I want to get a place for just Grey and me, and Chloe if she wants, to make new memories.

When I open the door, I see him on the couch watching TV. He hardly ever takes time to actually relax, so the sight of it makes my heart swell. He looks over his shoulder, and his eyes beam with light.

"Hey, baby." He stands and meets me in the middle of the living room. "I had one of the guys bring me home."

I wrap my arms around his waist and just take a moment to feel his warmth. It's been the best day. Nothing compares to having him here waiting for me when I get home.

I take a step back and smile. "Okay, are you ready for your surprise?"

"Let's see what you've got for me, little shadow." He looks at me curiously because I don't have anything in my hands, and I've already told him that the surprise wasn't anything sexual.

"You know how you got that tattoo over your chest for me?"

"Yes."

"Well, I got one for you, and don't worry, I was covered the entire time, and the artist was a woman. I know your psycho ass would want to know."

I pull down my cropped blouse to reveal the flaming heart over my chest. The inside of the heart is bare, save the two initials, GH. The black outline of the heart is made up of shaded flames rather than the traditional straight outline of a heart. He walks over to me and inspects it closer before looking up at me with so much vulnerability and compassion.

"You got this for me?"

"You're my everything, Grey, and I don't plan on spending a day without you again."

"You put my initials on your chest."

"I did." I square my shoulders and stand proud. "Everyone should know who I belong to."

His eyes light up with fire. The next thing I know, he's throwing me over his shoulder and marching straight to our bedroom. I giggle and bask in the reality that this is our life now. I get to spend every single day with the man who has always held my heart.

Epilogue

Greyson - Six months later

She looks so beautiful sitting there, drinking her coffee and snacking on one of the muffins I bought her. I still make sure that she has both daily. It's something special that I can do for her to make sure she knows what she means to me. It doesn't take much to make her happy, but I will spend the rest of my life trying to be the person who does it.

Ava put her house up on the market almost immediately after we met with Knox, and it sold quickly. We were both surprised at how much she was able to sell it for. She moved some of her mother's things into storage and is still working up the courage to go through everything. It's a lot for her to process, so she's taking it a little bit at a time, with me right there by her side.

Knox sent a ton of fabricated information regarding Gary Myers to Ava about a month after our meeting. It was more than enough evidence to prove that he was caught up with the wrong people before tragically perishing in the fire at Temptations. He didn't, but Mrs. Myers never questioned a single thing. She was just so grateful to know what happened to her son. The payout from Ava completing the job was massive.

With those funds, the money from the sale of her house, and what I've saved up over the years, we were able to buy a pretty nice place for ourselves. It's just outside of Dune Valley. Close enough that I can get back into town when I am needed by the Crimson Rose, and she can get back into town when her sister calls. Kai wasn't even the slightest bit upset about me moving out. He had Wrenly moved in just a few months later.

We've been operating on the hybrid model Ava suggested to Knox for the last six months, and it seems to be working perfectly. I'm no longer directly associated with the gang business, but I'm still the one they turn to when they need information tortured out of someone. It was truly a perfect solution—a meet-in-the-middle of sorts and one hundred percent my girl's idea.

The parts I partake in are enough to satiate my flaming urges. I've gotten a bit more creative with how I use the fire on my victims. It's also a bonus that I get to catch up with the crew when I go there. They all took the news exceptionally well. Nobody had anything to say about me stepping back. Maybe they were afraid of what I might do to them if they did. Kai stepped up as Knox's new right hand, and he's been excelling at it. They've managed to broker deals with several new buyers, and based on what he's told me, business is at an all-time high.

We've attended a few get-togethers for the Crimson Rose. I thought at first that Ava wouldn't want anything to do with the crew, but it's actually quite the opposite. She's made friends with some of the other members' wives, and while she is technically not and can't ever be a gang wife because I am no longer an active member, she's earned a new level of respect for them.

Matt is a full-fledged member now. He was initiated as soon as he and Chloe returned from their trip, which was supposed to last one month but ended up being three. They were just having so much fun that they didn't want to come back quite yet. If Chloe hadn't had college classes starting up, she would have likely wanted to travel longer.

Ava wasn't happy about her being away for so much longer. She missed celebrating her 18th birthday with her, which was pretty upsetting, but I had to remind her that it was good for Chloe and Matt to experience that together. She's gotten over it now that Chloe is back, but she has a strict rule that she is not allowed to leave town for her birthday next year. I guess Ava made her agree to let her throw a huge party to celebrate.

Chloe and Matt live in the house she grew up in. They remind me of what Ava and I could have been had I not tried to take the easier route and break things off with her. They seem so happy and so in love. If he ever hurts her, though, I will burn him to a crisp.

Ava started her new job at the police station as an office assistant. She's been fitting right in with everyone and has even considered taking the courses needed to become an officer. Knox thinks it's a fantastic opportunity because then he will have another friend on the inside. When he told her that, she just rolled her eyes at him.

Andrea and Mrs. Wolfe both left town not too long after graduation. They needed a fresh start, and Andrea wanted to go to college in South Carolina. Susan just couldn't bear being here in Dune Valley alone, so she packed up and went with her daughter. From what I've been told, Chloe still talks to Andrea occasionally, but it's sparingly.

What's left of the Cobras isn't much. We heard through the rumor mill that they get together here and there, but there is no formal organization. There is a very low probability of them ever climbing back up to the status they used to be at. Even if they did manage to crawl out of the ashes, the Crimson Rose has gained so much standing it wouldn't matter. Knox made sure to install a ridiculous number of cameras around the property, at the garage, and in the torture shed. He wasn't taking any chances after the incident.

I have a date night planned with Ava tonight, and I can't wait. I still have a reputation around town, so I was able to call in a favor with one of the guys who runs the local drive-in. I wanted tonight to be perfect. She has no idea what I have up my sleeve, which makes it all the better. I told her we were going to the movies, of course, but I have an extra surprise that she has to wait to find out.

I left her at the house a little bit ago to get ready. I needed to run into town and gather a few things. Blueberry muffins, check. Her favorite coffee, check. A few drinks for me, check. Before I know it, I'm back in the car and heading inside the house to escort her to the car for our date night.

THE AFTERTHOUGHT

She looks stunning, like always. Her fiery orange hair falls across her chest in perfect loose curls. She has dark eyeshadow and bright red lipstick. It accentuates the deep brown color of her eyes. I can't help but imagine those red lips staining my cock later. If everything goes according to plan tonight, she will definitely want to find a way to thank me. She has on one of her classic crop tops, a pleated black skirt, and tights that I will absolutely be ripping into before the end of the night.

All the things we need for the evening are already packed into the back seat of the car, so I turn on the ignition to make the short trip to the drive-in. We've made a point to start up our date nights here again throughout the summer. Tonight, I notice that there aren't as many people here as there normally are. That's a good thing. That means there will be fewer people to hear the way I make her scream when my cock is buried inside her.

After I pay the attendant, I pull right into the spot in the back row that we've claimed as ours. Nobody ever tries to park here anymore. I may have spread the word around town that if they do, they will regret it. This is Ava's favorite spot because it has the best view of the screen. I simply made sure she always has it. Once parked, I pull out everything to set up while she runs to the concession stand to grab a churro.

When she gets back, I'm already sitting in my spot, waiting for her to join me. I lift the blanket, prompting her to slide in next to me. The leaves have started to fall from the trees, and autumn is in full effect. My girl snuggles into the warmth of my hold without question. She fits perfectly in my arms.

I lean in and whisper in her ear, "You should have left the tights at home, little shadow."

She pulls back, eyes wide before they narrow. "Don't ruin my tights, Greyson."

"Oh, you can guarantee I am going to."

She rolls her eyes in annoyance, but I know she's not annoyed. My dirty girl is probably waiting in anticipation. I wrap my arm around her and pull her close, anxious to get on with the night. My nerves begin to get the best of me, but the warmth from her body has calmed me down enough to pull myself together without giving anything away.

The sun has finally set enough for the beginning credits of the movie to start playing, and instantly, she recognizes the song. Be My Baby by the Rosettes fills the speakers in the cars around us, and she looks over at me with nothing but complete shock on her face. "They're playing Dirty Dancing?"

"I might have pulled a few strings to get them to play your favorite movie." I grin and keep her close.

"Grey, this is too much."

"Nothing is ever too much for you, baby. Now, watch your movie," I tell her, reaching over to grab her coffee and handing it to her. She drinks what she wants and then hands the cup back to me, sinking into my hold. I place my hand on her thigh and slowly slide it up and under her skirt.

Her legs fall apart, giving me silent permission to continue with my mission. I run my finger across her center and feel the way she shivers beneath me. She stays quiet, ensuring nobody around us knows what's happening under this blanket. Again, I swipe my finger across her in a teasing manner.

"Grey," she whispers.

With that, I grip onto her tights and rip them wide open. She gasps, and I smile to myself. I love catching her off guard. I pull her panties to the side and immediately slip my fingers inside her. She tightens around them, just like I expected her to.

Her hands reach for my pants to unzip them and pull my cock out. Fuck, her warm hands feel so good wrapped around my length. She pumps me up and down, keeping the same pace that I am as I push my fingers in and out of her. I bring my thumb to rub on her clit, amazed at how wet she is.

I lean down to whisper in her ear. "Such a dirty slut letting me finger fuck you in public. Come over here and sit on my cock, baby."

"We can't," she protests.

"Ride my cock like my good little whore and make yourself come without any of these people hearing."

I can tell the words send a bit of extra excitement through her body, and she slides a leg over to straddle me, facing me with her warm cunt right next to my cock. To anyone looking at us, we would appear to be innocently making out. The blanket covers anything important, and just about everyone here makes out at some point.

"Do it, dirty girl," I encourage her.

She lifts herself up and sinks down on my cock slowly. Inch by inch, I fill her up, and she buries her face into my neck to drown out her moans. She moves her hips back and forth, finding the perfect rhythm that she needs in order to hit that perfect spot inside her.

"Eyes on me, little shadow," I tell her, and she lifts her head to look directly at me.

I see the way she bites her lip and feel the way her pussy flutters. I grip her hips to aid her movements, speeding up the process. Her favorite part of the movie is coming up, and I can't have her miss it.

Just when I think I might have to take control, her fingers dig into my back, and she clamps down around me. A moan leaves her lips, so I lean in to steal it with a kiss, letting her ride out the high she needs before her pussy finally releases its hold on my cock. I lift her up a few inches and slam into her over and over until I find my release inside her. Knowing my come will be dripping from her for the rest of the night makes me smile.

She slides off of me to fix her underwear, and I tuck my cock back inside my pants, quickly pulling up my zipper. I can tell that she wants to run to the bathroom to clean herself up, so I quickly squash that. "Leave it. I want you to feel me dripping out of you."

She opens her mouth to protest but closes it without saying anything. She just shakes her head and snuggles into my side. We finally made it to her favorite part of the movie. It's where

Baby is at the final show of the year with her parents, sitting in the corner, and Johnny comes in to tell them that nobody puts Baby in a corner.

When they start their dance, I see the way her eyes light up. She knows the whole thing by heart, but what she doesn't know is that I learned it for her. I watched this scene enough times to have it burned into my mind because I wanted to make today perfect for her.

I stand up and hold my hand out, prompting her to take it. She looks at me in confusion for a second before she reaches out to grab my hand. The two of us dance along with Johnny and Baby, and I can't help but admire the pure joy on her face. She is nothing but straight giggles. There's enough light from the concession stand nearby to make out every single line of her face.

As the song comes to an end, we skip the big jump. Instead, I fall to one knee, and her eyes almost gape out of her skull. She stands there in complete shock as I pull the ring from my pocket and reach out to grab her hand.

"I don't ever want to spend a single day without you, baby. You are the fire that burns inside of me, a light that I hope never gives out. Avalynn Blake, would you do the absolute honor of becoming my wife?"

Tears stream down her face, and she nods her head over and over again before the word I want to hear finally comes out. "YES!"

I slip the ring onto her finger and stand up to hug her tightly. I'm honestly scared for a moment that I'm going to break her, but she squeezes back just as hard. I don't know exactly what our future has in store for us, but I know we will go through it all together.

"I love you, little shadow."

"I love you too, Grey." Tears still fall from her eyes, but I know they are tears of joy.

I grip her chin and tilt it up, forcing her eyes to meet mine. "Forever my heart."

"Forever my always," she says with certainty, and I lean in to give her a kiss.

The End.

Acknowledgements

Thank you so much to all the readers who took a chance on this book. You are all making my dreams come true one page at a time. I am eternally grateful for every one of you.

Hubby, thank you for always supporting me. Late nights, off the wall ideas, weird things you don't want to know, you are there for every bit of the process and I love you so much!

Amanda, Amanda J, Haley, Jordon, Kayla, Nicole, and Sarah, I appreciate you and the time you put into this book more than you know. It wouldn't be possible without the input you provided. Through every character development and plot hole, I was lucky to have you all behind the scenes.

Maree, you outdid yourself with this cover and I'm in awe of your talent. Thank you for being such a big part of my author journey. Your kindness is unmatched.

Taylor, my amazing editor, I'm sorry for all the missing/messed up commas in this acknowledgement. I would be lost without having you there to polish off my books and make them perfect! Thank you, beautiful! You are amazing!

A special shout out to Motionless In White for being the main source of music to drown out my ears while writing!

About the author

K.M. Baker is a Dark Romance author who lives in a small town in Pennsylvania with her husband. She has three dogs, two German Shepherds and a Bichon Frise, who are like children to her.

Writing has always been her dream, but she never had the courage to do it until recently.

Most of her free time is spent reading all the spicy books she can get her hands on (the dirtier, the better). Outside of reading, she enjoys gardening, crafting, and taking her 1972 Sprint Mustang to car shows. Coffee, red wine, and blankets are some of her favorite things to indulge in. She is also very passionate about traveling!

Stalk Me:
Tik Tok: @K.M.Bakerauthor
Instagram: @K.M.Bakerauthor
Facebook: K.M. Baker's Bookworms
Email: KMBakerauthor@gmail.com

Also By K.M. Baker

Evading Darkness

Made in the USA
Columbia, SC
20 February 2025